The Long Way Home

A Bluff Creek Novel

Blessings!
Amanda Mason
Jeremiah 30:2

Copyright 2020 © Amanda Mason

Dedication

To my family for always believing in me and encouraging me to pursue my dreams.

To all CHD warriors, but especially those that have touched my life.

Table of Contents

The Long Road Home 1

Chapter 1 *Homecoming* 4

Chapter 2 Goodbyes 11

Chapter 3 *Choices* 20

Chapter 4 *Prodigal Son* 29

Chapter 5 *Blindsided* 42

Chapter 6 *Rage* 54

Chapter 7 *Confrontation* 64

Chapter 8 *Roadblocks* .... 71\

Chapter 9 *Opportunities* 89

Chapter 10 *Beginning* 94

Chapter 11 *Ultimatums* 104

Chapter 12 *Surprises* 117

Chapter 13 *Secrets Revealed* 129

Chapter 14 *Unknowns* 141

Chapter 15 *Hellos* 161

Chapter 16 *Trials* 170

Chapter 17 *Endings and Beginnings* 188

Chapter 18 *Betrayal* 199

Chapter 19 *Full Circle* 212

Epilogue 247

Chapter 1 *Homecoming*

"Count is all joy, my brothers, when you meet trials of various kinds." James 1:2

Jake Rawlings felt as empty inside as his gas gauge appeared on the dash of his shiny sports car. He chewed his lip nervously and glanced back up at the lonely road then quickly back to the gas gauge. The orange low fuel light taunted him while he silently threw up a prayer that he could make it to the nearest filling station. He didn't have a tremendous amount of faith that his prayer would be heard. It seemed none of his prayers had ever been answered the way he wanted them to be. He felt confident God was ignoring him so he didn't waste any time feeling bad about returning the favor.

"How do people survive in this place with no cell phone reception?" Jake cringed as his fiancée's shrill voice pierced his thoughts. "Jake, I have not had a signal in miles!"

"Whitney," he said, hating how weak his voice sounded, "I told you Bluff Creek is a little off the beaten path—"

"A little?" she interrupted. "It's not a little off the beaten path! It's miles and miles from the beaten path. People here probably don't even know the beaten path exists!"

He dragged his hand down his face and tried to tune out her continuous whining about the lack of 5G reception. He glanced back at his gas gauge and a sense of desperation threatened to engulf him. The last thing he needed to happen right now was to run out of gas, with no cell phone reception, on the side of a lonely country road with Whitney. The misery he would endure if that happened might just be what tipped him over the edge he felt so dangerously close to most days.

A small ray of hope burst in his chest as he saw a wooden sign in the distance. He knew without being close enough to read it exactly what it would say. And he also knew that just a mile down the road would be Watson's Service Station. At least that's the way it had always been when he grew up here, a local football hero and son of the town's beloved football coach. A sliver of doubt pierced his mind. He hadn't been home in years; what if things had changed?

"Welcome to Calumet County," Whitney read the sign as they approached. "Population 872. Home of Country Music Star Lane McCay." She snickered behind her hand and Jake cut his eyes at her. He knew without her speaking why she was laughing. Another smaller sign, one end broken and flapping in the wind, announced that Calumet County was also home to Jake Rawlings, High School All-American football player.

She giggled, cleared her throat, and tried to put on a serious face. "Tell me, Jake, will your throngs of fans be waiting for us at the edge of town?"

He tried to ignore her, but his silence seemed to encourage her. "You haven't visited in like what…eight years and your name is still on the welcome sign? I mean it's been a lifetime since you were named an All-American. Talk about not being able to let things go…but then again I guess they are trying to let your fame go. The sign with your name on it was broken." She adjusted her designer sunglasses and went back to tapping her phone.

"Ten. It's been ten years since I visited," Jake said under his breath and to no one in particular, following it with a bitter laugh. Little did anyone know that sign was a perfect representation of his life: broken and barely hanging on.

"Oh, well even worse. Ten years without a visit and they still have your name on their welcome sign. Sounds like this town is just a hub of excitement." She rolled her eyes as the sarcasm dripped off her tongue.

A sudden urge to defend his hometown welled up in him but Jake bit his tongue before he said something to her that might lead to even more trouble. He had visited Bluff Creek once after his life-altering injury, but Whitney did not know about that visit. It was a visit he didn't let his mind ponder for very long for fear of what emotions it might stir inside him. In life he had determined that emotions were a dangerous thing. He had known from an early age what kind of life he wanted, what kind of life he felt he was owed, and he was determined to have it no matter the cost. Jake Rawlings had learned the hard way you grabbed onto opportunity where you could and you held on for dear life. He had also learned the hard way that it was easier to just keep quiet than to try and fight with Whitney.

She opened the glove compartment and its contents spilled at her feet. She picked up the worn copy of *The Adventures of Huckleberry Finn* and shook it at him. "When are you going to read adult material? You've read this a million times and I've told you it's silly."

He glanced at the worn cover of the book and felt an affinity to it, not unlike that of an old friend. "Just put it back, Whitney," he mumbled, and she continued as if she hadn't heard him,

"I want to be back on the road by six o'clock tonight, Jake. You know I'm jeopardizing the Fleming deal by coming with you."

Jake took in a deep breath. If he had heard Whitney mention the multimillion-dollar real estate deal she was working on once, he had heard it at least ten times since they had left their beachfront condo that morning.

"Whitney, this is my grandfather's funeral. I told you that you didn't have to come, but you insisted. I can't demand that my family grieve around your work schedule."

"A grandfather you haven't seen in years. Do I need to remind you of that?" She pierced him with her gaze, which Jake avoided and instead stared out the windshield. "We will be on the road by six p.m. Daddy wants us back in town as soon as possible. We have an important meeting tomorrow with the investors on our deal and you do not need to leave The End Zone unmanaged for any longer than you have to."

Jake winced. "It's not unmanaged. Scott is running the bar while I'm gone."

Whitney scoffed. "Scott is exactly the reason you need to return as soon as possible."

The sports bar Whitney's father had helped Jake start several years ago was always a spot of contention between them, but never more so than when they discussed Jake's choice of employees. Scott Kilzner was also a former high school and college standout athlete who had seen his dreams end too soon. The two men had become fast friends after they met in physical therapy, having both suffered career-ending injuries. Scott did not have the social standing necessary to be considered an acceptable friend as far as Whitney was concerned. But Jake suspected that her dislike for his friend stemmed more from Scott's inability to tolerate her spoiled behavior. She had tried for years to extricate Scott from their lives. It was one of the few situations that Jake did not let her have the final word on, which fueled her dislike for Jake's best friend even more.

Ahead he saw the sign for Watson's Service Station and silently thanked God that some things never changed. He parked next to the gas pump and unfolded his long body from the car, stretching to his full 6'3" height. He rolled his neck and took in a deep breath of the clear crisp air. A feeling of belonging settled in his stomach, and it surprised him. He had purposefully chosen a life that had taken him far away from his hometown, so to experience a feeling of comfort and maybe even a little joy at being back home was not something he had expected. Before he could examine the emotion any further, Whitney jumped out of the passenger's seat.

"Stay in the car, Whitney." His voice was low and he hoped she wouldn't try to argue with him.

She scowled at him as she turned to walk toward the front doors of the service station. "I have to go to the bathroom," she threw over her shoulder.

His long legs ate the distance across the parking lot and he caught up with her right before she opened the door. He reached around her to grab the door, glared at her, then gave an exaggerated gesture for her to enter. Jake abruptly stopped when he crossed the threshold. It was as if he had stepped back in time. The service station had not changed one bit since Jake had been a boy. The tables and chairs along the front window were still a burnt orange color, the posters above the drink coolers were still the same faded ones from his youth, and the same worn bar stools were pushed up to the same old wooden counter, waiting for customers to take a seat. And to Jake's complete astonishment, Charlie Watson, who had seemed to be an old man when Jake was a boy, was still behind the counter.

"Well, I didn't think I'd ever live to see the day! Jake Rawlings in the flesh!" Charlie exclaimed and came around the counter to extend his hand to Jake.

Jake grasped the older man's hand and was pulled into a hearty hug as Charlie slapped Jake's back. "How are you, Jake? My goodness, it's been years since you've been home. I just hated what happened to you. Such a shame. You were headed for the big time."

Jake ground his back molars, Charlie's words were not unfamiliar ones. Jake had heard them many times and he still hated them as much today as he had the first time he heard them. The words, the looks of sympathy, the head shakes, and whispers were one of the reasons he avoided his hometown. He could not stomach the entire town's murmuring about what a shame he had gotten hurt, but more than that he could not take the look of disappointment in so many people's eyes, especially in those of his father.

"I'm doing well, Charlie, really well." Jake had become so accustomed to telling the lie he almost believed it himself. "I'm a little surprised to see you still here. Figured you would have retired by now." Jake pulled away from the clerk, but Charlie continued to grip Jake's hand firmly.

"Nawww, I don't know how to do anything but run this gas station. I guess I'll be here until the good Lord comes and gets me." Jake chuckled and Charlie quickly continued, "I sure was sorry to hear about Shep. He was a fine man."

"Yes, Charlie, he sure was." Jake's throat constricted as he spoke of his grandfather. He gathered his emotions quickly and reminded himself of the desperate situation he found himself in. "Listen, Charlie, in our rush to get here for Shep's funeral, I've…well, I'm a little embarrassed here." Jake stepped close to the older man and lowered his voice. "I've left my wallet at home. Does my dad still have that charge account here?" Jake's face flushed at the lie and a little part of him, buried way down deep, hated the deception.

"Do you really think I would charge you, Jake Rawlings, for a measly ol' tank of gas?"

"Excuse me!" Whitney's high-pitched voice echoed throughout the store as she stood in the middle of an aisle after circling the store for the third time. "Where is the bathroom?"

"Oh, it's around back." For his age, Charlie moved quickly behind the counter and retrieved a key on a heavy black chain. He moved toward Whitney as he held the key out to her. "Just right out the front door and go around the corner of the building." He pointed out the windows with his other hand.

She stared at the key as he held it out to her, momentarily refusing to take it, a disgusted look on her face. She finally reached out and snatched the offered key and glared at Jake as she stomped past him, muttering, "You have got to be kidding me!"

Jake and Charlie both watched her as she shoved the front door open, almost smacking the side of the building, and marched toward the outside entrance to the restroom.

"She's not spent much time outside the city," Jake mumbled, trying to make an excuse for Whitney's rude behavior.

Charlie waved his hand as if to dismiss the incident. "Now

what was you saying about needing gas?"

"If I could charge a tank on my dad's account—" Jake began.

"No need for that," Charlie interrupted. "You fill up your tank and it's on the house. Jake Rawlings, here in my store again. I just can't believe it! Come here, I want to show you something." The old man led Jake to the counter and pointed to the wall.

"You remember that picture?" The old man's eyes twinkled as he watched Jake's gaze land on the framed photo.

Jake leaned forward slightly and squinted to see the old photo hanging on the wall behind the counter. A picture of a young man in his football uniform, arm positioned to throw the ball down the field. Jake's mind wandered back to that time briefly and his face softened. "Yeah, I remember," his voice barely above a whisper.

"That is a picture of you throwing the winning touchdown the year we won state. I'll never forget that day as long as I live." Jake glanced at Charlie and he knew the older man had wandered back in time too. "Shep sure was proud of you."

Charlie's words hit a nerve deep within Jake and he wondered if Shep were here if he would still be proud of him.

The old man snapped out of his reverie and grabbed Jake by the shoulder. "You fill your tank up, Jake, and go say goodbye to Shep." He patted Jake's arm and walked around the counter.

"Thanks, Charlie. Means more to me than you know." Jake's shoulders slumped as he headed out the door.

"Jake."

Jake turned back to face Charlie at the sound of his name.

The old man smiled widely and said, "Welcome home, son."

Chapter 2 Goodbyes

"Do nothing out of selfish ambition or vain conceit. Rather, in humility, value others above yourselves." Philippians 2:3

Jake shook his head as he pumped gas and watched Whitney hold her phone at a variety of angles, walking around the filling station parking lot trying to obtain a sliver of service. He finally turned his back to her and leaned against his car, gazing out at the road in front of him. Home, he was home — one place he thought he might never be again.

From an early age Jake had felt different from those around him. As if the powers that be had destined him for something more than ordinary life in a small town. As a young boy, he had been a standout athlete. When others had to work hard to master athletic abilities and skills, it came easy to him. Maybe it was due to growing up with a father who was a well-known football coach, or maybe it was just in his DNA, but he had always stood out from the others. He had heard from others many times that God had blessed him with athletic ability. He scoffed at that sentiment now and thought that those who always talked about God had one thing right: He gave and He definitely took things away.

When he was still a child, murmurs of his abilities and speculations about how far he could go began. Jake had felt with every fiber of his being he was destined for greatness and so had his family and the town. People treated him differently;

old men slapped him on the back and spoke of him as if he were already a legend. Young children waited after games for him to sign their hats or jerseys or to just simply get a glimpse of him. No matter where he went in Bluff Creek, he never had to pay for anything; someone had always taken care of it for him. The attention was addictive and Jake enjoyed it immensely.

It had taken him a while to adjust to college life. He hadn't immediately experienced the hero worship he had back home, but never did he doubt his destiny. By his junior year he was once again back on top. He knew beyond a shadow of a doubt that he was headed straight for the NFL and becoming a household name.

Jake's performance in the opening game of his senior season ended up on a sports highlight reel. The media buzz surrounding him rose to a frenzy after his impeccable performance in game two. Three games into the season, there were rumors of NFL scouts; everything that Jake had always dreamed of was within his grasp. He continued to play with a focus and energy that amazed not only his opponents but also the variety of NFL scouts who had reached out to him. Once again people waited on him after his games to get an autograph, every restaurant he entered someone was there to pick up his tab. His life felt like it had righted itself, like it was back the way it should be.

Six games into the season, a fierce tackle had broken his leg and crushed his dreams. He had refused to listen to the doctors when they told him he would never play the game he loved again. But after several surgeries and disappointing results in his therapy, Jake had sunk into a dark, lonely place, shutting out everyone and everything he had once held dear. The loss of the future he had felt destined for was a crippling blow to him. His pride hurting, he refused to see teammates and friends who tried to visit him. He hated the sympathetic look in their eyes and their cliché platitudes trying to convince him that things would be okay and that God had a plan. He wanted to let them know that he had also had a plan, and now it was ruined. He didn't want another plan, he wanted the one he had dreamed of his entire life. The one that left him a football star and the lifestyle that came with that. He had dreamed of the day that he would visit his hometown and have people stare at him in envy as he led the perfect life. Now he would never have people looking at him and admiring his life.

But worse than all of that, worse than every sympathetic look he had ever received combined, was the look of utter and complete disappointment he saw in his father's eyes. In fact, he despised it so much that he began to avoid spending time with his father altogether. It didn't take long for him to realize the doctors had been right and he would never play again. He dropped out of college right before the last semester of his senior year began. He distanced himself from anyone who might remind him of what he had lost, letting his anger fuel him. Pride kept him from showing any weakness; the last thing he wanted was for anyone to see inside his hurt. He refused phone calls and he could still remember sitting quietly on his couch while his father knocked repeatedly on his door, imploring him to let them inside. Anger and pride would not let him open up and let his father in. He would show them all. He would prove to everyone that he was still destined for success. In those moments he promised himself that when he returned to Bluff Creek, the sympathetic looks that overtook people's faces when they saw him, the solemn whispers behind hands and sad shakes of heads, would be replaced with envy and admiration.

He had known Whitney before his accident, but had reconnected with her after he had distanced himself from his family and friends. She didn't look at him with sympathy or pity in her eyes and she lived the lifestyle that Jake had always dreamed about. Whitney Peterson's father owned the premier real estate agency for the Gulf Coast. He negotiated multimillion-dollar beach home development deals before most people got out of bed in the mornings and had the glamorous lifestyle that went along with such high-stakes real estate investments. Mike Peterson, or Mr. Peterson, as Jake still called him even after dating his daughter for several years, was a commanding presence. He knew how to work a room and cut a business deal and was like no one Jake had ever met before. The Petersons had wealth, prestige, popularity, and respect, the exact life Jake had felt had been robbed from him. He had pursued Whitney, and hindsight being what it is, he wasn't sure what drew him—her or the opportunities that being with her offered to him. Honestly, it wasn't something he liked to think about too long.

He pulled down the quiet tree-lined street he had grown up on as he heard Whitney mumble the word *Mayberry* under her breath. He pulled his car into the driveway, the same driveway he had pulled into a million times as a kid, and studied his parents' bungalow-style house with its deep front porch and towering trees in the front yard. Conflicting emotions warred inside him. He couldn't help but feel a tug of pleasure at being back in his childhood home. He had too many wonderful memories to feel anything but some happiness at returning.

But he also knew that staying away as long as he had would have an impact on his welcome. It's not that he didn't speak to his parents. There were the occasional phone calls, text messages, and social media posts that kept him in contact; more with his mom than his dad. His parents had visited him and Whitney at their beachfront condo last summer and while his mom had seemed thrilled to spend time with her only child, he couldn't help but feel the disappointment emanating from his father, and honestly Jake had felt some relief when his parents had left.

"Quaint." Whitney pulled her designer sunglasses to the end of her nose and studied the house.

"Whitney." He turned to glare at her. "Don't do that."

"What?" She turned to him defensively.

"You know what. Don't act like everything is beneath you." He jerked his car door open, suddenly eager to be out of the car.

Whitney quickly jumped from the car and marched around the hood to face him. "Don't you forget that this isn't who you are anymore." She poked her perfectly manicured nail into his chest. "You are Jake Rawlings, a successful businessman, who just happens to be engaged to an equally successful, up and coming real estate mogul. We are destined to be a power couple. We are not destined for small homes on side streets of small towns."

He closed his eyes tightly, shaking his head, but before he could respond he opened his eyes to see his mother step out onto the porch, a tight smile on her face, followed by his father. Something innate in him drew him to his mother. He stepped around Whitney and quickly walked to the top of the steps, pausing only briefly before he stepped into his mother's outstretched arms.

"It's good to have you home," Mary Rawlings whispered, clutching her son as if at any moment he might vanish into thin air. Jake held her close, trying not to think about why he did it. Was he glad to see his mother, or was he avoiding the commanding presence of his father, Coach Jim Rawlings, standing behind her? Before he could decide if he could get by with avoiding his father for the entirety to his trip, Jim cleared his throat and stretched out his hand as his mother released him.

"Son."

Jake took his father's hand and gave a curt nod. "Coach." For a brief moment, he thought his father was going to pull him into a hug, but before the coach could act, Whitney cleared her throat loudly behind them. Jake was simultaneously relieved and irritated.

"Hello," Whitney sang out in a singsong voice, quickly stepping forward and taking over the situation. "It is so good to see you again, Mary." She quickly hugged his mother and gave her an air kiss. "And my, my, Coach, you are looking as fit as ever." Whitney patted his father's arm and Jake cringed. She was completely oblivious to Coach's steely gaze as she took his arm and turned him toward the front door. "Coach, I am just so sorry to hear about your daddy. I understand Shep was quite the character." Jake winced at her sugary tone, knowing his father was a no-nonsense man and wouldn't be moved by her act.

"He was definitely one of a kind," Coach responded and then

added as he glanced at his son, "Too bad you didn't get a chance to meet him."

Jake bit the inside of his cheek to keep from responding and held the screen door open for his mother. He was surprised to see not much had changed on the inside. The stairway in the foyer still held a gallery of pictures featuring him at various stages growing up. The family photo, including Shep, taken during Jake's senior year of high school, still hung over the fireplace. Jake stopped to study the picture, and was momentarily overcome with grief. His grandfather had been an intricate part of his childhood. Unfortunately, Jake's self-imposed exile from Bluff Creek had kept him apart from Shep, along with the rest of the family.

He jumped as his mother touched his arm. "He went peacefully in his sleep." And then she quietly added as her fingers lightly touched his cheek, "He loved you so much."

As he placed his arm over her shoulders and squeezed, he looked up and met his father's gaze across the room. Jake couldn't quite decipher the look in his father's face; for a moment he thought his father was going to cross the room and join them, but instead he cleared his throat and announced, "It's about time to go. Shep was always there for us, we need to be there for him."

Jake couldn't help but take the comment as a personal shot at his absence from the family. He dropped his arm from his mother's shoulders and went to retrieve his suit from the car, not even trying to keep the screen door from slamming behind him.

****

Jake's feet hurt from standing for hours beside his parents receiving what seemed to be every citizen in three counties; his cheeks hurt from the fake smile he kept plastered across his face. His mother stood between Jake and his father, silently forcing them to be civil. To the outside observer they looked like a loving, yet grieving family; Jake felt, however, that on the inside they were barely able to stand being in the same room together. He glanced over at the front pew to see Whitney frantically typing on her cell phone. When there was a lull in the line of people wanting to pay their respects to Shep, Jake quickly strode to her, sliding in beside her.

"What are you doing?" he hissed quietly, glancing around the room to see if anyone might be watching them.

She looked at him as if he had sprouted two heads and answered an octave too loud, "I'm checking my email because we are finally in the one place in this Godforsaken town that has decent Wi-Fi. Did you know your parents don't even have Wi-Fi?"

"Whitney, we are at the funeral home for my grandfather's visitation. Put the phone away." He glanced to see if his parents were watching him and jumped, startled, as Mary sat down beside her son and patted his arm. "I've got to sit down for a minute. Have you ever seen so many people? Everybody loved Shep."

He slipped his arm around his mother's shoulders. "They sure did."

"And your father, a lot of your dad's players have come through to pay respects."

Jake picked at imaginary lint on his pants; he didn't want to think about the way all his father's players loved and respected him. He had once been so proud to be Coach's son, but that was before — before he had crushed not only his dreams, but also his father's by getting hurt.

"Jake." His mother turned to face him but before she could finish, Whitney's phone rang out, causing heads all over the funeral home to turn in their direction.

"I have got to take this," Whitney announced. At least she had the decency to walk into the hallway before she answered, Jake thanked God for small miracles. His mother cleared her throat and he turned his head to meet her gaze.

Mary opened her mouth to speak and then stopped, dropping her gaze to her lap and then looking back up into her son's troubled eyes. He knew immediately why his mother was concerned.

"She's just different, Mom. She wasn't raised in a small town where everybody and their brother shows up at the funeral home and stays for hours. Her dad raised her and he has taught her to be an amazing businesswoman, but maybe he didn't focus on manners or tact so much." His voice trailed off, but then he quickly added, "But she's good person, Mom, and she's going to be your daughter-in-law." he leaned forward, resting his forearms on his knees, wondering who he was trying to convince more, his mother or himself.

Mary patted his back. "I'm sure she's lovely...in her own way."

He leaned back and turned to his mother, and something behind them caught his eye. He suddenly felt as if all the air had spontaneously left the room. He dragged in a deep breath and it felt as if it caught in his throat. The room tilted on its axis and the air temperature skyrocketed as sweat beaded on his forehead. He reached up and loosened the collar of his shirt, trying hopelessly to draw in another breath. His face must have shown his distress, and his mother turned to see what had caused his reaction.

"What is she doing here?" he whispered harshly as he ducked his head.

"Who?" his mother asked sweetly, trying to smother the smile playing across her lips.

He cut his eyes. "You know who, Mom. Jules, what is Jules doing here?"

"Oh, you mean Julie?" She turned to watch the figure in question approach Coach at his post beside Shep's casket. "Well, like you said, son, it's a small town, everyone is here."

"Did you call her? Did you tell her?" he accused.

"What? No!" His mother turned back to him. "I know you've been gone a while, but surely you haven't forgotten how quickly word travels in Bluff Creek."

It took Jake a minute to respond. "Wait...are you telling me Jules—" He stopped and corrected himself; she had only been Jules to him, but she hadn't been his for a long time, "I mean

Julie, lives in Bluff Creek?"

"Yes, she moved back about three years ago to take over the diner when Etta died."

"Etta died?" Jake's heart sank as he thought of the tough little woman who had run the town's only restaurant for as long as he could remember. Etta was Julie's only living relative that he knew of. "Why didn't you tell me?"

"I called you, dear. You were in Hawaii; you didn't answer."

He glanced nervously toward Julie, still standing arm in arm with his father in front of Shep's casket.

"Why don't you go say hello?" his mother encouraged, nodding toward the casket.

"No!" he said a little too forcefully.

"Jake," his mother admonished, "you two were inseparable for years, it would be rude not to speak to her."

"I think I'll check on Whitney." He stood quickly and almost didn't hear his mother mumble under her breath that she was sure Whitney didn't need anyone checking on her. He ignored his mother's comment. He had to get out of that room before his past caught up to his present.

Chapter 3 *Choices*

"For there is nothing hidden that will not be disclosed, and nothing concealed that will not be known or brought out into the open." Luke 8:17

She had known he would be there. No matter what had happened between him and his parents, she knew he couldn't stay away when it came to Shep, even if it was to say goodbye. She had been privileged with a front row seat to the close relationship Jake had enjoyed with his grandfather as he grew up, having spent many days with Jake and Shep on the riverfront farm the family owned and that Shep had lived on until his age had caused him to move to town. The moment she had heard about Shep's passing her thoughts had turned to Jake. She knew no matter the anger she carried toward Jake, she would always have a soft spot for him too.

She had spotted him the moment she had entered the room, sitting beside his mother, his long arm slung loosely around her shoulders. The sight of him had stopped her in her tracks. She had rehearsed this moment over and over in her mind for the past six years. Would she rail at him, taking all the hurt and pain out on him, or would she pretend to be indifferent and hide the struggles she had faced since he left her? Each day over the past six years seemed to bring a different fantasy about how she would greet him when at last they were face to face again.

She was prepared — outwardly she appeared cool and calm; inwardly she was a mess. In the end, it didn't matter because he left the room, relieving them both from the awkward reunion.

Coach had pulled her into his arms and whispered how much Shep had loved her. A tear slipped from her eye as she pulled back and whispered to Coach how special Shep had been to her. Since she had taken over her grandmother's diner, Shep had eaten lunch there almost every day. She had few memories growing up in Bluff Creek that didn't include Shep and the entire Rawlings family. When Julie was the tender age of eight, her mother had dropped her at her grandmother's for the summer and had forgotten to return to pick up her only child. Etta Wooten had raised her only granddaughter as best she could while running the only diner in Bluff Creek. There had been many late nights spent doing homework and falling asleep in the storeroom while the last of the day's customers lingered over the diner's famous apple pie and coffee.

It was that same summer when she found Jake Rawlings hiding behind the dugout in the local park reading *The Adventures of Huckleberry Finn*. At the time she didn't understand why he had been so upset when she walked up to him and said hello. He had panicked and tossed the book into the bushes a few feet away. She had retrieved it and tried to return it to him as he profusely refused to acknowledge it was his. She called his bluff and pointedly told him she had seen him reading it just mere minutes before. He glanced around nervously before demanding her sworn oath to tell no one she had caught him reading. He had explained he was a jock, after all, not a bookworm. Julie hadn't understood why he couldn't be both and had told him as much. She guessed he hadn't trusted her not to tell somebody about his secret bookworm status, because beginning the next day, and for every day the rest of the summer, he showed up at the diner and the two had become inseparable.

Sometime between summer break and school starting, she had started eating dinner with the Rawlings at least once a week, oftentimes staying with the family until Etta closed the diner and came to pick her up. The boys at school tried to tease Jake about having a girl as his best friend, but when you are the cool kid and your dad is a legendary high school football coach, you didn't get teased very often or for very long. Everyone seemed to accept that Jake and Julie were the best of friends, and no one batted an eye when in high school they became more than friends and began dating.

She had always known he felt pressure to be an athlete simply because of who his father was. He felt he was expected to excel on the field, and every action off the field should be made to improve his play. By the time they were in high school, he was being recruited by colleges. She knew that wanting to get an offer from the right school added to the pressure that he felt. He often told her that she was his safe space; the one person who never expected anything from him. She simply accepted who he was and allowed him to let his guard down and be himself. He didn't have to be Jake Rawlings, superstar football player, when she was around; he could just be Jake Rawlings, a teenager who loved football and secretly loved to read.

When he had left town to go to college, they had committed to making their long-distance relationship work. But with his commitments to the team and her attending a smaller college closer to home and working in her grandmother's diner, the relationship had suffered. Julie remembered counting down the days until he would be home for their first Christmas break. Each day leading up to his return had seemed to stretch well beyond twenty-four hours. She lay awake at night, dreaming of the reunion. She could almost feel his arms around her as she anticipated his return.

She had expected him to immediately stop at the diner when he got into town; instead he called her several hours after his arrival. The moment she stepped foot into his house, she knew something was different. She had thrown her arms around him, so happy to be back in his embrace, and he had quickly detached himself from her. For the two weeks he had been home, they rarely spent time alone, but instead always had one of his friends with them or his parents or even Shep. She pushed her worries out of her mind and tried to focus on the positives of the visit, telling herself that he had a small window of time at home and everyone wanted a piece of his time and attention. She had spent hours planning the perfect present for him, a scrapbook that highlighted all his accomplishments on the football field since he was a little boy. He had given her a university sweatshirt.

At the end of the two weeks, as he was packing his car to return to school, he had broken the news to her that he thought they should end their relationship. She would never forget standing in his driveway as he stood there, fists in his jeans pockets, shrugging his shoulders and avoiding her tear-filled gaze. He had told her he needed to focus on football if he ever hoped to make it to the NFL, and that he couldn't do that as long as he felt obligated to her. To this day she hated the word *obligated*. She had put up a brave front and had kept from having a complete meltdown in his driveway, but as soon as he had pulled away and was out of view, she had collapsed. She couldn't control her body as it crumpled on the concrete beneath her feet. It may have been mere moments, or it could have been hours, before she felt Coach's gentle hands lifting her up and carrying her inside. As weeks stretched into months, the one person that Julie had believed would be in her life forever faded into nothing more than a painful memory.

After weeks of Etta assuring her she would be fine without him, Julie had transferred to a bigger university, hoping to immerse herself in school and forget about her heartbreak. And for three years, she had attempted every day to embrace her current life and forget about how she thought her life would turn out. She had embraced every opportunity that college had offered her; internships, traveling abroad, and even meeting a handsome young law school student named Eric.

Eric had been exactly what her broken heart had needed. He had been sweet and attentive. He had been patient and romantic. And while Julie's head told her that she should be madly in love with him, her heart constantly reminded her that he was not Jake. Mad at herself for not being able to let Jake's memory fade, she dedicated herself to being the perfect girlfriend. But no matter how hard she tried, something was missing from the relationship. As Eric hinted of future, long-term commitments, she panicked and suddenly made plans to attend graduate school.

In the fall of her senior year, news spread quickly of Jake's career-ending injury. She had watched it repeatedly on the ESPN highlight reel, cringing each time and chewing her fingernails in worry. She stalked the internet looking for updates on his condition and reached out to everyone she knew in Bluff Creek who might have news of his condition.

Guilt ate at her as Eric set about planning the perfect holiday for her while she secretly sought news of Jake and his injury. By mid-December, Julie had given Eric a halfhearted excuse about spending a quiet Christmas with her grandmother before graduating and heading to grad school. Julie headed home to Bluff Creek before Eric could attempt to join her, secretly hoping to find news of Jake. She would never forget the night that plan had finally fallen into place.

The streets were crowded as the Christmas parade made its way through town. Julie had stood outside the diner with her grandmother just as she had for so many years. And while she kept her eyes on the festivities, she couldn't help but scan the crowd for the tall familiar frame of Jake Rawlings. She mentally chastised herself for letting someone she hadn't spoken to in three years take up so much of her thoughts. She told herself that it was friendly concern, nothing more. They had been friends long before they were anything more, she convinced herself.

Finally, she caught a glimpse of him across the street. His tall athletic frame was easy to pick out among the crowd of onlookers. She shuffled back into the crowd so she could watch him without being noticed. He was standing with a few of his buddies from high school, one of whom must have said something amusing as a smile broke over his face. Only Julie couldn't help notice that it didn't quite reach his eyes.

After the parade passed them by, the onlookers began

making their way to the town square for the lighting of the Christmas tree. Julie quickly moved into position far enough behind Jake that she could watch him without being noticed. When they arrived at the town square, she guided her grandmother, Etta, to the opposite side from Jake and tried to slip into the shadows.

She had turned to speak to someone she had gone to high school with, and when she turned back to the Christmas tree, her eyes collided with his. They held each other's gaze across the town square; time seemed to stop and everyone around them faded away. He never took his eyes off her as he made his way across the crowded space, stopping mere inches from her.

"Hey," he whispered, his voice thick with emotion.

"Hey," she replied, her voice soft and wavering. She straightened her shoulders and cleared her throat. "How are you?" She glanced down at his leg, still encased in a brace.

"It's healing. Doc says hopefully I won't limp the rest of my life." She couldn't help but notice the bitterness that he didn't even try to keep out of his voice.

"Jake, I'm so sorry. I know this is hard for you." Involuntarily she reached out and touched his hand. Warmth spread up her arm and through her body.

He studied her for a long time before he spoke. "You want to get out of here? Go someplace we can talk?"

She caught her breath at his question, but quickly nodded her head in agreement. He never let go of her hand as he led her through the shadows of the crowd. Neither of them spoke as they wound their way through empty streets until they reached his truck. He opened the door and gestured for her to climb in. At first the conversation was awkward, each wary of the other. But as he drove the dirt roads they had cruised as teenagers, they both loosened up, they both relaxed, and the easy companionship they had enjoyed since they were children slowly returned. He told her about the pressures of college football, admitting to her how hard it was to go from somebody everyone knew to a virtual nobody. She couldn't help but wonder if those insecurities had been the driving force behind their breakup. She told him about Eric, feeling a small sliver of pleasure when Jake stiffened as she mentioned Eric wanted to get married some day. When Jake finally stopped the truck, they were sitting in the driveway of Shep's riverfront farmhouse.

"Shep moved to town a few months ago," Jake explained. "Mom and Dad wanted him closer to them so they could keep an eye on him. He's not getting any younger."

"I can't imagine Shep letting anyone keep an eye on him." She laughed nervously.

"Want to go in? I know where he hides the key." Jake studied her intently as he wound his fingers into hers. The emotions that passed between them in that gaze didn't require words. She knew exactly what he was asking. She also knew exactly what would happen if she agreed, and in that moment she wanted nothing more than to be with Jake. She nodded her head and he moved as quickly as he could to open the door for her. He captured her hand again as she exited the truck and neither of them spoke as he found the hidden key to the back door.

As soon as they entered the darkened house, Jake turned to face her, never releasing her hand. He traced the planes of her face, feathered his fingers down her throat, and pulled her close to his body.

"I've missed you," he whispered before he dipped his head and lightly kissed her lips. Her body responded to the light touch of his lips. Desire sliced through her body as she stepped closer to him and wrapped her arms around his waist. Their eyes met, and her stomach dropped at the intensity of his gaze. He unwrapped her arms from around him and as he took her hand he took a step down the hallway. She was grounded to the floor, unable to follow him, and when their arms stretched between them, he turned and met her gaze. Years of unspoken words passed between them in those brief moments.

He pulled her arm toward him and slowly motioned his head toward the bedroom door she knew was just down the hall. For a moment she wavered, dropping her gaze to the floor. Images of Eric floated through her mind; the pain Jake had caused when he broke up with her tried to surface, but when she looked back up into his piercing eyes, all she could feel was the love she had felt for him since they were kids. The wave of emotions for him engulfed her and before her rational mind could take over, her feelings won out and she took a step toward him.

As they stepped into the bedroom, he turned to her, catching her up in his embrace. He dipped his head and whispered how beautiful she was; how much he had missed her. His lips met hers and they both poured all their jumbled emotions into the kiss. He stepped back and looked intently into her eyes, as if asking her to continue. She chewed the inside of her lip, and she could hear the voice of reason telling her to back away and slow things down. She contemplated what life had been like without him, and realized how she had been longing for him since they had broken up. No matter what happened in her life, she always thought about him and what he was doing, how he would react to events and decisions in her life. In that moment she decided to take what he offered, something she had never taken from him before or from anyone, for that matter. She threw caution to the wind and stepped into his embrace.

The next morning she had found him in the kitchen gazing out the back door toward the river that lay at the edge of the pasture, sipping a steaming cup of coffee. She had slipped her arms around him and pleasure was immediately replaced with sickening dread when he stiffened and stepped out of her embrace.

"Hey…I found some coffee in the pantry," he had said as he refused to meet her gaze and busied himself pouring her a cup. He kept himself at arm's length when he offered the cup. He took a deep breath, looked back out the window over the pasture, and began, "About last night…"

She swallowed hard as the room began to spin and a roaring filled her ears. She saw his mouth moving but couldn't decipher what he was saying. His words finally found their way through the noise and she heard him say, "I think we should just chalk last night up to a great memory and go back to our normal lives. My life is complicated right now…and I…"

He faltered and she quickly gathered herself. "Please take me back to Etta's."

Some emotion she didn't want to examine too closely flashed over his face before he answered, "Of course."

She didn't speak as they drove back to town and he pulled into Etta's driveway.

"Jules." His voice sounded strained as he stopped the truck and turned to her.

She held her palm up toward him and tried to make her voice sound light. "Don't, Jake. Let's not do this. Like you said, last night was…." She choked on the words and couldn't get another sound to come out of her mouth. Without looking at him she had opened the truck door, straightened her shoulders, and never looked back as she marched toward her grandmother's home.

Today, as she dressed to attend the funeral, fear and old memories threatened to overtake her. She questioned every decision she had made, from that painful moment in Shep's kitchen until now. She glanced at the Bible verse from the book of Joshua taped to her mirror.

"Have I not commanded you? Be strong and courageous. Do not be afraid; do not be discouraged, for the LORD your God will be with you wherever you go."

She closed her eyes and willed herself to believe God's promise, but as always in the back of her mind she doubted. Could God be with someone who was a liar? Who continued to lie every day of their lives? She pushed down the guilt that threatened to consume her. She did what she had to do. She did what was necessary; she just had to keep telling herself that.

Chapter 4 *Prodigal Son*

"For what will it profit a man if he gains the whole world and forfeits his soul…"Matthew 16:26

Jake absently rubbed his aching leg as he sipped coffee in the early morning dawn. He had risen before anyone else in the house and quietly slipped outside to enjoy the stillness of the morning from his parents' front porch. He soaked up the quiet as the entire town seemed to still be asleep except for him, and the calmness of his surroundings helped soothe him. He hadn't slept well and this morning he felt restless and anxious. As much as he wanted to blame it on Whitney's disastrous behavior when she found out that not only would they be spending the night, but that his parents were decidedly old-fashioned and had prepared Jake a bed on the couch for the evening, deep down he knew it had more to do with seeing Julie than anything Whitney had done. He was used to Whitney's spoiled behavior and for the most part he ignored it. He was not used to seeing a grown-up and gorgeous version of his high school sweetheart and he didn't like his reaction.

The moment he had seen her last night, his mind had immediately gone back to the last time they had been together. Regret and agony warred inside for supremacy when he thought about that morning. If he closed his eyes, he could still remember exactly how it felt to see her across the town square that night. When their eyes had collided, his heart had pounded so loudly that he couldn't hear, couldn't think, all he could do was move toward her. Every pain, every emotion, and every trial he had gone through in the time since high school had seemed almost healed in her presence. In those hours he had stolen away with her, he had forgotten his troubles, he had forgotten his crushed dreams. For a moment he had been just a guy laughing and talking with the girl of his dreams and everything about it had felt right. Her laugh, her touch, the way she slid her eyes up at him, fueled a desire in him that he had never experienced before.

During their courtship, they had never crossed that line. Both had been raised in homes where church attendance was mandatory, along with the idea that the intimacy found between two people was best saved for marriage. After four years away from home and from his church upbringing, his moral compass had drifted slightly from due north. He knew in that moment that he had never wanted anything or anyone as much he wanted her.

He had awoken the next morning, sat up on the edge of the bed, and hung his head. She would expect things from him now. Things he just couldn't give; things like a home and life in Bluff Creek. When he thought about a simple life, working every day at some job he hated and coming home to an ordinary house on a street like his parents', he started to feel suffocated. There was no way he would come back here and be faced daily with the disappointing looks that reminded him of his failures.

And while a successful life as a professional athlete was no longer attainable, he had glimpsed a life with Whitney far beyond what anything in Bluff Creek offered him. A small voice inside of him had tried to reason with him; had tried to tell him he could have a good life with Julie right here in his hometown. But the stronger voice of pride told him he couldn't live the rest of his life with everyone in town looking at him with disappointed eyes and talking about what his life could have been like if he had made it to the pros.

He had left the bed and quickly dressed. He briefly

contemplated leaving while she was still asleep, but decided even he wasn't that much of a coward. With his mind made up he refused to let doubt creep in, no matter how hard it tried. When she had stepped behind him that morning and wrapped her arms around him, he had momentarily wanted to give in and wrap himself up in her embrace. He almost tossed the world's opinion of him aside along with his overabundance of pride and grabbed hold of the happiness that she offered him.

But something stopped him and he had jumped headfirst into his decision to distance himself from her. He didn't want to think about the times since then that he had wondered what would have happened if he hadn't taken that path. What would have happened if he had returned her embrace and led her back the bedroom like his heart longed to that morning?

But instead, he had crushed her and the last time he gazed into her eyes, he had seen the disappointment in them. The same disappointment he saw when he looked into his father's eyes; the same disappointment he received from the majority of residents of Bluff Creek. He had gritted his back teeth as he pulled from her driveway, determined that one day he would come back to this town and the disappointing looks he received from everyone would be replaced with pride and maybe a little envy once again.

The clap of the screen door brought him out of his reverie, as his father stepped onto the porch. They nodded to each other as Coach took a seat in the rocking chair and mumbled, "Morning."

They sipped their coffee quietly and Jake rolled his shoulders, feeling the tension rise in his body in the presence of his once beloved father.

"Sleep good?" his father asked and Jake jumped at the sound of his voice.

"Um, yeah," Jake responded, studying the dark liquid in his cup to keep from meeting his father's gaze. "You?" he asked and his father nodded his reply. They sat silently for a few moments and Jake couldn't help but reflect how much things had changed between them. When most of his friends had become rebellious and resentful of their parents as teenagers, he had seemed to be closer than ever with his father. They shared a love for sports and a dream for Jake to play in the NFL. Jake didn't like to think about how much it hurt that his father had loved the dream of the NFL more than he had loved his own son. When he could take the silence no more he cleared his throat. "How's the team going to be this year?"

His father glanced up at him and then out toward the street, studying some unseen object. "Pretty good, I think. Got a few key players returning and a few promising freshmen."

Jake nodded. "Gonna make a run for the championship?"

A smile broke on Coach's face as he lifted his mug and winked. "That's always the plan."

Jake asked about the some of the assistant coaches for his father's high school team and was surprised to find out several had retired in recent years. He hadn't thought about his father being old enough to retire, but he mentally calculated his dad's age and realized he could have retired years ago. They spoke easily of the program that his dad had led since before Jake's birth, reminiscing about events, winning moments, and people who had come through the program. Jake's heart warmed as it seemed the disappointment from his father waned for the moment.

When Whitney breezed through the front door exclaiming she had looked everywhere for him and planted a much too long kiss on his lips, Jake didn't even try to hide his annoyance. He glanced up at his father to see the twinkle that had sparked in his eyes during their conversation was gone, and the familiar disappointment was back.

His father stood and cleared his throat as Whitney snuggled a bit too close to Jake's side. "Funeral is at eleven. I guess we need to be there early." Jim hesitated at the door and turned back to them. "Jake." He swallowed hard as he met his son's expectant gaze.

"Yeah, Dad?" Jake leaned forward, shaking loose from Whitney's snare.

"There is a will...Shep's will. There will be a reading. You need to be here for that."

Jake nodded, but before he could speak Whitney snaked her arms around his neck and interjected, "So will that be done sometime today, Coach? We really need to get back on the road."

Jake had seen the look that stole across Coach's face before. It was the look he had reserved for players who had just used up their last bit of goodwill with him. The coldness that crept in Jim's eyes caused Jake to sit up straight and remove Whitney's arms from around his neck.

"No, Whitney." Coach's voice was emotionless. "Today we are going to bury my father, one of the greatest men I have ever known, and the will reading will be done after a respectful amount of time. If you need to get on the road, please don't let us keep you from it."

Whitney's mouth fell agape as Coach let the screen door slam behind him. "Well, that was rude." She huffed as she rearranged her bathrobe, oblivious to Jake's incredulous gaze. When she finally looked at Jake's face she threw her hands up and questioned, "What?"

Jake was at a loss for words as he stood and headed for the door his father had just slammed, stopping briefly before he entered. "Are you really that self-absorbed? Just when I think there is nothing else you can do to surprise me, you take your insensitivity to a whole new level!" And for the second time that morning the screen door to the Rawlings' home slammed shut, breaking the calm silence of the street.

****

The entire town turned out to lay Shep Rawlings to rest. The names and faces of those offering condolences ran together as Jake stood beside his parents yet again in front of Shep's casket. Whitney had the decency to stay off her phone for the most part, but he could tell by her demeanor she was pouting over Coach's, as well as his, treatment of her earlier.

Minutes before the service began he saw Julie slip quietly into the last pew in the room. He quickly turned his gaze to the elderly woman reaching for his hand and tried to force his mind to focus. As the older woman, who had apparently been his second grade teacher, droned on about Shep and what a wonderful person he was, Jake's mind raced, unable to comprehend anything the woman said. Julie was obviously avoiding him. She had walked easily into Coach's embrace the evening before, which caused Jake to wonder how close his parents were with his former girlfriend. Did she still hate him, or had time softened her anger toward him? As the funeral began, the unanswered questions bombarded him. While he tried to focus on the minister's words, all he could think about was if he was consuming as much of Julie's thoughts as she was of his.

After the service and burial, Jake's family and what seemed to be the majority of the town were invited to the basement of the local church for a meal. Jake filled his plate and took a seat at a corner table, still unable to get Julie off his mind. When he realized how often he had been scanning the crowd for a glimpse of her, he focused on his food and tuned out the conversation around him. A passing comment by his mother brought his attention back to the conversation at hand.

"Wait, what did you say, Mom?" He stopped eating and turned to his mother.

"I said, it sure was nice of Julie to provide all this food."

"Julie provided all the food?" Suddenly his mouth seemed dry and his appetite diminished.

"Well, the diner did, but it was Julie's idea." His mother swirled the ice in her cup and reached for the pitcher of tea at the center of the table. Before he could stop himself he grasped her hand to stop her. "Why would she do that?" he asked.

"Well…I don't know, son. Shep ate lunch there every day. I guess she was just trying to be nice." Mary shrugged and reached for the tea again.

Jake met his father's steely gaze from across the table. He knew his father wanted to comment on the situation, but instead he looked from Jake to Whitney, who once again had buried her face in her phone, shook his head, and pushed his chair back. "I need some air," Coach announced as he tossed his napkin on top of his plate and quickly left the room.

****

"Thursday?!" Whitney shrieked.

"SHHH, keep your voice down." Jake knew his tone was harsh but his ability to tolerate Whitney's outbursts had been waning lately. He grabbed Whitney's elbow and guided her across the church parking lot to his car. The sun had dipped deep and cast long shadows over the parking lot as the final mourners left the church.

"Do you realize it is only Monday? Thursday is three days from now." She wrenched her arm from his grasp and planted her feet, refusing to take another step.

Jake glanced around the parking lot nervously, hoping no one was watching them. He then gritted his teeth and seethed, "I am well aware of the order of the days of the week, Whitney. What do you want me to do? That's the day the lawyer has available to read the will. I can't change it." He stood with his hands on his hips and watched her as she chewed her lip. He knew her well enough to know she was contriving a plan.

She took quick paces back and forth in front of him, talking to herself. "If we leave now, we can be home before midnight. I can ask Daddy to push our meeting to tomorrow afternoon, and if the lawyer here can move the will reading to one o'clock on Thursday, we can come and go in a day. Not ideal, but it will work." She tapped her lips with her index finger, all but ignoring Jake in her planning process.

"I'm not leaving today." The words slipped past his lips before he really considered them, but Jake felt tired and the weight of his life pressed on him, causing him to blurt them out. When he thought about the problems waiting for him back in the city, he wanted nothing more than to escape them for a few days, even if that meant looking his father in the eye every day, knowing the disappointment he saw there was reserved solely for him. "You can take the car and go home today, but I'm staying here until Thursday."

The finality in his tone stopped her in her tracks. "Not leaving?" she repeated, coming to a stop in front of him.

"I'm staying here with my family for a few days. You can go home and I'll come home on Friday." He saw the indecision in her eyes and knew immediately that she didn't like his plan. Since the news of Shep's passing and being home, it seemed as if a spotlight had been held on Whitney's bad behavior. Most of the time he overlooked her obnoxious comments and spoiled tendencies, but lately he couldn't quite let them go as easily as he once had. He wasn't exactly excited about being back in his hometown with his parents for a few days, but he needed this time apart from Whitney to do some relationship assessment. The fact that it allowed him to avoid his mounting problems with his business was a bonus. He pulled her to his chest and wrapped her up in his arms, and immediately felt disgusted with himself, but pushed those feelings aside. "Look, I know you need to work and I need to try to mend some fences with my family."

She leaned away from him and stuck out her bottom lip. "I just don't like leaving you here. This isn't your home anymore; you belong with me."

He stepped back and dropped his arms from around her. "It's just for a few days, Whitney."

"What about The End Zone?"

"I'll call Scott; I'm sure he can keep an eye on things until I get back."

Whitney rolled her eyes at the sound of Scott's name. "Daddy didn't help you get The End Zone open just so Scott can run it into the ground."

Jake shoved his hands in his pockets and rolled his shoulders, trying to choose his words carefully. "Scott can handle it for a few days."

"I don't know about this, Jake... How are you going to get home?"

"I'll get Dad to drive me down after the will reading." Jake surprised himself when he heard the words rolling off his tongue. The lies just kept coming to him so easily.

Whitney continued to pout and Jake could tell her mind was searching for an alternative solution that suited her. She finally replied with a huff, "I guess I have no choice."

Jake didn't want to think about the thrill of excitement that raced through him when she conceded, nor did he want to think about the fact that before too much longer he would have to face his relationship issues. For now he was content with knowing he would have the week to hide from all of his problems.

****

Jake lazily pushed his feet against the wooden porch, putting the porch swing into motion. He stretched his arms over his head and could not remember the last time he had felt so relaxed. In the two days since Whitney had left, Jake felt as though he had been rejuvenated by his surroundings. On Tuesday, he had spent the entire day out at Shep's farm on the river. He had fished a little, hiked paths along the river he hadn't been on since he was a kid, and overall enjoyed just being alone. He thought about Shep and the relationship he had shared with his grandfather and when regret tried to eat at him, he intentionally pushed it away. He had avoided the house, knowing if he stepped a foot inside, that the memories of his night with Julie would threaten to ruin his newfound peace. He knew at some point, he might have to deal with those memories, but for now he would keep them pushed aside.

On Wednesday he had slept in and spent the morning in his childhood home, enjoying the peace and comfort he found there. He had visited his mother at work, her face beaming when he strolled through the door, and had walked around the town square visiting various stores, some old, some new, for the rest of the afternoon. Now he was relaxing on his parents' front porch after eating one of the best home-cooked meals he could remember. He studied the quiet street and briefly thought how nice it might be to live there. He immediately sat up and stopped the swing as the traitorous thought invaded his mind.

He had a business to run and a fiancée who would definitely not agree with him on the prospects of living in Bluff Creek, but still he couldn't deny the peacefulness that he felt at being home.

The peacefulness was interrupted when his father let the screen door close loudly behind him as he took a seat in the rocking chair across from Jake. Coach took a deep breath and released it. Jake had avoided being alone with his father as much as possible the last few days. While his mother acted thrilled that he had returned, Coach still seemed to be giving Jake the cold shoulder. He watched the older man slowly begin rocking and waited with bated breath as Coach took a sip of his iced tea. Just when Jake was about to break the silence and ask his father what he wanted, Coach spoke quietly.

"Will reading is tomorrow."

Jake stopped the swing altogether. "Yes sir," he responded and waited for Coach's next move.

"Whitney coming back?" Coach cut his eyes from the amber liquid in his glass he had been studying to his son.

"Uh, no, I think I convinced her to stay at home."

Coach nodded his head and Jake couldn't decide if it was in approval or disdain.

"I went out to the farm yesterday." Jake hated how small talk seemed so strained with the man he had once found so easy to talk to.

Coach nodded his head and studied his glass again. "I've been meaning to find someone to take care of it, maybe rent the house, but I haven't."

Jake studied his dad and suddenly realized his father looked old. "It looked like everything was holding up good to me."

Coach nodded. "Shep would kill me if he thought I let the place go to ruin."

"You've been busy, Dad." Jake let the name slip off his tongue and a warmth spread through him. He had always vacillated between calling his father "Dad" and "Coach." Since Jake's injury, he had always called him Coach.

"Yeah, well, that's true. But aren't we all?" Coach gazed

down the street at nothing in particular.

"How's the team looking? Big game next week, right?" Jake asked, trying to guide the conversation topic to one they could discuss without much emotion.

"Yeah, first game of the season…" Coach kept his gaze on something down the street and Jake knew his father had something on his mind before he continued, "Jake…I… uh…"

"Yeah, Dad?" Jake leaned forward, hating all the hope and emotion he heard in his voice. He was a grown man, with a business and a fiancée, he didn't need his dad's approval, but obviously that didn't keep him from wanting it.

Coach dropped his head and studied the floor of the porch for a long time, leaving Jake gripping the edge of the swing, waiting for him to speak.

"Jake…" Coach began again and then swallowed hard. He looked up at his son and then hurriedly said, "The team sure would love it if you came by practice tomorrow. I know it would mean a lot to the boys."

And with that he quickly stood and disappeared back into the house. Jake sat in the swing watching the screen door slam and his father's back retreat into the house. He couldn't deny that he felt a sense of disappointment and an unrelenting feeling that his father had something else to say. What he couldn't decide was if he really wanted to hear it or not. His phone buzzed in his back pocket and interrupted his thoughts. Expecting it to by Whitney, he immediately decided to ignore the call. To his surprise Scott's number lit up his home screen.

"Hey, man," Jake answered.

"Jake." Scott's voice sounded tight. "Can you talk?"

"Sure. Is everything okay?" Jake began to run through worst-case scenarios in his mind.

"You tell me," Scott countered. "Some guys came in here looking for you."

Nervousness sliced through Jake's stomach. He glanced through the screen door to make sure his parents were out of ear shot, but lowered his voice anyway. "Who was it? What did they say?"

"There was three of them, but one did all the talking. He said his name was Nick and that I should give you this message word for word."

Jake stilled himself, closing his eyes and gritting his teeth. "What was the message?"

"You have one week. That was all he said, that you had one week."

Jake cursed under his breath and closed his eyes. "OK, Scott, thanks for telling me."

"Jake, are you in trouble? These men didn't exactly look like choir boys." Concerned etched Scott's voice.

"It's nothing, Scott, don't think another thing about it." Jake pinched the bridge of his nose and tried to sound nonchalant.

"Jake, if you are in trouble let me help you," Scott pleaded.

"You're helping me by running the bar while I'm away. Thanks again." Jake quickly ended the call, standing to pace the front porch.

He had never had any career plans other than being a professional athlete. After his injury and beginning a relationship with Whitney, she had insisted he go to real estate school and join her father's business. He had barely attended the classes and had fully expected to fail the state licensing exam, but by either a miracle or influence from Whitney's father, he had passed. Six months into his real estate career, without one single sale or prospect of a sale to his credit, he had been approached by Whitney's father. The real estate mogul had picked up a dilapidated beachfront restaurant in an area that was being revitalized. He offered to help Jake renovate the property to get a sports bar started, believing with Jake's popularity it would be a great success.

Jake didn't really have a passion for starting the sports bar, but it sure seemed better than attempting to sell real estate. He agreed and began the work to restore the bar. And while the bar was up to date in every way and appeared to be a smashing success if you judged it by the lines of people waiting to get in, Jake had no experience running a business. Each month when he sat down to balance the books, it seemed as though the bar fell deeper and deeper into debt. He studied the numbers until his head hurt, but was still unable to understand how he could continually lose so much money.

He knew he was in over his head when his payroll checks began to bounce. Faced with angry workers and threats to cut off his water and electricity, he was desperate. He refused to go to Whitney or her father. He could not handle one more person looking at him in disappointment. He had always known guys around the football programs he was associated with who bet on games. Unable to comprehend any other way out of this mess, he took a thousand dollars from the cash register after the bar closed one night and placed a bet with a bookie, known only as Nick. The gamble had paid off and he had been able to keep the water and electricity on.

Unfortunately, while betting on everything from college football to professional hockey had bought him some time, his business skills kept digging a deeper hole for the bar. His luck finally ran out when he lost thousands on a professional baseball game. Barely able to keep the lights on in the bar and meet payroll, there was no way he could cover his gambling loss too. He had put off the local bookie as long as he could, paying him a few hundred dollars along the way to keep the heat off of him. Apparently Nick's patience had worn off, and he was demanding full payment of $20,000 in one week. Jake was broke and had coasted into town on fumes, lying to get a tank of gas. There was no way he could come up with $20,000 in a week's time. He hadn't been able to pay himself a salary from the bar in months and had run up his credit cards to maintain his lifestyle and hide his dilemma from Whitney.

He glanced around his parents' street, unable to find the peace he had felt just moments before. Something in his life had to change, that was apparent. It seemed he had reached the end of his rope.

Chapter 5 *Blindsided*

"There is a way which seemeth right unto a man, but the end thereof are the ways of death."
Proverbs 14:12

  Jake sat nervously tapping his foot and glancing at the clock on the wall of the lawyer's office waiting for the last will and testament of Shepard Hudson Rawlings to begin. He, along with his parents, sat in a quiet conference room waiting for Shep's lawyer to join them, as minutes seemed to stretch into hours. Internally Jake warred with himself. After the phone call from Scott, he hadn't slept, trying to figure out his next move. He knew avoiding the gambling debt was no longer an option. He had to make some decisions and he had to make them quickly. Waves of guilt swept over him as he secretly hoped Shep had left him enough money in his will to pay off this debt. He had promised himself, Shep, and God—not that Jake felt he was listening—that he would never gamble again and would sell the bar if they just saw fit to get him out of this mess. Footsteps on the other side of the door caused Jake to raise his head just in time to see Shep's lawyer, the only lawyer in Bluff Creek, Clay Phillips, hold the door open for Julie Wooten to enter the room.
  As soon as she stepped across the threshold, Jake found it hard to take a deep breath. He looked at her, but she refused to meet his gaze. Nodding a greeting to Coach and his mother, she sat on the opposite of the table, giving all her attention to Clay.

Jake fixed his gaze on his father, trying to see if Julie's presence was a surprise to him, but Coach seemed to be avoiding eye contact.

"Sorry to keep you all waiting, but now that everyone is here, we can get down to business." Clay shuffled a stack of papers and smiled sympathetically at the family. "Part of Mr. Rawlings' wishes were that the four of you named in his will would all be in a room together and that I would cover what were his last wishes. Before I begin, I will say that he mentioned numerous times how much he loved each of you present today and that he wished nothing more than that you would be happy and find joy in your lives." Clay glanced around nervously. Anyone who had lived in Bluff Creek knew the history between Jake and Julie; Clay was no exception. Jake couldn't help but feel a little sorry for Clay being placed in such an uncomfortable position.

Jake fought to keep his eyes focused on Clay; the calm, half smile plastered on his face belied the turmoil inside of him. For the life of him, he could not figure out what Julie was doing here. Obviously Shep had mentioned her in his will, but why? Had she grown that close to the older man since her return? Jake glanced to his left to try and read his mother's expression. But Mary also avoided her son's gaze, telling him that Julie being present was no surprise to her.

Clay cast glances around the room one more time and cleared his throat. "Well, let's get started, shall we?" He paused briefly before he continued, "I won't bore you with a lot of legal jargon. I understand that you all have been through enough in the last week so I will attempt to do this as quickly as possible. Coach, you and Mary have been left Shep's house in town. He held several shares of stock in the local bank along with some bonds; that and the cash in his checking and savings account are all yours."

Clay paused for a moment before he continued.

"Julie, you are listed next." Clay looked up and smiled at Julie and Jake felt a stabbing pain of jealousy that he quickly tried to shove away. He didn't take the time to examine whether the jealous feeling stemmed from the way Clay smiled at Julie or the fact that his beloved grandfather had mentioned her first in his will. He pushed the emotion aside and concentrated on breathing in and out as if he weren't a complete mess on the inside.

"Julie," Clay placed both palms on the table before he continued, "Shep did want to me to say that he was particularly fond of you and your family. And he also wanted me to say that your family has made the last years of his life very enjoyable. With that being said, Shep had one certificate of deposit at the bank in the amount seventy-five thousand dollars, in which you have been named beneficiary. It will mature on the seventeenth of next month, and at that point, you can do whatever you like with the money."

Jake's mouth dropped. He stared at each face in room, and each face, he felt, purposely avoided him. He felt anger rise in his chest.

Clay paused to clear his throat, glanced around the room, and then continued, "Jake."

Jake heard his name being called, but his mind was spinning. His eyes met Clay's and he could see the lawyer's mouth moving, but the roaring in his head and the tightness in his chest kept him unable to decipher the words.

"Jake," Clay repeated, "are you ready?"

Jake opened his mouth to speak, but nothing came out. He felt as if he had been punched in the gut, losing all breath in his body. He cleared his throat, trying to grasp some semblance of calm. He quickly glanced at Julie, who had kept her eyes glued to Clay since the reading had started, and nodded his head for Clay to continue.

Clay turned in his chair to face Jake. "Shep wanted you to have the river farm—all one hundred twenty acres, and all the contents of the house and outbuildings. This bequeath is valued at several hundred thousand dollars, and it belongs solely to you." Clay paused and studied Jake intently and enunciated each word that followed. "Provided you can meet one condition."

Jake's mind raced, and suddenly his mouth became as dry as the creek bank behind Shep's house in the middle of a July heat wave. He couldn't wrap his mind around what was happening and why Shep had left him a farm he had no use for and had left Julie the money he so desperately needed. And now his inheritance had conditions? Desperation welled up in Jake's chest and threatened to overtake him.

"Wait, I'm confused…" Jake stumbled over his words; his tongue seemed thick and stuck to the roof of his mouth. "What are you talking about …a condition?"

Clay straightened his tie and looked uncomfortably around the room. "Jake, the river farm and the contents of the house and buildings are solely yours provided that you make Bluff Creek your primary residence for the next six months."

Mouths collectively dropped around the room, but Julie's gasp turned all eyes toward her. Ever so briefly her eyes met Jake's and the emotion he saw in them and felt in his own body was more than he could handle in this moment. Her face reddened and she quickly dropped her eyes to the floor, refusing to meet anyone's gaze.

Jake blinked, trying to focus on Clay's words. He glanced over at this parents, who were looking at him with a combination of shock and expectancy. He looked again at Julie, who still refused to meet his gaze. He felt as if he was in an alternate universe. His mind struggled to find words to speak but he finally croaked out, "Wait…what? I don't understand."

Clay took a deep breath and loosened his tie. "Jake, I knew this would cause some problems, but Shep was insistent that this is the way he wanted his will written up."

Jake fell back in his chair and rubbed his forehead, trying to grasp what had just happened. He leaned forward, arms stretching across the table. "What is this? I mean…I don't understand. Clay, this has to be some kind of joke."

Clay looked at Jake sympathetically. "No jokes here, Jake. This is what Shep wanted, no, let me say this is what he demanded." Clay leaned forward, folding his arms and resting them on the table. "Look, Jake, I tried to advise him that this was... unheard of, but he insisted."

Jake looked around the room, meeting no one's gaze as the walls seemed to close in on him. Everyone present had received what he needed from Shep—cold hard cash—all except him. He needed the cash his parents or Julie had inherited to pay off his gambling debt and get his feet back on solid ground. As it were right now, he didn't have enough cash to purchase gas for the trip home. He dropped his head to the back of his chair and stared at the ceiling, internally chiding himself for ever getting his hopes up that things would work out in his favor. They never did; why would they start now?

"Jake." Clay stood and placed papers in front of him on the table. "I took the liberty of making you a copy of the will. I assume you will want to have other lawyers look at it."

A ray of hope sprang in Jake's chest. "Do you think there is a loophole?" he blurted out.

Clay studied him for a moment before answering, "I seriously doubt it, Jake. Shep has had me working on this particular part of his will for about two years now. He wanted to make sure there was no way you could bypass his conditions."

Jake studied the papers in front of him, anger welling inside of him at the cruel joke fate was dealing him.

"What if I don't do it? What if I refuse?" Jake couldn't keep the bitterness out of his voice.

Clay glanced around the room and Jake couldn't help but think he was the only one in the room not in on this injustice that he was being served. Clay took a deep breath. "If you choose not to meet the condition of the will, you forfeit your inheritance. Jake." Clay waited until Jake met his gaze. "If you don't do this, you will get nothing."

"What happens to the farm if I don't meet these conditions?" He spat out the last word as if it were poison.

Clay met his gaze and never wavered. "Julie gets the farm if you don't meet the conditions of the will."

****

Julie couldn't keep her body from shaking as she gripped the steering wheel of her car, which was parked behind the diner. She couldn't get out just yet; she had to compose herself first before she went inside and faced Marti, her best employee and best friend. She had been in shock the week before when Clay Phillips had been eating lunch at the diner and asked her to stop by his office to discuss a legal matter. She had panicked, with a million disastrous scenarios running through her mind. In the last six years, Julie had lived in fear that the decisions she had been forced to make in a time of panic and stress would finally come full circle. She had planned to make sure that never happened. Her plans had included staying as far away from Bluff Creek and the Rawlings family as possible.

But life had thrown her one too many curve balls for that to happen. The grandmother who had taken her in when no one else cared about her had needed her. Against her better judgment she had returned to Bluff Creek, taking care of her dying grandmother and then Etta's diner after she passed. It hadn't taken Shep long to become a fixture in the diner, eating at least one meal there a day. They had grown close, but had never spoken about Jake. She couldn't get the image of his shocked face when he had heard Clay explain Shep's last wishes. She had refused to look at him for fear that one look in his pain-stricken eyes would disintegrate all her resolve to stay away from him.

Her hands still shaking, she loosened her grip on the wheel, looked at her reflection in the rearview mirror, and tried to fix her makeup. When the Rawlings family had left the room, she had wept openly. Shep must have realized what a struggle the last few years had been for her financially, how she had prayed for a way to make ends meet. Now he had given her a gift she had never dreamed of.

A tap on the driver's side window caused her to jump and let out a scream. She turned her head just in time to the see the boyish face of her entire world break into a giggle. She opened the door as he squealed, "Mommy!" and jumped in her lap. She held him tight. She finally had the money to give him the life he deserved and make sure all his medical needs were taken care of. And while she and Shep had never discussed her son's paternity, Julie couldn't help but wonder if Shep had somehow known who her son's father was. She saw Jake every time she looked in her son's eyes, or watched him cock his head while he was concentrating. In her mind, there might as well have been a neon sign over his head that blinked continuously stating that he was Jake Rawlings's son. She had never told anyone, not even Etta about their one night together nor had she revealed to anyone who her son's father was. But she couldn't help but think that Shep must have somehow figured it out. And if Shep had figured it out, had he told anyone else?

Fear gripped her and she hugged him tighter. She wasn't exactly proud of her decision to keep her son's paternity a secret, but so many things had led to that decision, and fear had played a big role.

The moment she had returned to school after her Christmas break, she had ended things with Eric. Two months later she had finally accepted the truth that she was pregnant. She occasionally still saw Eric around campus, and didn't want to hurt him by being open about her pregnancy and the circumstances surrounding it. She had decided that she would finish the semester and take the next one off. It was only four months, and she was confident she could hide her pregnancy. She had told no one but Etta, and even then had refused to reveal who the father was and Etta had assumed that the child belonged to Eric. Confronted with the shock of an unexpected pregnancy, she had decided that she would wait until after the semester ended before she told Jake.

In early April she had been scheduled for a routine ultrasound. She had no idea something might possibly be wrong with her baby. She was young and in good shape and of course Jake had always been the picture of health. She had been devastated when the doctor had explained to her that her baby had a heart defect. Essentially he would be born without a heart valve and would need open heart surgery as soon as he could tolerate it after his birth. She had been devastated and had called Etta in a panic. Her grandmother had gotten in her car and driven all night to be by her side.

Unable to concentrate on her classes, she dropped out by the middle of April. She and Etta had rented an apartment within five minutes of the best pediatric heart hospital in the state. Etta had refused to leave her side and had spent the next five months making sure Julie and the baby had the best care available. Doctors repeatedly told Julie to prepare for the worst. Despite Julie's constant prayer that God would take care of her baby, she found herself in a constant state of worry and panic. In those months, she convinced herself that there was no reason to tell Jake about the baby until she knew that everything was going to be okay.

Early one August morning, Huck Isaiah Wooten made his entrance into the world. He had been rushed immediately into ICU and after a few weeks of intensive care, he was ready for his first surgery. The next few months passed by in a haze. Julie was intent only on Huck and the rest of the world faded away as if it didn't exist. She argued with herself that she had too much to deal with at the moment to tell Jake the truth. She would wait until after the next surgery, but the next surgery came and went and she had another excuse for not telling him. She lived in the ICU pod with her baby, never wanting to leave his side. Now, a little over five years later, except for the occasional trip to the cardiologist and the massive scar that dissected his chest, he was a normal little boy and captured the heart of everyone he met. He definitely had gotten his personality from his father.

When Etta had called her with the news of her cancer diagnosis, Julie knew she had to come home and take care of her. Her grandmother had been her lifeline during Huck's birth and subsequent surgeries. In the week before the move, Julie had lain awake at night anticipating all that could go wrong when she brought her little boy back to Bluff Creek. Would the Rawlings take one look at him and know beyond a shadow of a doubt that he was their grandson? And if that happened, would they want to take him from her? Would they tell Jake he had a son? She had kept up with news concerning Jake from a distance through mutual friends and late night social media stalking. She knew that he appeared to lead a charmed life, just like he had always planned. Her life was anything but charmed.

When they had been teenagers they would dream about their life when he was a professional football player and she was his wife. They had dreamed of exotic vacations, a large home, and fine cars. He seemed to be living that dream without her now. She worked hard in Etta's diner trying to make ends meet and take care of her dying grandmother. If he knew about Huck and her financial struggles would he try to take their son away from her? It was a fear she lived with every day. She would do what she had to do to take care of Etta, but as soon as possible she would take her son and leave Bluff Creek.

Much to Julie's horror, Shep was a regular customer in the diner, sometimes showing up for both lunch and dinner. Try as she might to keep Huck hidden in the back office of the diner, the curiosity of the young boy had him sneaking out front every chance he got. It wasn't long until the news was all over town that Etta's granddaughter was back and had a child in tow and no ring on her finger. Shame burned inside Julie and the fear threatened to overtake her. She could take Huck and leave town never to return.

And just as she had decided that was exactly what she must do, the town busybody had come to her rescue. Mrs. Amelia Johnson was a Sunday school teacher, wife of a city councilman and the biggest gossip for three counties. When she knocked on Etta's door with a plate of homemade cookies and a look of sympathy in her eyes, Julie had known exactly why the woman was visiting. Her visit had little to do with Etta's health and more to get a firsthand look at the mysterious child of Etta's wayward granddaughter. Julie had braced herself in the coming days for the Rawlings to storm the diner or Etta's home and demand that she turn Huck over to them. She prepared for the worst, the looks and whispers from townsfolk who had surely heard Mrs. Johnson's story by now.

But much to Julie's surprise, as the days went by she began

noticing how people looked at her sympathetically and several regular customers discreetly slipped her extra tip money. One such customer quietly whispered to her one day that she hoped Julie's ex-fiancé, Eric, suffered every day of his miserable life for abandoning her and her sweet little boy. Julie had never been able to get Etta to admit that she had fed Mrs. Johnson the story, but in the moment she was grateful, even if she did feel the smallest twinge of guilt over besmirching Eric's reputation.

Huck had begun hanging out more and more in the front of the diner and even sat with certain regular customers while they ate. Huck had warily eyed Shep as he had visited the diner for lunch one day. Etta was becoming increasingly ill and Julie had taken over running the diner completely. For weeks Huck had inched closer and closer to the older man when he came in for lunch, until one day Julie noticed her son sitting at a table with Shep, heads hunkered close together, deep in conversation.

Fear had gripped Julie and refused to relinquish its hold. What if Huck did something that would cause Shep to know that Jake was his father? She comforted herself with the lie that Etta had woven and set into motion. The two had struck up a quick friendship, and it wasn't long before Shep had asked if he could take Huck fishing or on some other adventure around town. At first Julie had said no, but as the bond between Shep and her little boy grew she had a hard time keeping her resolve. She had been back in town for months, and everyone now accepted that Huck was Eric's child.

Julie never asked but always listened when customers in the diner spoke of the Rawlings. From what she could gather, Jake had abandoned his parents along with Shep and had never returned home after the Christmas following his career-ending injury. She began to relax and reasoned that she if she allowed Huck to spend time with Shep she might be righting some of the wrong she felt in her deception. Shep had never mentioned Huck's paternity and had never given any indication that he might believe the young boy might be Jake's son. Huck spoke nonstop about Shep but when he also mentioned stopping by football practice, Julie's heart stopped. She had curbed some of

Huck's outings with Shep after that.

She was startled out of her reverie when Huck placed both of his hands on her cheeks, turning her eyes to meet his.

"Momma, why are you sitting in the car?" Huck shoved his blue plastic-framed glasses up his nose and patted her face.

"Oh, I was just thinking about what kind of pizza I wanted to order for dinner tonight." She watched as his face lit up.

"Cheese?" he squealed.

"Of course!" she replied with equal enthusiasm, trying to hide her concern as she studied her son; to her it was obvious who his father was. From the curve of his jaw, to the line of his lips, to the cowlick at the crown of his hair, he screamed of Jake's DNA. And while the town had easily bought the lie that Huck had been fathered by Julie's ex fiancé, would Jake? He was the only other person in the world who knew about that night at the farm. Would he take one look at her son and know beyond a shadow of a doubt that he was his father? If Jake accepted the terms of the will, he would be in Bluff Creek for at least the next six months. Could she keep Huck from him for that long? She briefly thought about leaving town, but she had the diner to consider and Huck had just begun kindergarten.

From the look on Jake's face today, he was none too happy about the conditions surrounding his inheritance. And from the looks of his fiancée, she couldn't quite imagine her moving to a small town, even temporarily. Julie felt confident he would not abide by Shep's last wishes. But then again if Jake didn't accept the terms, he would receive nothing from his grandfather. Julie had noticed the sports car parked in front of the funeral home the other night, and the expensive suit he had worn to the meeting today. She doubted he needed anything financially. He might want the farm for sentimental reasons, but she could never imagine him living here permanently.

She smiled down at Huck again. She would just have to keep him away from Jake. No way would the man she had witnessed today spend one more day than he had to in this town; just a few more days and life could return to normal and she could drown out the voice of her conscience nagging her that regardless of his actions, Jake deserved to know he had a son and Huck deserved to know he had a father.

Chapter 6 *Rage*

"My dear brothers and sisters, take note of this: Everyone should be quick to listen, slow to speak and slow to become angry." James 1:19

Jake pushed the gas pedal to his mother's SUV, zooming precariously down a dirt road, heading nowhere in particular. Rage fueled by desperation boiled inside him, causing him to press the pedal even harder as he punched his dashboard. What had Shep been thinking leaving that much money to Julie and leaving him in essence with nothing? What would he do with a 120-acre farm? And how could he wait six months to get the money he so desperately needed? He sped down back roads that he hadn't been on since his youth, winding roads that dissected one another, and without conscious thought, he found himself at Shep's farm, which he guessed was now his farm, at least for the time being.

He sat in the car for some time looking out over the fields, contempt building in him. He finally opened the car door and stood, looking around at his inheritance. The house he had spent so much time in as child looked old and lonely. He leaned against his car and studied the night sky. Anger continued to churn in his stomach. Was this some cruel joke fate had played on him? What had he done in life that had caused God to keep everything he needed just out of his grasp? First he had lost his dreams and then at every step since, life seemed to be waiting to throw him another curveball. His financial woes could no longer be swept away, but he was at a loss on how to handle them. He shoved his body away from his car and screamed at the darkened sky, "Why? What did I ever do to deserve this?"

He waited momentarily, as if expecting an explanation. He stomped around his car, desperate to find some outlet for his rage. A loose board on the barn flapped in the wind as if taunting him. He grabbed the board with both hands, trying to pull it loose from the dilapidated structure. In his current state of mind, he felt confident he could tear the entire barn down, board by board. He gritted his teeth and pulled with all his might, but when the board refused to budge, he took a step back, clenched his fist, and punched the board with his entire body weight behind the blow.

The pain that immediately shot up his arm cut through some of his anger momentarily but then fueled it to an entirely new level. He grabbed the board with both hands and pulled with an intensity he hadn't felt about anything in years. He twisted at the waist, trying to pry the board loose. As he twisted, the final nail slipped from its hold, and he along with the board fell hard against the ground. Searing pain burned through his knee. He rolled from side to side, writhing in pain, flashing back in his mind to the last time he had felt such pain in his leg. The time when all the dreams he had held dear had died.

He wasn't sure how long he lay on the ground, waiting for the pain to subside. He was finally able to use the cursed board that had started it all to scoot himself up enough to get to his feet. He attempted to place some weight on his knee and while the pain caused him to clench his teeth, it wasn't so bad that he couldn't hobble to the house. He found the hidden key in the exact spot it had always been, and refused to think about the last time he had been in Shep's house. Refused to think about the feelings he had once had for Julie; all he felt for her now was animosity. He limped to the only piece of furniture left in the house, a straight-backed chair sitting in the middle of the empty kitchen, and heavily sat down. He felt his pants tighten around his swollen knee and grimaced; he knew from experience he needed to ice and elevate the injury. He struggled to get out of the chair and limp to the refrigerator, only to find it empty. He slammed the door shut and, leaning back against it, slid to the floor. He rubbed his forehead and laughed bitterly. He thought about what he had imagined his adult life would be when he was a kid. Never in his wildest dreams did he ever consider he would sink this low.

Sometime in the night, he scooted away from the fridge and stretched out on the cold hard floor. He awoke with a start, briefly unaware of his location. The pain in his hand and knee quickly reminded him. The sun beamed brightly through the kitchen window, allowing him to assess the damage to his knee. The swelling seemed to have subsided somewhat, but it was still too painful to attempt to bear his entire weight. He scooted to the counter and pulled himself up, using the counter to bear part of his weight. He limped to the back door, easing himself down the steps. He let the back door slam shut behind him, not even attempting to lock it. Folding himself into his mother's compact SUV presented itself as near impossible. He ran the driver's seat as far back as it would go and screamed through gritted teeth when he finally was able to swing his legs into the car.

He cursed his own temper that had been the source of this accident every time his leg throbbed. He glanced at the clock on the dash that told him it was 9:15 a.m. and he hoped that the one and only doctor that he knew of in Bluff Creek was still in business.

****

"Doesn't look like you've done any permanent damage." Dr. Carnahan viewed the X-rays of Jake's knee while Jake sat on the examining table, head leaning against the wall. Jake felt relief and with that came an overwhelming sense of exhaustion. The anger and adrenaline he had been running on since the will reading yesterday had long since passed.

"You want to tell me what happened?" The doctor turned to

eye Jake over the top of his glasses.

"I fell," Jake responded flatly, closing his eyes momentarily.

"Did you hit your hand too when you fell?" The tone of Dr. Carnahan's voice told Jake he didn't believe him. Jake's eyes flew open and he turned his hand to see dried blood covering busted knuckles.

"Uh, yeah, I guess I did," he mumbled.

Dr. Carnahan studied him before rolling a stool closer to the examining table and sitting down. "Jake, I hate what happened to you." He nodded his head toward Jake's swollen knee. "I always enjoyed watching you play."

"Thanks, Doc." Jake hated the sympathetic tone in the older man's voice.

"Always thought you'd make it to the pros….guess God had different plans."

"Well, I wish He would tell me what they are." Jake didn't even attempt to keep the contempt out of his voice.

"Have you asked Him?" The doctor stood and leveled his gaze on Jake. "If you ask Him, I bet He will tell you."

"No," Jake said flatly and returned the man's gaze. "We don't speak too much these days."

The doctor held Jake's gaze for several seconds before nodding to his bleeding knuckles. "I'll get my nurse in here to clean that up. Some of those cuts look pretty bad. Keep them clean. As far as the leg, rest and elevation to keep the swelling down, alternate ice and heat, which I expect you already know."

As the doctor reached the door he turned and spoke before leaving the room. "Jake, when God closes a door, He always opens another one, you just have to look for it. Stop pouting in the hallway and look for the open door."

****

Jake's stomach growled loudly as he left the Bluff Creek Pharmacy after getting his prescription for pain pills filled, asking them to mail the bill to his parents' house. The steady throb in his knee reminded him that he needed to consume the medication as soon as possible, but first things first, he had to eat. He had been too overcome with anger to remember to eat dinner the night before. If experience had taught him anything, he knew if he didn't eat soon, the pain meds wouldn't be in his body long enough to dull the ache in his knee and give him the oblivion he craved right now.

Etta's Diner sat across the street and offered him the only option for a quick meal that wouldn't require him trying to drive with his knee so swollen he could barely bend it. He stood staring down the street as if another restaurant would mysteriously appear before he finally squared his shoulders and limped across the street.

Marti Cooper stopped in her tracks, nearly dropping the pot of steaming coffee she was using to refill one of the regular customers' mugs, when Jake Rawlings walked through the front door of the diner. She watched as he glanced around and proceeded to limp to the end of the counter. As he slipped onto an empty barstool as far away from other customers as he could get, Marti glanced back at the kitchen nervously. She knew Julie would be back in the office poring over paperwork and working on a supply order. She prayed that she could get Jake in and out of the diner before Julie took a break and came out front.

She set a coffee cup in front of him and began pouring him a cup. "You look like ten miles of rough road," she offered.

He cut his eyes up at her. "Good to see you too, Marti."

She studied him for a moment and then pointed one red-tipped acrylic nail at him. "If you've come for breakfast, the special is on the board; if you've come to cause trouble, you can head right back out the door."

"Are you this nice to all your customers?" He sipped his coffee.

"Just the ones I know won't tip well." She leveled her gaze on him.

He rubbed his hand down his face. "I'm not here to cause trouble, just to get breakfast."

"Looks like you've already found trouble." Marti nodded toward his bandaged hand before turning away from him.

He sipped his coffee, thankful she had finally left. Marti had been a classmate of his and Julie's, and was well known for her sharp tongue. Jake usually enjoyed the banter, but he just didn't have it in him today. He wanted to be left alone to eat his breakfast, pop a few pain pills, and then sleep for hours. Maybe when he woke up this would all have just been a horrible nightmare.

Marti refilled his coffee cup a few minutes later and set a plate of sausage, eggs, and toast in front of him. He nodded his thanks and barely took a breath as he inhaled his food. Marti filled his cup for the third time and placed his check on the counter beside his plate. His chewing slowed and a sickening feeling settled in the pit of his stomach. He reached for his wallet and looked for cash, even though he knew there would be none there. He flipped through the array of credit cards and tried to pick the one he thought would have the best chance of being accepted. The food he had just devoured sat like a rock in the pit of his stomach as Marti picked up his check and card and walked toward the cash register. He watched her out of the corner of his eye and silently prayed that the card would work. If he had ever done even one thing right in his life, maybe God would hear this one prayer. He knew the minute he saw Marti frown and try to swipe the card again that God indeed had not answered his prayer.

"Figures," he muttered under his breath and contemplated quickly exiting out the front door, but with his knee still throbbing he knew his chances of a clean getaway were slim. He was already reaching into his wallet, hoping to find another card that would work, when she came back to stand in front of him, snapping his rejected card loudly against the counter as she announced, "Declined." He thought he detected a hint of laughter in her voice, but he suppressed the urge to meet her gaze as he handed her another card.

Marti sashayed back to the cash register, and Jake knew she was enjoying the predicament he found himself in. He also knew the minute the second card was declined by the expression on her face. Heat rose up his neck as he considered his options. He had no cash and apparently no working credit card. He hadn't spoken to either of his parents after the will reading yesterday, and while he obviously didn't have a ton of pride left, what he did have wouldn't let him call them.

And just when he thought things couldn't possibly get any worse, the kitchen door swung open and Julie stepped into view. He quickly averted his gaze and frantically searched the restaurant, looking for anyone who might come to his aid. Out of the corner of his eye, he could see Marti whispering to Julie and then nodding in his direction. His stomach lurched when Julie took the card in hand and headed his way. What small shred of pride he had left swelled inside of him and he leveled her with a steely gaze. He was Jake Rawlings, beloved hero of this town at one time, and he would not give her the satisfaction of seeing him broken or submissive.

Julie had thought about what she would say to him if she ever spoke to him again. But never in her wildest dreams did she think it would have been, "Your card has been declined."

He took the card she held toward him and rifled through his wallet again, hoping to find something that he knew wasn't there. After several minutes Julie cleared her throat. "It's on the house, don't worry about it." She began clearing his plates.

Embarrassment boiled inside him, and Jake could feel the heat rising up his neck. He didn't even attempt to curb his anger when he spoke. "Well, that's awful nice of you. Seeing how Shep just left you a small fortune that's the least you can do."

"Jake," she began, but before she could finish, he continued with his tirade.

"Tell me, how did you manage that anyway? Convincing an old man to leave you that much money. Did you give him some sob story? Make him feel sorry for you?" And even though he knew he should stop, he continued in a mocking tone, "Poor Julie, all alone with no family. Is that the angle you used? Or did you use another angle? Flirt with the old man a little—"

"Get out of my restaurant," she spat between gritted teeth.

"You might not have any family left, Julie, but that doesn't mean you can poach mine." He let his words hang in the air and he knew he was being a jerk but something in him refused to stop.

"If you care so much about your family, maybe you should spend more time with them." Julie turned on her heel, straightened her shoulders, and headed straight for the kitchen.

Jake watched her back as she disappeared behind the swinging door. He knew he should call her back and apologize; he had been beyond rude. And while he couldn't understand why Shep had left her such a large sum of money, he knew Julie well enough to know she hadn't manipulated the old man into including her in his will. He gingerly tested part of his weight on his swollen knee and stood to leave. Only then did he notice that everyone in the diner was staring at him. He lifted his chin and limped out the front door, chewing two pain pills as he went. At least sleep would give him a brief escape.

****

Julie's hands were shaking so hard she could barely hold onto Jake's plate and coffee mug as she took them to the dishwasher. Before she could safely exile herself in her office, Marti busted through the swinging door.

"Are you okay?"

"I'm fine." Julie waved her hand as if to dismiss the notion as silly.

"You don't seem fine, Julie." Marti followed her into her office and sat down across from, reaching out to take Julie's shaking hand in her own.

Julie couldn't keep the tears from slipping from her eyes and her voice shook as she spoke. "I thought he might be upset that I was mentioned in Shep's will, but it's not like I asked for it. I had no idea until Clay told me."

"I know, Julie, I know." Marti squeezed her hand gently and tried to voice the question that had been plaguing her. "Julie…what exactly did Shep leave you?"

Julie looked down and refused to meet her best friend's gaze. She contemplated how Marti would react when she found out the exact terms of Shep's will. Julie knew that when the terms of his will became public knowledge many people would have the same questions as Jake. Why had Shep left her so much money? Dread filled her as she untangled her hands from Marti's and dropped her face in them.

"Seventy-five thousand dollars." Her words came out garbled from behind her hands.

"What did you say? Sounds like you said seventy-five thousand dollars." Marti chuckled, but when Julie raised her head to meet her friend's eyes, laughter was forgotten. Her face blanched as she whispered, "You did say seventy-five thousand dollars."

Julie straightened her spine and wiped her tears. "And that's not all, he left Jake the farm, but on the condition that Jake has to live here in Bluff Creek for six months. If he doesn't, the farm is then mine."

Marti pinched the bridge of her nose, rubbed her hand down her face, and then spoke softly. "So when are you going to tell him?"

"Tell who what?" She leaned away from her friend, dread filling her chest.

"When are you going to tell Jake that he is Huck's dad?" Marti asked matter-of-factly.

Julie's face paled and her heart jumped into her throat. She had never discussed the issue of Huck's father with anyone. "How did you know?" Her voice was barely a whisper.

"I didn't." Marti let her words hang in the air. "After the way Huck took to Shep, the thought crossed my mind but I just didn't think it was possible, but after this…it was a hunch, but I didn't really know until just now. Why else would he leave you that much money?" Marti leaned forward and caught Julie's hand again. "Julie, if I figured it out, others will too. Jake will eventually. You have to tell him."

Julie bit her lip and tried to control the fear that was coursing through her body. "After the way he's acted, he doesn't deserve to know Huck."

"Oh, honey," Marti whispered, her voice filled with

compassion, "that's not something you get to decide alone."

Chapter 7 *Confrontation*

"Be on your guard! If your brother sins, rebuke him; and if he repents, forgive him." Luke 17:3

Jake had let himself back into his parents' home and slept for the rest of the day. He awakened to the smell of food cooking wafting from the kitchen. He gingerly tested his knee and limped into the kitchen. His mother grinned as he entered the room. He couldn't help but notice that Coach kept his back turned to him while stirring something on the stove. When he hobbled to the table to take a seat, Mary cried out.

"What happened to you? Is that your bad knee?" She rushed to his side to help him ease into the chair.

"I fell, Mom, that's all." He grimaced as he bent this knee and hoped she didn't notice.

Coach eyed him suspiciously from across the room and muttered, "Pretty hard fall looks like."

He ignored his father's comment and reached for the basket of steaming rolls his mother had just set on the table. He watched silently as his parents finished bringing dishes to the table. He began dishing heaping helpings of pasta onto his plate only to realize his parents were staring at him, waiting for him to take their outstretched hands to bless the food.

After the blessing, Jake ate hurriedly with his eyes down, trying to avoid any conversation with his parents. The tension was palpable in the room and he knew they both wanted to discuss not only the will reading but where he had slept the night before.

"Jake," his mother began tentatively, "have you considered what you are going to about the conditions of Shep's will?"

Jake slowed his chewing and looked from his mother to Coach. So much for small talk, he thought. "Well, Whitney's dad has a team of lawyers...I'm going to have them take a look at it, see if there is a way out of the six-month residence condition."

Jake watched his mother and father share a look before his mother continued, "Jake, six months isn't that long and it would be nice to have you around more."

"Mom." Jake fell back in his chair. "I have a business to run and a fiancée, I can't spend the next six months living here." Silently he added that he also needed the money the sale of the farm would bring him and wondered if the way his dad coughed at the mention of Whitney was pure coincidence or something more.

Mary pushed the food around on her plate with a fork and didn't meet his gaze as she repeated, "Just would be nice to have you around more."

Jake reached over and covered his mother's hand with his own. "I promise Whitney and I will spend more time here. We've got a wedding to plan and I'm sure that Whitney would want your help." He knew the words were a lie as he said them so to try and change the subject he continued, "I don't know what Shep was thinking...leaving me the farm on the condition that I live here." He studied both his parents before he asked the question that had been bothering him since yesterday. "And why did he include Julie? I mean, it's been a while since she was a part of our lives—"

"It's been a while since she was a part of *your* life," Coach interrupted. "She's been a part of Shep's life ever since she moved back here when Etta got sick."

Jake rubbed the back of his neck and gave a bitter laugh. He and Coach eyed each other, both refusing to look away. "What's so funny?" Coach's voice was low and measured.

Jake leaned back in his chair and tossed his napkin on the

table. "Oh, it's not funny. Not funny at all...the way my family has decided to choose...to side with my high school girlfriend over me."

"Who's picking sides, Jake? I didn't know we had to pick sides." Coach leaned forward, resting his forearms on the table.

"Oh, you've picked sides." Jake scooted his chair back and attempted to stand, but his knee buckled underneath him, forcing him to sit back down with a hard thump. The display of weakness angered him and he took it out on his father. "You've picked sides ever since I couldn't play football anymore...any side that wasn't mine."

"What are you talking about?" Coach asked in an incredulous tone.

"I'm talking about how you haven't looked at me with anything but disappointment since I killed your dream of having a son in the NFL." Jake could see the shock on his father's face but he refused to analyze that and continued, "You know, Dad, I don't know what hurts more... the fact that you loved the dream of the pros more than you loved me, or that you turned the whole family against me, including Shep, because of it. And this will? It's like one last kick in the gut from beyond the grave, one last opportunity to let me know what a disappointment I am to this family."

Coach looked up at the ceiling and took a few moments before he responded, "Are you kidding me right now? Tell me you don't truly believe that garbage that you just spewed."

"Come on, Dad, you cannot deny that every time you've looked at me since my accident, you've had disappointment in your eyes."

Coach leveled his gaze on his son and studied him for several moments. Jake began to wonder if his father was even going to respond, but eventually his father spoke in an unnervingly calm voice. "Son, if I have ever been disappointed in you, it was never, ever over football, but in the man you've turned into since your injury. We didn't raise you to treat people the way you do; we didn't raise you to turn your back on your family or to be so bitter and entitled, and we sure didn't raise you to cause a scene the way you did in the diner this morning."

"Jake!" Mary exclaimed, breaking her silence, obviously hearing about the diner incident for the first time. "What happened?"

Jake held his father's steady gaze for several moments before turning to his mother. "Nothing, Mom. Just had a discussion with Julie about how surprised I was to find out she had been mentioned in Shep's will, that's all."

"It was more than a discussion from what I heard," Coach said flatly. "And why don't you tell us what really happened to your leg? A simple fall wouldn't cause that much damage or bust up your knuckles like that." Coach nodded his head toward Jake's bandaged hand.

Jake closed his eyes and shook his head. "And you wonder why I don't come home. This is why." Jake stood abruptly and the pain that shot through his leg caused white spots in his line of vision.

"Don't turn this around on us, son." Coach stood just as quickly, facing his son. Mary reached over and took her husband's hand.

"Jim, please don't do this," she whispered desperately.

"No Mary." Coach held his son's gaze. "I'm tired of walking on eggshells around him. I'm tired of hoping one day he will let us back into his life. But mostly I'm tired of watching him treat everyone who cares about him like dirt on the bottom of his fancy shoes."

"Oh, that's rich, Dad, that is rich." Jake laughed bitterly as he turned and hobbled out of the kitchen.

"Don't walk away, Jake," his father spoke behind him. "You need someone who loves you enough to tell you the truth."

"Jim, please," Mary pleaded and Jake could tell without looking at her that she was crying.

"Someone who loves me enough? What did you love more, Dad, be honest, me or the dream of the NFL? Because from where I'm standing, you didn't want to have anything to do with me after that dream crashed and burned." Jake knew he had raised his voice, but the emotion behind his words fueled him.

"I always loved you, son, always. Yes, I wanted you to make it to the pros, but only because that is what you wanted. That was your dream... and well… you were my dream…mine and your mother's. We would have moved mountains for you, to see you happy, to see your fulfill your dreams."

Coach followed him into the living room as Jake stood leaning on the couch for support. Coach's words dove deep inside his soul and touched a spot that had been raw for many years. They were the words that he didn't know he desperately needed to hear, but pride and anger kept him from allowing them any foothold inside of him.

Coach continued, "Maybe we spoiled you. We prayed for years for a child before you came along. You were our dream, son, and an answered prayer…a blessing. Maybe we sheltered you, petted you. That's the only explanation I can think of for the way you have behaved since the injury…like a spoiled little boy who didn't get his way. God has other plans—"

"Well, excuse me if I don't see it that way and I don't want to hear about God's plans. So far they have been nothing but a disappointment." Jake's tone was bitter as he interrupted. He and his father stared at each other, the only sound in the room Mary's occasional quiet sob.

"I won't have you talk that way in my house," Coach finally said quietly.

Jake nodded. "Well, that's fine, Dad, I have my own house, remember? And a hundred twenty acres that I have no idea what to do with."

Jake hobbled up the steps to retrieve his belongings. He could hear his parents speaking in hushed tones as he threw clothes in his bag, hobbled back down the steps, and let the door slam behind him. It was time to see if his future father-in-law's lawyers could get him out of this mess.

****

The First Community Church of Bluff Creek was open daily

from 2 p.m. until 5 p.m. for parishioners to come and pray, talk to the pastor, or just sit in the peace and quiet of the church nestled among towering shade trees at the end of town. It was one of Julie's favorite places and in times of great stress in her life she had found a peace here that she couldn't seem to find anywhere else. Today, however, the peace she desperately needed eluded her. When she first arrived she sat in her usual pew, halfway up the aisle, and tried to find the right words as she silently spoke to God.

In her mind she went through all of the reasons she had used for not informing Jake that he had a son. The reasons she had comforted herself with for years suddenly seemed flimsy and unsubstantial. She put herself in Jake's shoes and when she began to feel something akin to sympathy for him, she immediately replayed their conversation from that long-ago morning in Shep's kitchen. She replayed his words over and over in her mind and tried to reason with God that she had every right to keep Jake in the dark about his son. She had been raised in church and she was raising Huck to understand the value of church attendance, but more importantly the importance of a relationship with God. She had not always relied on her faith the way she should have. In fact, prior to Huck's birth and Etta's illness, she had given little thought to her relationship with God.

But in those desperate places where she had no hope and no control over what was happening in her life, she had cried out to God and he had met her there, in those dark places. Caring for her in numerous ways and guiding her in His timing. As she looked back over the last several years, she undoubtedly could see God's hand in her life. Her prayer life had become an important and vital part of her daily routine. But now as she prayed, she didn't like the answers she was receiving. She wanted to pray that Jake would just go away, that he would leave Bluff Creek, never to return, and she would no longer be faced with having to tell him the truth.

But as hard as she tried to pray Jake out of their lives, she just couldn't find the words, couldn't finish the prayer. One of her

favorite verses from Isaiah kept floating through her mind:
> *"For My thoughts are not your thoughts,*
> *Nor are your ways My ways," says the Lord."*

She wanted to argue with God, try to convince Him that the situation should be handled the way she wanted it to. Her life and how God had guided her was her testimony, and the guilt she felt over keeping Huck from his father weighed on her. Deep down, she knew it was one area of her life that she had not given God control over.

Faced with the reality of what she would have to do, she stood suddenly and walked down the aisle of the church, pushed the heavy wooden doors open, and stepped outside into the deep shade provided by ancient trees in the front yard. She walked over to her favorite bench and sat down. She didn't want to think about what would happen when Jake found out Huck was his son. Fear crept through her as she suddenly thought about what would happen if Jake tried to take her son from her.

And then just as quickly as that thought came, another flitted through her mind and took hold: What if Jake rejected their son? What if he wanted nothing to do with Huck? Anger replaced the fear in her body as she thought about her precious boy and how much he meant to her. And what about Jake's fiancée? How would she handle a rambunctious five-year-old? Julie shook her head, trying to clear her mind. She couldn't allow anyone, not even his biological father, an opportunity to hurt her child. He had already been through so much at a young age, she would not subject him to further pain.

Chapter 8 *Roadblocks*

"'For my thoughts are not your thoughts, neither are your ways my ways,' declares the Lord."
Isaiah 55: 8-9

     Jake unlocked the back door of The End Zone and stepped into the darkened kitchen. The bar didn't open for another several hours and Jake always enjoyed the stillness of being alone in the building. Whitney had met him with an excited squeal when he had finally made it back to their beachfront condo late Friday night. Charlie Watson had been more than excited to give him a ride halfway, then he had Ubered the remainder of the trip. Her excitement had quickly diminished when he had explained the conditions of Shep's will to her. Despite Jake's protests that it was much too late to phone her father, she had immediately called Mr. Peterson. He now had a team of lawyers going through Shep's final wishes with a fine-tooth comb. Jake felt confident if there was a way out of this mess, Mr. Peterson could and would find it.

     Jake stepped around the bar and sat heavily on the nearest barstool. The past week played like a highlight reel through his mind. Had it really been less than a week since he and Whitney had traveled back to his hometown? He thought about the funeral and all the people he hadn't seen in years who had immediately treated him as if he had never left. The warmth it brought to his heart was quickly diminished when he thought about the last conversation with his parents. No matter how hard he had tried to keep his parents at arm's length, he knew deep down that their opinion of him and his life still mattered to him. He heard the back door creak open and turned to see Scott letting himself in.

"Hey."

Scott jumped at the sound of Jake's voice and let the door close with a loud thud.

"You scared me, man." Scott walked over to the bar and slapped Jake on the shoulder. "I wasn't expecting anyone to be here."

"I'm back…for a little while anyway." Jake sighed and reluctantly recounted the details of Shep's will to Scott.

Scott proceeded to brew coffee as he listened to his friend. When Jake finished his story, Scott set two cups of steaming liquid on the bar and studied Jake for a few moments before he spoke.

"Are you kidding me right now? That sounds like something off television, not real life." Scott sipped his coffee.

"I wish I were kidding." Jake crossed his arms and leaned them on the bar. "But no, unfortunately, this is my life, just keeps going from bad to worse."

"What did Whitney say about all of this?" Scott raised an eyebrow; he had never tried to keep secret the fact that he didn't care for Jake's fiancée.

Jake cleared this throat and dragged his hand down his face, "She flipped out. Called her daddy. He has his lawyers going over the will trying to find a loophole."

"So that's what you want? To get out of it?"

"Yes," Jake said forcefully. "My life is here, my fiancée, my business." He paused briefly and then confessed, "I promised myself after I got hurt, that I wouldn't let that injury keep me from the life I've always dreamed about. I can't do that in that town."

Scott studied him and Jake felt as if there was something his friend was trying to put into words. Scott dropped his eyes and studied the bar, considering his words carefully before he met

Jake's gaze again.

"Speaking of your life and your business, Jake…I've uh…I've been looking over the books."

Jake leaned back and crossed his arms, waiting to hear what Scott said next.

"A wine vendor came in demanding payment, Jake, I didn't know what to do. He was going to cancel our order. I tried to call Whitney, but she didn't answer my call. So I wrote the check and then I went to record it…Jake, I didn't mean to snoop, but one thing led to another and…" Scott let his voice trail off and searched Jake's face.

"And?" Jake supplied.

Scott squared his shoulders and spoke with no hesitation. "And this bar is broke."

Jake slumped his shoulders, contemplating his current situation. He mentally tried to prepare an argument that would convince Scott that he was mistaken, but honestly, he didn't have the strength at this point to carry on the charade. He decided he was tired of lies, and the truth might be a nice change for once. "Scott, to be honest, we are probably worse off than just broke."

"Jake, what happened? Our business is pretty good, the location is great. I mean, what's going on? There is no way the bar should be in this bad of financial condition!" A dam seemed to break in Scott as he let all his questions pour out.

Jake rested his chin in his palm and stared into his coffee cup before answering quietly, "I don't know. This place," he looked around the bar, "it was Mr. Peterson's idea. I never really gave it much thought, he said we could make a lot of money and I just kinda went along with it. I didn't know anything about running a bar…I still don't. And the books, they are just…well, I never could make heads or tails of them." Jake finally met his friend's gaze and was amazed at how much better he felt sharing his woes with him.

"Those guys that have been coming in here looking for you…" Scott trailed off.

In that moment Jake felt exhausted. He had finally confessed the truth, so there was no need to keep trying to hide from Scott. "I owe them money. I couldn't cover payroll one week and the electric company was threatening to shut off service. I was desperate." Jake glanced around the empty bar, unable to meet his friend's gaze or to stop the confession of all his transgressions once they had started. "I placed a bet with them and I won enough money to cover both." Jake straightened his spine and picked up his coffee cup. "Thought I could make some quick cash, but as usual, my luck ran out and now I owe them money. A lot of money." He drained his cup, letting the hot liquid burn his mouth and throat.

Scott studied him quietly for a moment before responding, "How much money?"

Jake let his fingers circle the rim of his now empty cup and looked out into space. "It really wouldn't matter if it were a little or a lot...I don't have either. I coasted into my hometown on fumes and had to lie to get a tank of gas. I conned an old man to drive me halfway home, Ubered the rest of the way, and lied to Whitney about leaving my wallet at my parents' house so she would pay for that." He clenched his fists and thought about the terms of Shep's will; bitterness welled inside of him. "I should have plenty of money to pay off my debts and put gas in my car, but Shep decided instead to leave the bulk of his estate to my parents and my high school girlfriend."

"Jake." Scott squared his shoulders and waited for his friend to meet his gaze. "I've got some money saved up, let me help."

"No." Jake shook his head and hoped his tone left no room for argument, but just for good measure, he repeated, "No."

"Come on, man," Scott countered, "I love this place and I've been thinking I need to do something more with my life than just bartending. I wouldn't be loaning you money...think of it like me buying into the business, becoming a partner."

Jake pinched his lower lip between his thumb and forefinger and contemplated the offer. Before he had an opportunity to speak, some of the wait staff breezed through the back door calling out greetings, several offering condolences over the loss of his grandfather. He took the distraction as an opportunity to avoid Scott's offer. As much as he wanted the gambling debt to go away, he couldn't quite put his finger on why Scott's offer didn't appeal to him. He strode to the office and attempted to busy himself with paperwork, but his mind would not cooperate. His thoughts drifted to the words he had spoken to his parents and a pang of guilt swept over him. His mind then drifted to Julie, and the hurtful things he had purposefully said to her increased his guilt threefold.

He cleared his throat and shook his head as if to will away the unfamiliar emotion of guilt, but it hung on. He took a deep breath and ran his hands through his hair. He was usually good at pushing emotions to the side, but today he couldn't seem to do that. The more he tried to avoid thinking about his parents and Julie, the more they invaded his thoughts. He finally left the office for the busyness of the bar, hoping it could distract him. The bar was in the middle of a busy lunch rush, so Jake assisted with food delivery and behind the bar and his thoughts focused on the task at hand. He was so consumed with his work, he didn't even feel his phone vibrate in the back pocket of his jeans. It was well after the rush had ended and he had taken a seat at the end of the bar that he dragged his phone out of his pocket and saw a missed call from Whitney's father.

Hope sprang in his heart as he quickly redialed the number, confident that Mr. Peterson would have good news for him.

"I want to meet the lawyer that drew up this will." Mr. Peterson didn't bother with any greetings as he answered the phone.

"Okay." Jake faltered, unsure of the path the conversation was about to take.

"I want to meet them and I want to hire them, because this thing is ironclad. My team of lawyers have been going through this thing since Whitney sent it over last night and unfortunately, there is no loophole, Jake." Mr. Peterson could never be accused of sugarcoating anything.

"Are you sure?" Jake's stomach fell and he rubbed his forehead roughly.

"If there was a way out, they would have found it. According to my team you have two options."

Jake waited for Mr. Peterson to continue, but was met with only silence so he asked the question he didn't want to hear the answer to. "Which are?"

"You either live in Mayberry for six months and then you can sell the land, or don't live in Mayberry for six months and let it revert to…" Mr. Peterson paused and Jake could hear shuffling on the other end of the phone. "Julianna Wooten. Who is that, a cousin?"

"Not hardly," Jake mumbled, and rolled his shoulders trying to loosen the tightness that had settled there.

"Anyway, there it is, Jake, the black and white of it. I say let this Julianna have it. No need letting this interfere with your life."

Jake mumbled his thanks and tapped the button to end the call. He sat at the end of the bar and contemplated his options. The crux of his problem came down to money or lack thereof. He needed money to pay off his gambling debts and avoid physical harm from his bookie's hired men. He needed money to get the bar operating in the black again and to pay off the wad of credit cards in his wallet that he had been using to maintain his lifestyle.

He thought about Scott's offer, but knew immediately that he was unlikely to accept. He doubted Scott was willing to invest the amount of money Jake needed, and in any case, while he might be at rock bottom, the sliver of pride he still had refused to let him accept help. He would figure out a way out of this on his own and get his life turned around. He had promised himself that he would be successful no matter what it took. He never wanted anyone to look at him with disappointment in their eyes again.

Which brought him back to his parents. If he gave up the farm, he felt like it would be the last nail in the coffin of the relationship with his parents. And then there was Julie; she had already received so much from Shep, why should he help her get even more? If the farm reverted to Julie, there was no clause forbidding her to sell it. Jake knew that the prime river bottom property would bring a good price if sold, leaving Julie with even more of the inheritance he believed should have been his.

Somewhere in the depths of his darkened thoughts, the plan emerged. He only needed to hang on six months and then immediately sell the farm. The sale should generate enough money to pay off his debts and put The End Zone in the black. He would double down on his efforts to become a successful business owner once this was all over. His path to success was once again illuminated and he would stop at nothing to reach the top.

****

Julie sat in her usual pew at church and chewed her lip. She tried to concentrate on the pastor's message, but her mind was focused on her son sitting two pews in front and across the aisle from her with Jim and Mary Rawlings. Several months ago, Huck had begun asking to use the restroom during the service as an excuse to slip into the back pew of the church with Shep. Julie had been shocked this morning when her son had asked if he could sit with Coach.

"Momma," he had loudly whispered in his sweet five-year-old voice, "I want to sit with Coach this morning. He looks sad since Shep went to live in heaven."

Julie had blanched at this declaration. She glanced up just as Coach and Mary had made their way down the aisle. Coach had smiled and given Huck a small wave, but Julie couldn't help but notice that the smile looked forced. Numbly she had nodded as Huck clambered down from the pew and all but ran to the Rawlings. Coach and Mary had both gushed over him and joyously welcomed him to sit with him. Mary had turned to give Julie a smile over her shoulder.

Guilt rose up and threatened to consume her. What would they think if they knew the truth? That the little boy who now sat between them was actually their grandson. Would they hate her? Would they try to take Huck from her? She second-guessed every decision she had ever made concerning Huck in the span of that church service. She vacillated between blurting the truth out to the Rawlings as soon as possible and planning her escape from Bluff Creek with Huck in tow, never to look back and risk her son being taken from her.

Her heart pinched as she watched Coach helped Huck find the correct page in the hymnal or flip the pages of Huck's children's bible to the passage being discussed in the sermon. Guilt weighed heavily on her; what had she done? She had kept Huck away from grandparents who would have loved and adored him. And why? Why had she really kept Huck's parentage a secret? Why had she allowed everyone to believe that Eric was Huck's father? She tried to tell herself it was fear; fear of Huck's illness, fear of Jake's reaction or possibly rejection, but when she got right down to it, she knew it was out of anger. Anger and hurt over Jake's behavior the morning after their night at Shep's farm. Without actually speaking the words, she had basically said, "Watch this, Jake," concerning their son.

Shame washed over her as the pastor ended his sermon with a call to parishioners to come to the altar to pray. She never hesitated as she stepped out in the aisle and walked to the front of the church. She wept openly at the altar and pleaded with God to show her what to do. She wasn't sure how long she had been kneeling there when she felt a soft touch as someone's arm wrapped around her shaking shoulders. She looked up to meet the concerned face of Mary Rawlings kneeling beside her, with love and sympathy shining in her eyes, and in that moment Julie had never felt more ashamed of her decision. She tried to reason that she hadn't technically ever lied. When she had returned to care for Etta with Huck in tow, everyone had assumed his father was the promising young lawyer that Etta had bragged about. Julie had never told anyone that Eric was Huck's father, not even Etta, but she sure hadn't corrected anyone's assumptions either.

When the service ended, Julie made her way to the towering trees in the churchyard and took a seat on her favorite bench. Huck made a habit of visiting the playground after church and Julie enjoyed the quietness of the afternoon and watching her son. The quiet was quickly interrupted when Marti spotted her and made her way over to the bench.

"You okay?" Marti asked as she sat beside Julie.

Julie studied Huck for a few moments before answering, "Yeah, I'm fine."

Marti followed her gaze to Huck and then asked gently, "What are you going to do?"

Julie didn't have to ask her what she was talking about. "Well, I thought about leaving. I have seventy-five thousand dollars to start over with. I could sell the diner and just leave this place."

"And go where, Julie?" Marti interrupted. Julie shrugged her shoulders and glanced back at Huck while Marti continued, "It just seems to me that once you start running away from problems, it's hard to ever stop."

"I didn't say that was what I was going to do, Marti, I said I had thought about it." Julie swung her gaze to her friend. "I just don't know what to do…I mean, I don't want to leave. This is my home; Huck's home."

"If you are staying, you have to tell the truth about Huck," Marti whispered harshly. "People are going to start talking. It's already out that you were mentioned in Shep's will; Jake's little outburst in the diner caused that. When people find out how much he left you….tongues will start wagging, you know that."

Fear gripped Julie as she thought about what would happen when the truth came out. "I could deny it. Etta already told everyone that Eric was Huck's father, I can't help what people say."

"Julie." Marti waited until her friend turned her eyes toward her. "You know you can't lie any more about this. Look, I don't even like Jake so if *I'm* saying what you are doing isn't right…"

Marti's voice trailed off as she watched Jim and Mary Rawlings exit the church hand in hand. Her eyes turned back to Julie. "Julie, you know it's not just Jake that you are lying to here."

"I never lied!" Julie replied hotly.

Marti took her hand gently. "By not telling them the truth," she nodded toward the Rawlings, "you are living a lie."

Julie sighed and ran her hand through her hair. She knew Marti was telling her the truth, but at the same time a fear so intense that she shook settled into her bones.

Marti slipped her arms around Julie's thin shoulders. "This has got to be exhausting, living this way, constantly worrying about what will happen if anybody finds out."

Julie sat quietly for a while, looking out over the churchyard but seeing nothing. Her mind was in the past, five years ago to be exact, as she quietly spoke. "At first I thought I would just never come back here. Huck and I would just live far away from here…but when Etta got sick and she refused to leave I knew I had to come home. She was always there for me, I couldn't abandon her when she needed me the most. I thought we could come home long enough for Etta to get better…but then she didn't and the medical bills kept piling up. Not just Etta's but Huck's too. When Etta died, I had the diner to think about. It provided a good income for us, and Huck could go to work with me, so I decided we would stay for one year and then we would sell out and leave. But then one year turned into two and then…well, here we are…"

"Here we are," Marti repeated, "and here is an opportunity for Huck to have a family, just like you always wanted. Don't keep it from him."

Chapter 9 *Opportunities*

"…But when he was yet a great way off, his father saw him, and had compassion, and ran, and fell on his neck and kissed him." Luke 15:20

    Coach Jim Rawlings sat in his office with his offensive playbook open on his desk. He stared at the pages without seeing anything. He leaned back in his chair, released a pent-up breath, and closed his eyes as he pinched the bridge of his nose. He crossed his arms and stared out the window that looked out over the Bluff Creek High School football field. His normal focus and drive seemed to have disappeared. He could not keep his thoughts harnessed no matter the amount of effort.

    It had been a week since Jake had stormed out of their home and Coach had replayed the scene in his mind over and over. The part of him that desperately missed and loved his son regretted the words he had spoken, but another part of him knew that it was long past time to confront Jake on his childish behavior. He thought back to the days he had spent with his son on the very field outside this window. What had he said or done that would have led Jake to believe that the inability to make the pros would cost him his father's love? Nothing was further from the truth. Jim Rawlings loved his son with all his heart, which at the moment was broken over the distance between them.

    He had spoken at length with his pastor about the strained relationship with his son. The pastor had led him to the chapter of Luke and the story of the prodigal son. The Bible verses told the story of a son who left his family in search of fame and fortune only to return destitute, expecting his family to disown him and treat him no better than their servants. Instead the father had met the prodigal son and given him fine clothes and jewelry and held a feast in his honor. Jim knew exactly how that father felt. What he wouldn't give to have Jake back in their lives. Not only did his own heart hurt over the relationship, but to watch the heartache quietly carried by his wife added to his own pain. He had promised her on the day they married that he would always take care of her and do everything in his power to make her happy. But there was nothing Coach could do to alleviate the pain Mary felt at having an estranged child. He dropped his forehead against the window and prayed the same request he had been praying for years; for God to restore the bonds between the Rawlings and their son.

Coach jerked his head up as a quick knock on the door followed by his defensive coordinator entering the office interrupted his prayers.

"Got those game films you wanted, Jim." Doug Elliot, Jim's defensive coordinator for over twenty years, stepped into the office, laying the films on Jim's desk before taking a seat.

Coach nodded his thanks and turned back to gaze out the window.

Doug studied his back for several moments before asking, "You all right, Jim?"

"Fine, fine…I'm fine." Jim glanced over his shoulder as he spoke.

Doug straightened in his chair. "You know, Jim, with everything that is going on right now, no one would blame you if you took some time off."

Coach turned back to his desk, picking up the films and tapping them gently against his palm. "I can't take time off, got too much to do to get ready for the rest of the season." His team had barely squeaked out a win over their biggest rival to open the season. Coach blamed himself for the less than stellar performance. He had been too distracted by his personal problems to prepare the team properly.

"Jim, it's a lot… losing your dad and all. I know how close you were with Shep. I'm here if you need me."

"I need you to get our defense ready." Jim chuckled, knowing that Doug was one of the best defensive coordinators in the state.

"Don't you be worried about us, we will be ready; you just have your offense ready to go."

Jim grinned and waved a finger between them. "This is what I need, not being at home with nothing to occupy my mind but worries."

Doug rubbed the pad of his thumb across his chin. "You know Jim, we still have that open coaching position that you haven't filled yet."

Coach leaned back in his chair and rubbed his eyes. "It's just slipped my mind, Doug. I can't seem to get all my ducks in a row." Coach chuckled to try and lighten the mood, but his voice held a note of discouragement that only a friend of over twenty years could notice.

"Well, I was thinking with Jake back in town, maybe he would want to help us. I know the boys would love having him around, he's somewhat of a legend around here."

Coach grimaced and looked down at this desk, unable to meet his friend's gaze. "Jake left town last week, Doug, and I'm afraid he won't be back."

Doug leaned forward, a puzzled look on his face. "You sure about that? I saw him at the hardware store yesterday and overhead him say he was staying at Shep's farmhouse for the next few months."

Coach jerked his head up. "You sure that's what you heard?"

Doug nodded confirmation and Jim was up and walking toward the door. "Excuse me, Doug, I've got something I have to do."

****

Jake looked around the kitchen of the farmhouse and

mentally inventoried his meager furnishings. After deciding his only option was to ride out the six-month provision and then sell the farm, Jake had taken anything of value in his possession, including his engraved high school state championship ring and the diamond earrings he had given to Whitney as a Christmas present, and pawned them. Mustering all of his courage, he had visited his bookie. With a thousand dollars cash and the promise to pay back double what he owed in exactly six months along with monthly payments to be paid from the bar, he had been able to narrowly escape bodily harm and convinced the gambler that within six months he would be able to make good on his promises. He had made sure to drop Mr. Peterson's name in the conversation to reassure the man that he had a man of means and power in his corner. He wasn't confident until he was back in his car and headed for Bluff Creek that his idea had worked. He knew he would wind up paying them an exorbitant amount of money by the time it was all over, but he decided keeping his face from being mangled and all his limbs intact was worth it.

    August brought sweltering heat to the south and the stuffiness of the kitchen did nothing to improve Jake's mood. He glanced out the window to see a breeze blowing the low-hanging limbs in the backyard trees and decided it might be cooler outside. He stepped out the back door and down the steps, finding a seat underneath the ancient tree in the backyard and leaning his back against the trunk. For someone used to the noise and clamor of the city, it felt eerily quiet. He had spent one night back in Bluff Creek and he already felt restless. How could he make it six months? He shook his head, trying to dislodge the thought. He had to make it; this was his only option.

    The crunch of gravel in the driveway brought him to his feet and he made it around the corner of the house just in time to see Coach's truck parking beside his sports car. He took a deep breath and readied himself for the confrontation he felt sure was coming.

    Coach exited his truck, letting the door slip from his hand while he took in his surroundings. His gaze finally landed on his son and he raised his chin in greeting. Jake mimicked the gesture and watched as his father took a few steps in his direction.

"Heard you were back." Coach ended the silence.

Jake gave a short laugh. "Well, that didn't take long, just got back yesterday."

"News travels fast around here."

Jake nodded his agreement.

"So I guess you are planning on accepting the conditions of Shep's will?" Coach tried to keep his voice even.

Jake shrugged his shoulders. "What choice do I have?"

Coach put his hands in his pockets and shrugged too. "Could've let Julie have it."

"And let her get more of what should have been mine? No thank you." Jake didn't even attempt to keep the bitterness out of his voice. Silence stretched for what seemed like eternity before Coach spoke again.

"You think you deserved that money Shep left to her?" Coach's voice was quiet and measured. Jake thought about his father's question before he answered, "Just as much as she did."

"Son, we don't deserve anything in this life. If I regret anything, it's that I didn't teach you that."

Jake closed his eyes and shook his head, but before he could respond, Coach continued, "Jake, I wanted to talk to you about something you said." Jim searched his son's face and Jake could see the emotion playing in his father's eyes. He nodded for his father to continue. "Okay."

Coach cleared his throat, took his hands out of his pockets, and crossed his arms. He swallowed and took a step toward his son. "Jake, I was hurt when your knee blew out and I was hurt even more when they told us you would never play football again…but not for the reasons you think."

Jake studied his father but didn't respond.

Coach uncrossed his arms, dug his fists in his pants pockets, and shrugged his shoulders. "I was hurt and disappointed because I knew you were. I knew that had been your dream for so long and all I ever wanted was for you to be happy…it hurts to see someone you love hurt so much. Maybe I didn't do such a good job of letting you know that and you thought I was upset or disappointed in you, but that just isn't the case. I don't care if you are a football player or a real estate agent or a bartender...I love you, son. I always will and I will always want to be in your life. I'm sorry, Jake, for anything I've ever done or said that made you think otherwise." There was so much more that Jim wanted to say, but he stopped to gauge his son's reaction.

Jake rubbed the back of his neck as he contemplated what to do with his father's words. Before he could respond, Coach spoke again and Jake couldn't help but think he had never heard his father talk so much or emotionally all at the same time.

"I hope that this six months will give us a chance to heal, a chance to become a family again. Maybe that was Shep's plan all along." Coach's words seemed to hang in the air, and the hopeful look in his eyes broke something deep inside Jake.

"Maybe so," Jake finally responded after studying the toes of his shoes for several long moments. "I'm sorry for the things I said the other day...to you and Mom. I just..." He shrugged and let his voice trail off. In that moment, the disappointment and bitterness he had carried for so long seemed unbearably heavy and he wanted nothing more than to lay it down.

"I understand, Jake. There has been a lot of hurt thrown in your direction...sometimes we take that out on the ones that are the closest to us. We've got six months to sort it all out."

"I just felt like I always disappointed you. Not just with football, but with every decision I've made since then." Jake could hardly believe he was speaking those words to his father as they suddenly tumbled out of his mouth.

Coach's lips set in a grim line as he mulled Jake's words. "Jake, you're a grown man so I'm not going to lie to you. I have been disappointed with some of the decisions you have made...the main one being your decision, whether you meant to or not, to distance yourself from me and your mother." Coach stopped and Jake couldn't help but think there was something else that his father wanted to mention but held back. Coach cleared his throat and continued, "But just because I might not like a choice you make, doesn't mean that I will ever stop loving you or wanting to be a part of your life. You are my son, Jake. Your mother and I, we love you more than you could ever imagine. Without you around…well, our family just isn't complete. It's like a hole inside us that we can't fill up."

Jake suddenly found himself stepping forward into his father's embrace. They hugged fiercely for several moments before parting and while Jake couldn't swear to it, he thought he saw his father wipe a tear from his eye. Something inside of Jake, maybe the bitterness or the anger, he wasn't sure, but something tight inside him loosened just a bit.

They stood, their gazes locked, neither able to say more. Coach finally broke the silence. "You are more than welcome to join your mother and me for dinner tonight."

Jake looked around the yard and wiped the sweat off his brow. He thought about how hot it was inside the house and all he had to eat in the house were chips and room temperature bottles of water. His mouth involuntarily watered at the thought of his mother's cooking and he could almost feel the cool air from his parents' comfortable home. "That sounds good," and before he could stop himself he added, "I haven't had a chance to get the electricity turned on here so it's a bit warm in the house." Jake didn't bother to add that he probably didn't have enough money for the security deposit, much less the money to pay the monthly bill. His plan hadn't included much beyond getting out of the city with his body parts still intact.

Coach glanced at the house and then back to his son. "No reason you can't stay with us until you get things set up here. The way I read the will and the residency requirement, it stated in Bluff Creek, not necessarily the farmhouse."

Jake bit his lip and mulled his father's words over in his mind. "After everything we said to each other, you would let me back in your house, just like that?"

Coach grinned and nodded. "Yes, son. You apologized. I apologized. Maybe we both said things we regret. As far as I'm concerned, it's water under the bridge. You'll understand one day when you have a son of your own."

****

After a wonderful dinner, a comfortable bed, and a breakfast fit for a king the following morning, Jake decided that the next six months might be the best of his life. His mother had been overjoyed to see him and didn't even try to contain her giddiness at the thought of him staying with them for the next six months. There was a tenuous peace between him and Coach and for now he would take it and not press the issue.

But by the end of the week, Jake was bored out of his mind. There was no way he would make it six months without finding something to occupy himself. He found himself eagerly awaiting his mother's arrival home from work just so he had someone to talk with. On Friday afternoon, she rushed through the back door, throwing a quick hello in his direction as she bounded up the stairs. She returned to the living room a few minutes later, decked out head to toe in blue and gold, and stopped to stare at Jake as if he had sprouted two heads.

"Jake!" she cried. "What are you doing?"

Jakes eyes darted left and right, trying to determine if there was some reason his mother was acting as if he had completely lost his mind. Before he could speak she threw her hands up. "Are you not going to your father's game tonight?"

"Um… I…I really hadn't thought about it," Jake stammered.

"What?! It's Friday night, the entire town will be there." She rounded the couch and sat down beside him, taking his hand. "I know it would mean so much to your father."

A lump formed in his throat as he nodded. "Okay…sure, I'll go," he croaked out. His mother's beaming smile was enough to warm up the coldest of hearts. He jogged upstairs, quickly found a BCHS T-shirt in his father's closet, and followed his mother out the door.

He had forgotten the intense, electric atmosphere that accompanied a high school football game, but the minute he stepped through the gates, he was quickly caught up in the excitement. He followed his mother through the gate and was met with a throng of people waving hello or slapping his back in greeting. He couldn't help but be amazed at how easily this town had accepted him back into their arms as if he had never left. Mary led them to the same seats she had been sitting in for years. He had sat in these very seats as a child, watching his beloved father on the field. Later he had looked up from the sidelines as a player to see his mother beaming with pride. He greeted the other fans sitting around him and took his seat beside his mother and his eyes searched the sidelines to find his father. He watched his father more than he watched the actual game, the intensity he showed, the singular focus he had; Jake couldn't help but admire him.

Right before halftime, he noticed Julie sitting in the front row of the bleachers with Marti beside her. He wasn't sure why he was surprised to see her; it appeared the entire town had turned out for the game. Once his eyes found her and could study her without being noticed, she became his focus. She grinned at something Marti said and he couldn't help but think about how beautiful she looked. She had been a cute teenager, but the years had been good to her and she had become a stunning woman. Her light brown hair fell in gentle waves below her shoulders, and when she absently reached up to guide a wayward piece behind her ear, he felt his hand ache to do the same. The urge to touch her shocked him. He quickly glanced around the stands to see if anyone had noticed his study of her. Everyone around him seemed focused on the game so he felt safe in letting his eyes find her again.

He wasn't sure how long he watched her. He watched her speak to those around her, watched her jump to her feet and clap along with the rest of the stadium full of fans. He grinned inwardly as she stopped a vendor to get cotton candy and he remembered her sweet tooth. With several minutes still on the clock, Jake watched a small boy run up to her and throw his arms around her neck. He watched her lift the small boy into her lap, his face animated as he spoke, pushing his plastic glasses up his nose several times, holding a football under his arm and wearing a worn BCHS T-shirt. As the clock ran down, most of the fans began leaving the stadium. As the crowd moved to leave, he lost sight of her and without really thinking about his actions he stood quickly to try and find her again. He stood on the bleacher in front of him and craned his neck.

"Did you see someone you know?" His mother stepped up beside him and took his arm.

"Uh…yeah… I thought I did, but I guess I was wrong." He turned to his mother and helped her gather her things. As he and Mary left the stadium, he was stopped several times by well-wishers expressing their happiness at seeing him back in his hometown. He tried to focus on each person who spoke to him, but his mind was occupied trying to catch sight of Julie again. He caught a glimpse of her holding hands with the little boy, walking in the parking lot. He quickened his pace trying to find her again; his mother caught him by the elbow and stopped him in his tracks.

"Jake, let's go to the diner like we used to when you were little! Remember? You know your father will be here for hours, let's do it! My treat."

He studied his mother for a moment, her eyes bright with excitement, and he momentarily forgot about his personal oath to never darken the door of the diner again after his outburst. "Sure, Mom. Why not?"

The diner was crowded, but there was no sign of Julie. Jake tried to ignore the hint of disappointment he felt when he realized she wasn't there. He turned his focus to his mother, but they were continuously interrupted by people stopping by to let him know how happy they were to see him and to offer their condolences at Shep's passing. If he didn't know any better he would think that some of them actually meant those sentiments. He let his mother talk him into sharing a hot fudge sundae with her after their meal, and he couldn't help but feel joy as her eyes danced as they dug into the ice cream and spoke about the game Coach had just won, but there was one thing he just couldn't get out of his mind.

"Mom, tonight at the game… I saw Julie with a little boy…"

A nervous energy surged through his body as his leg began to involuntarily shake beneath the table.

Mary wiped the mouth. "I'm sure that was her son."

Jake felt his mouth suddenly become as dry as cotton, his heart pounding in his chest. "H-Her son?" his voice barely a whisper.

Mary mistook the look of fear on his face as one of hurt and reached across the table to take his hand. "I thought you knew she had been engaged?"

"Uh, yeah, I did hear something about that…" Jake found it hard to draw enough breath into his body to force the words out.

"Well, from what I understand, he abandoned them. I think the little boy had some health issues when he was born and from what I was told, the fiancé just couldn't handle it and left them."

"Oh," was the only response Jake could make. He tried to determine what he was feeling. Fear had settled in his bones when he had first witnessed the little boy climb into Julie's lap. He immediately thought of their night at the farmhouse and began trying to speculate how old the little boy was. He did feel relief now that he knew the truth, but a small part of him felt a combination of disappointment and jealousy.

Later when he lay awake in his bed, staring at the same ceiling he had his entire childhood, he couldn't deny that tonight had been enjoyable. His mother's happiness had been contagious, and when he had felt a tinge of that same emotion, he realized it was foreign to him. He thought about his life with Whitney, their condo, the bar, and he tried to conjure up that same happy feeling he had felt tonight sitting with his mother in his hometown, sharing an ice cream sundae.

He sat up quickly and walked to the window when he realized he couldn't. While he stared down at the familiar scene below him, he confronted himself with the question he had never really asked himself. Was he happy with the way his life had turned out; happy with his decisions? He released a breath and leaned his forehead against the glass. The answer was easy really. No, no, he wasn't; and for years he had held onto the demise of his football career as the reason his life had not turned out like his childhood dreams. He felt tired. Not sleepy, but bone-wearying tired. For some reason he could hear Shep's voice in his mind, repeating one of his favorite sayings, *"It takes a lot of energy to stay mad."*

He rubbed his hand down his face, hoping this thoughts would clear. He didn't want to examine his life too closely. He didn't want to realize it was not at all what he wanted. He had focused on a path and he was too far in to change that path now. Marrying Whitney offered him a life he couldn't have here. Owning the bar gave him the prestige he couldn't have here.

For some reason he briefly wondered what Julie would think about his life. He rolled his neck, not wanting to remember how he had watched her this evening at the game. Why had he been so focused on her? And what was the overpowering need to touch her? He had long since pushed her memory to a place in his mind that he refused to go. He associated her with the dreams that died with his football career, never to be resurrected. But if he were being honest with himself, he could admit that he thought of her more than he probably should. It didn't take much to bring her to mind; he didn't have many memories growing up that didn't include her. And in his darkest moments, he would let himself think about that night at Shep's farmhouse. He could remember every moment, every touch, and every breath with intense clarity. And just when he began to realize he had never had that type of connection with anyone, he would slam the door shut on those memories. Looking back didn't help him attain the life he wanted; the life he deserved.

He straightened his shoulders and pinched his eyes closed. His future was with Whitney, far away from Bluff Creek. His lot had been cast and he had headed down a road that there was no turning back from. He took a deep breath and decided that once the farm was sold and he had the money he needed, he would have that feeling of happiness. He just had to keep to his plan and not get distracted by silly memories.

Chapter 10 *Beginnings*

"But the father said to his servants, 'Quick! Bring the best robe and put it on him. Put a ring on his finger and sandals on his feet." Luke 15:22

Jake followed the smell of frying bacon to the kitchen of his parents' home early Sunday morning. He stopped in the entranceway and watched his parents as they cooked breakfast together. He couldn't help but notice the easy, relaxed way they interacted with each other; the soft muddled tones of their voices, the laughter, and the way they made a point of touching each other as they worked together. He thought of his own relationship and could never imagine himself and Whitney sharing such an intimate moment together completing such a mundane task as cooking. He shook his head and decided right then to stop comparing life in Bluff Creek to his life with Whitney. Whitney might not be very domestic, but she had other qualities that made her valuable to his life. He cleared his throat and took a step inside the kitchen before he could compare his relationship to that of his parents any further.

"Well, good morning." Mary smiled and quickly crossed the kitchen to embrace him. "We thought you might like some breakfast." She steered him toward the table as Coach began setting dishes of sausage, eggs, potatoes, and steaming biscuits in front of him.

"I'm going to have to step up my workouts if I keep eating like this every meal," Jake announced to no one in particular as he buttered his biscuit. His parents exchanged a look and Jake knew something was on their minds.

"Jake," his mother began, "you know you can stay here as long as you like. You are always welcome, but…well, what are your plans for the next six months, besides just working out and eating all our food? You've been here a week and honestly I think I'm going to have to buy a new couch you've spent so much time on it." Mary laughed and Jake felt some of the trepidation leave his body.

"I…I really hadn't thought too much beyond deciding to come back here and live for six months." Jake cleared his throat. "I mean I will have to go back and check on the bar sometimes, but…I guess I hadn't gotten that far."

"Sitting around here could get mighty boring for the next six months," Mary offered and cut her eyes toward her husband.

Jake glanced at Coach's face in time to catch a look of uncertainty, maybe even a hint of insecurity. Jake had never known his father not to be full of confidence. A man of his word, when Jim Rawlings spoke you could believe every word of it and you knew he had thought about his words before he spoke them. Apprehension slid up Jake's spine.

"Uh, Jake." Coach cleared his throat. "I was wondering if you…well…I have an open coaching position and…I couldn't pay you much, but I thought you might…" Coach's eyes searched his son's as if looking for the exact right choice of words. "Well, I thought it might help you pass the time while you are here."

Jake slowly chewed his food. He looked at his mother just in time to catch a look of triumph in her eyes before she dropped them to her plate. He slowly began to realize that his mother had totally set him up and maybe Coach too. To his surprise, his initial instinct was to jump at the chance to help his father coach. To be around the game he loved again, not to mention the promise of some sort of pay, sounded like a win-win situation to him. He swallowed before responding, trying not to appear too eager. "Sure…that sounds good to me."

Coach's smile brightened. "We can go watch film today if you want."

"After church, of course," Mary interrupted and then turned her gaze on Jake. "You are planning on attending church with us today, aren't you, Jake?"

Jake began coughing, his mother question catching him off guard and causing him to swallow a mouthful of food. The tone of his mother's question left no room for anything other than agreement. He hadn't been to church in years, and had not planned on attending any time soon. When he finally composed himself, he gazed from his mother to his father's expectant eyes and tried to formulate some type of answer that would appease them. He rubbed his hand roughly across his chin, trying to think of some valid reason for not attending church with them, but unfortunately he was coming up empty. He released a breath and nodded. "Sure." What could it hurt, he internally argued with himself? He would only be here for a little while and he could attend church to make his mom happy.

An hour later, his stomach sank and his heart started beating double time when he followed his parents past Julie seated with her son to take their own seats in church, and he quickly realized what his church attendance could hurt. His eyes found her the minute he entered the building, drawn to her like a magnet. She didn't see him as she spoke with other churchgoers seated around her. He was bombarded with well-wishers as he walked down the aisle with his parents, but out of the corner of his eye, he continued to watch her. He knew the moment she realized he was in the building. Her body stiffened and she became engrossed in reading the church bulletin. Heat rose up his neck as he smiled and shook hands, trying to focus on each individual who spoke to him.

By the time he sat down beside his mother in the pew two rows up and across the aisle from Julie, he could not recall one thing he had said to anyone since he had entered the church. He hoped he hadn't said anything inappropriate, but more than that he hoped no one had noticed how distracted he had been by her presence. What was wrong with him? Whatever they had shared together had been over for years. He reasoned that what he felt was guilt over the way he had treated her in the diner. It stood to reason that they would run into each other over the next six months, and when they did, he would apologize.

Julie fidgeted in her pew and smoothed her dress for what had to be the thousandth time. What was Jake doing in church? She briefly chided herself that she should be glad when anyone attended church, but she couldn't find the joy in this particular visitor. Try as she might, she couldn't stop her eyes from glancing his way repeatedly. When they stood to sing, his tall athletic frame towered over his petite mother; when they were seated his long muscular arm relaxed on the pew behind his mother's shoulders. Warmth spread through her treacherous body as she thought about how it felt to sit close to him, how it felt to have his arm casually rest on her shoulders. She squeezed her eyes shut and tried to force her mind to concentrate on the message and not on Jake Rawlings.

Jake rubbed his palm down his jean-clad thigh. Was she looking at him? Had she noticed him at all? He rolled his neck and tried to concentrate on the service, but instead all he could do was wonder if the blue dress she wore made her eyes sparkle the way they used to when she would wear his blue football jersey. He straightened in his seat and doubled down on his efforts to listen to the pastor.

Julie chewed her lower lip. Why did he have to look so good? Why couldn't the years have been hard on him? Seeing him looking relaxed as ever in his white button-down shirt and jeans, Julie had to admit that he was even more handsome than when they had dated. She ran her fingers through her hair, suddenly very aware her appearance. Most mornings were a struggle to get both herself and Huck ready to leave the house; she had barely brushed her hair this morning. She stopped herself just before digging into her purse for lip gloss. She pressed her fingertips to her mouth and prayed that God would help her pay attention to the sermon and not Jake.

Five minutes into the sermon, Jake had given up all attempts to pay attention and had let his mind wander. It was a luxury he didn't usually allow himself, but he figured if he let himself go just this once and got it out of his system, he could end this fascination he had with Julie. His mind drifted back to church services years ago when he also struggled to pay attention because of her. But she had been sitting beside him then, holding his hand or tucked close to his side.

He closed his eyes and could almost feel her hand in his. He remembered walks after church, his hand in hers, to the diner where Etta would feed them a meal fit for a king. He let his mind go back to fishing trips with Shep at the farm, where he and Julie spent more time laughing than fishing. Football games, where he would gaze up from the sidelines until he found her in the stands, holidays spent with family, the moment he realized as a fourteen-year-old boy that he felt more than friendship for his best friend, the first time he kissed her, all played through his mind like a highlight reel. But when his mind tried to drift to the last night he had spent with her at the farmhouse, the night that he had never told anyone about, he straightened his spine and refused to let himself go there. She was the past, Whitney was his future, and if he was going to survive the next six months and get his life back on track, he would do well to remember that.

As the pastor began summarizing his message, uneasiness crept into the pit of Julie's stomach. What if Jake took one look at Huck and instantly knew the child was his son? She began gathering her things so she and Huck could make a quick getaway immediately following the dismissal prayer. Jake's presence in town caused a pit to form in the bottom of her stomach, but if she knew anything about this older version of the person she once loved she knew he wouldn't stay here in Bluff Creek. He never did. All she had to do was avoid him today and she felt confident he would be out of their lives again. Guilt tried to inch its way into her subconscious, a voice inside her kept trying to convince her that Jake deserved to know the truth, that Jim and Mary deserved to know about their grandson, but a much louder voice of fear drowned all that out by telling her that if he knew, neither her life nor Huck's would ever be the same. For now Julie was content with letting fear win.

****

The next day, Jake met his father at the high school football field to begin his new assistant coaching position. Jake had reasoned that it would be something to fill his time and allow him to be around the game he loved, but he had no idea the emotions it would stir in him. He stepped onto the field and felt the lush green grass beneath his feet; he took a deep breath and let the familiar scents fill his lungs. He closed his eyes, lifting his face up and letting the warm late summer sun warm his face. He wasn't sure how long he had been standing there when he finally opened his eyes to find Coach standing beside him. Jake flinched. He had been so caught up in his emotions he hadn't even heard his father step up beside him. Coach reached out and squeezed Jake's shoulder. "I feel the same way about this place, son, the exact same way. There is no feeling like stepping out on this grass for the first time each season."

Coach's excitement was contagious and Jake felt more invigorated than he had in years. Jake watched the players as they took the field for warm-ups, and being unable to stop himself, he jumped in and joined them. Jake threw himself into the practice, helping the first- and second-string quarterbacks just as his dad had asked him. He showed them techniques and practices that he had learned during his college days. He enjoyed the looks of admiration and hero worship he received from the players, but more than that he had never felt such pride as he did when a technique he showed the team's quarterback helped him in a play. The young man approached him to thank him for his help and when Jake glanced over at Coach, he could see the pride in his eyes. He continued to throw himself into practice, sprinting down the field alongside players.

He was so engrossed in his coaching that he almost missed the glimpse of the woman running alongside the south end zone. He did a double take and realized it was Julie, her long brown ponytail streaming behind her as she jogged to the corner of the bleachers. He watched her as she bent down and dragged a small figure from behind the shrubbery lining the end of the field. She held her son tightly, then quickly held him at arm's length, bent over to look in his eyes. Jake could tell by her body language that she was upset. Concern for her and her boy rose up in his chest and he briefly contemplated if he should go check on her. Just as quickly as the thought came, he pushed it aside. She obviously had things under control as she turned on her heel and marched her son away from the field.

Jake fell into a comfortable rhythm over the next week. He enjoyed helping his father coach more than he truly wanted to admit. Each morning he would drive out to the farm, spending time nailing tin back on the roof of the house, outbuildings, and barns. He went through the items in the buildings, deciding what he would keep and what he would need to get rid of. He spent his afternoons and evenings coaching and spending time with his parents.

The routine was familiar and soothing, so much so that he pushed to the back of his mind the troubles he had with money and The End Zone and was able to truly live in the moment. That is, until Saturday afternoon. He had just finished another delicious meal prepared by his parents and was enjoying the evening sun as he sat in his parents' porch swing. His phone buzzed in his pocket and the feeling of dread that overtook him when Whitney's face appeared on his screen was something he knew he would eventually need to deal with.

"Hey, Whit, how are you?" he answered, hoping his voice sounded happier than he felt at the moment.

"Well, I *was* really good, I mean I woke up in the best mood this morning." Her tone was sugary sweet tinged with sarcasm. Jake took a deep breath to fortify himself for the tirade he was sure would be quick to follow.

"Oh yeah? That's good," he replied.

"Yeah, and all I could think about all day was that you would be here this afternoon and how good it would be to see you, but then I checked the GPS on your phone and I realized that YOU ARE STILL AT YOUR PARENTS' HOUSE!" By the time she was finished she was screaming so loud Jake had to hold the phone away from his ear. He waited until she was quiet before he spoke.

"You have GPS on my phone?" he asked incredulously. The silence that met him caused him to glance at his screen to make sure they were still connected.

When she spoke her voice, eerily quiet, dripped with venom. "That's what you want to focus on right now? I just can't believe how insensitive you are being. We haven't seen each other in over a week and all you can focus on is that I have GPS on your phone?"

"Well, yeah, Whitney, I think that's something I should know about, I don't think that's too much to ask." Jake stood and walked to the edge of the porch, hoping his parents couldn't overhear his conversation.

"Jake, seriously. Let's focus on the issue here, which is why you are not in your car heading home right this minute."

Jake pressed his forehead against the porch post and tried to think of a reason why he hadn't even considered going back to the condo for the weekend. But the anger that he felt over his every move being watched by Whitney overrode his guilt at not planning to see her this weekend.

"Well, as you can see from your GPS tracking, I've been pretty busy this week and we had an away game last night. We got in late and I spent the day helping my dad break down film." He didn't even attempt to keep the anger from his voice.

"So pretending to be a coach for this little football team and hanging out with your dad is more important than spending time with your fiancée? Is that what you are saying?"

Jake ground his back molars. "Don't do that, Whitney. Don't belittle what I'm doing here and make it sound like it's a waste of time."

She scoffed into the phone. "What are you doing there, Jake? Sounds like you're trying to recapture some of your high school glory days to me. It's a joke. That job is a joke and everyone knows it, including you."

"It's not a joke, Whitney, not to me. It makes me happy," and because he was angry and just couldn't stop himself he added, "Happier than I have been in a long time."

"Oh, so what now? Are you going to go back home and be, what, a part-time high school football coach? Is that what makes you happy now? Because the entire time I've known you, you have said you couldn't stand living in that town with everyone knowing everyone else's business."

Jake stamped his foot against the porch and looked up to the sky. Was Whitney right? For the moment it was fine, everyone knew it was temporary. Would he ever be able to overcome the desire for people to admire him, look on him as the picture of success? He doubted it, and while he knew he was far from successful, he had been able to construct quite the charade. A charade that would quickly fall apart if he moved back to Bluff Creek.

"Jake?" Whitney questioned impatiently after several long minutes.

"I didn't say that...I didn't say that I was going to stay here and coach football, it's just been a nice change of pace. Besides, I didn't even finish my degree so I couldn't be a real coach even if I wanted to."

"Oh, well that makes me feel really good, to know that you're choosing me because you don't have a degree to do the other." He could practically feel her bottom lip pouting out over the phone.

"That's not what I said, Whitney." His patience was wearing thin. "I was just..." His voice trailed off and he rubbed his hand over his eyes. "I don't know why I said that. I'm not staying here and I'm not choosing you because I don't have other options."

He waited for her to respond and was about to ask her if she had heard him when she responded, her voice childlike, "So when are you coming home?"

He rolled his eyes and let out a breath. "Not this weekend, we'll have to just wait and see about next weekend." And knowing she wouldn't like his answer he quickly added, "It's just six months, honey. We can handle this for six months."

She huffed into the phone, but finally responded, "Well, I guess what they say is right, love conquers all. We love each other so you are right, we can make it through this, and I want to set a wedding date for as soon as this six months is over."

Beads of sweat popped out on his forehead and suddenly he found it impossible to swallow. Panic overtook his body and his only conscious thought was to escape this conversation before it went any further.

"Sure, Whit. Look, I gotta go, I'll talk to you soon," he said hurriedly, but before he clicked the button to end the call he quickly added, "And take that GPS off my phone, now!"

Chapter 11 *Ultimatums*

"Hatred stirs up conflict, but love covers over all wrongs." Proverbs 10:12

"We've got quite the crowd gathered today." Doug slapped Jake on the back as he stepped inside the coach's office moments before practice started on the following Monday. "Guess word got out about you helping your dad coach. That's something everybody wants to see."

Doug had not only been his father's defensive coordinator for the past twenty years, but also a close family friend, and Jake considered him more of an uncle than anything else.

Jake rolled his eyes as Doug continued to tease him. "Hey, Jim, maybe we should start charging admission? That might get us enough money for those new uniforms."

"Ha-ha, very funny." Jake picked up the playbook and took a step toward the door.

Doug rested his hip on Jim's desk and continued, "The funny thing is that it's mostly women out there, Jim." And while he addressed Coach, his eyes never left Jake's face.

"And they are all dressed up, look like they just left a beauty pageant or something. I've never seen anything like it." Doug smiled innocently, but his eyes danced as he enjoyed teasing Jake. "Wonder what they are looking for?"

"Well now, Jake is an engaged man," Coach offered. "Right, Jake?"

"Right." Jake suddenly felt uncomfortable and desperately wanted to leave the room.

"Maybe we should make an announcement?" Doug offered. "Let all these ladies know that they can only look, no hope for anything else."

Jake left the room to the giggling sound of Doug and Coach. The ribbing took him back to his teenage years when Coach Doug loved nothing more than to tease and embarrass Jake. He shook his head as he walked to the field, but the feeling of belonging and love he felt when the older man teased him was welcome.

Jake hated to admit it, but Doug wasn't wrong about a crowd gathering at practices. He had noticed only a handful of parents hanging around the fence that surrounded the field last week; today there had to be at least twenty people watching from the fence and bleachers. He didn't want to think about why they might be here. He definitely didn't want to believe Doug's theory. He stepped onto the field and took a moment to scan the crowd, a habit he had developed years ago. An emotion he might label as disappointment in any other situation settled in his stomach.

Years ago he had always searched for a brown-haired, green-eyed beauty with eyes only for him, but of course she wasn't there now watching him. He remembered how proud he had been that she was sitting in the stands watching him. He briefly wondered if he would have felt the same pride at Whitney being in the stands for him or if he would have to have been constantly worried about who she might offend with her rude attitude.

Jogging over to the players as they began warm-ups, he decided to ignore the crowd that had gathered and do the job his father had hired him to do. He was successful at ignoring the crowd until he looked up to actually see that the brown-haired, green-eyed beauty had appeared at practice, but instead of watching him, Julie frantically paced the end zone, pushing aside the shrubbery and glancing around nervously. He tried not to stare but it was apparent to him that she was desperately looking for something or someone. She made one more trip down the end zone and, not finding what she was searching for, she quickly jogged away from the stadium. Try as he might to focus on the task at hand, he couldn't stop his mind from worrying about her. He glanced back to the end zone to see if she had returned just in time to glimpse someone dash from under the bleachers and jump into the end zone shrubbery.

Jake signaled for the quarterbacks to take a water break and jogged to the end of the field. He could see the shrubs shaking slightly. He walked quietly over and bent down, where he met large green eyes framed with blue plastic glasses. His stomach fell and he knew instantly that he had just come face to face with Julie's son, no doubt about it. He had gazed into similar green eyes too many times not to see the resemblance. The small boy jumped and Jake couldn't help but smile at him.

"Hi," Jake began but the boy refused to respond; instead he just stared at Jake. He decided to take another approach. "What are you doing hiding in the bushes?"

The little boy gulped and pushed his glasses back up his nose. "W-watching practice."

Jake knew by the quaking in his voice that the boy was frightened by his presence, so he got down on all fours to make eye contact with him.

"Watching practice, huh?" Jake knew he had found what Julie had been frantically searching for earlier.

"Y-yes sir." The green eyes seemed to grow larger.

"Does your momma know you're watching practice?" Jake raised an eyebrow.

Green eyes grew wide as he stammered, "I-I-I missed the bus."

Jake sat now, his legs crisscrossed, and scooted closer to the boy. "You missed the bus? What does that have to do with watching football practice?" Jake was enjoying this exchange more than he cared to admit.

The small boy gulped and cleared his throat. "I missed the bus and was walking to the diner. I saw the football team on the field and just wanted to watch a minute."

"Okay…but does your momma know where you are?"

"No." Green eyes looked at the ground and his voice was small.

"No," Jake repeated. "Did you know she was here looking for you a little while ago?"

The boy never raised his head as he whispered, "Yes." He looked up to meet Jake's gaze and the words began tumbling out of his mouth. He spoke quickly, running words together, never stopping to take a breath. "I just wanted to watch. All the kids at school say you are the best football player that ever lived and I just wanted to see you. But she won't let me come to practice now that Shep went to live in heaven and I don't think that's fair and I wanted to watch you so I hid when she came. And now I know I'm in trouble so I might as well stay and watch practice anyway."

Jake nodded his head, impressed with the young man's reasoning, but knowing how frantic Julie had appeared earlier, he knew he had to get him home. "Why don't you let me take you home and I'll help explain things to your mom."

The young boy studied him apprehensively and Jake thought for a moment that he was going to refuse him. Finally he began making his way out of the bushes and stood quietly in front of Jake. Jake glanced back down the field and bent down to look the young boy in the eyes. "I'll be right back, don't move." He jogged down to tell Doug about finding the young boy and taking him home. Jake knew from the smirk and glint in Doug's eye that this would be the next thing he teased Jake about, but for now he couldn't think about that.

"Come on, buddy, my car is parked right over here." Jake took the young boy by his shoulder and attempted to guide him toward his car but was brought up short when Huck wouldn't move.

"My car is right here." Jake pointed to his car sitting in the parking lot.

Huck kicked at the ground around him. "Momma says I can't get in a car with a stranger."

Jake's head jerked back as if he had been slapped and studied the boy. Huck was small, and the plastic-rimmed glasses made his green eyes luminous. The unsure way that he kept kicking at the dirt at his feet tugged at Jake's heart. He squatted down to look the boy in the eye. "So I've heard that you hung out with Shep a lot."

Huck's head jerked up at the mention of Shep's name. "I did." His voice was so small that Jake read his lips more than heard the words.

"Well, I did too when I was your age. I guess you could say he was my best friend."

Green eyes grew wide. "He was my best friend too." And then Huck quickly added in a whisper, "I miss him."

The boy's words dove deep inside Jake and he felt his own heart break from the emotion they caused. Suddenly a knot developed in his throat and he struggled to swallow it before he responded, "Me too, kid. Me too."

Jake studied Huck for a long moment before continuing, "Well, if we were both Shep's best friends, now that he's gone, I guess we could be each other's best friend."

Huck looked at Jake out of the corner of his downturned eyes, studying him as if to determine if he were trustworthy or not. Jake continued, "I don't have a lot of friends around here anymore. I could really use one."

Huck finally nodded his small head in agreement and Jake's face broke into a smile.

"Well, since we are friends now, will you let me give you a ride to the diner?"

Huck looked around as if searching for the answer or maybe his momma. He twisted his small mouth, contemplating Jake's question deeply, but finally answered, "I don't know…my momma might not like that."

Jake stood to his full height and took in a deep breath. On the one hand, he had to admire the kid's willingness to obey his mother on this issue and he thought if he had a child he wouldn't want them climbing in the car with just anybody. He looked back to find green eyes looking up at him. A tenderness tugged at Jake and he released the breath he had been holding.

"Well, the diner isn't that far, would you let me walk with you there?"

A toothless grin split Huck's face and he replied excitedly, "For sure."

A dam seemed to break in Huck as they walked to the diner. He peppered Jake with question. Apparently his return to Bluff Creek had caused quite the stir in the local elementary school, with tales of his football prowess growing with each retelling. Jake chuckled at some of Huck's questions and tried to correct the exaggerations.

"Tony says that you were going pro? Is that right?"

Amused, Jake thought as often as Huck had mentioned the other boy's name, Tony must know more about him than he knew about himself. "Well, Tony is kinda right…I wanted to go pro, but I had a leg injury and I couldn't play anymore."

"Did you cry when you couldn't play anymore?"

"Yeah, buddy, I sure did." As the diner came into view, Jake stopped. He contemplated letting Huck walk the rest of the way by himself, but knew that would be a cowardly thing to do. He was doing Julie a favor. She should be thrilled that he had brought her son home, maybe thrilled enough to forget his behavior in the diner the other day. As they approached the building, Julie rushed out the door, falling to her knees in front of Huck and pulling him into her arms. Jake stood to the side, feeling awkward, as if he were intruding on a family moment. Julie pulled back and took Huck by the shoulders. "Where have you been? I've been scared to death!"

Huck grinned at his mother and excitedly explained, "I'm sorry, Momma. I missed the bus and then I went by the football field and Jake said he would walk me home."

Jake smothered a grin at the way Huck whitewashed the events of the afternoon, but as soon as Julie turned her angry eyes up to him, the grin disappeared.

"Momma, do you know Jake? He was Shep's best friend too. He's the one that everybody has been talking about at school, the best football player ever—"

"Go inside, honey." Julie pushed her son behind her but her

eyes, wide with anger, never left Jake's.

"But Momma," Huck began but was quickly interrupted.

"Go inside, son." Julie gritted her teeth and her tone left no room for argument.

Huck turned dejectedly, shoulders sagging, to Jake. "Bye, Jake, see you around."

Jake squatted down to his level. "Bye… Hey, I don't think I ever caught your name."

"H—" The young boy was quickly interrupted by a loud and angry Julie. "Get inside now!"

Huck ducked his head and shuffled into the diner. Jake watched him until he was gone and then stood to face Julie, her hands on her hips, fiery darts shooting from her eyes.

"What do you think you are doing?" she spat, her voice low and venomous.

Jake stood his mouth open, shocked at her anger directed toward him. He finally gathered himself together enough to answer, "Bringing your son home." His own anger growing at her behavior, he couldn't stop himself before he added, "You're welcome."

Julie glanced up and down the street, breathing deeply as if trying to calm herself. Finally she spoke. "He has some health issues…when I can't find him…" She shook her head and her words trailed off. Jake watched as she rubbed her hands together, both of them visibly shaking, and he felt a stab of sympathy for her which quickly dissipated when she added, "Thank you for bringing him home, but I would appreciate it if from this point forward, you didn't associate with my son."

Shocked by her reaction, Jake stood, rooted to the ground, staring at her for several moments before turning his back on her. He had every intention of walking away and never looking back. In fact, he took several steps before turning around. The anger raging inside him wouldn't let him stay silent. Hands on his hips, he faced her. "You know, I did you a favor, bringing him home…I saw you searching for him at the field and I knew you were worried so I brought him home and this," he waved his hand between them for emphasis, "this is what I get?" He thought about his next statement only briefly before he spat it out. "What happened between us, Julie, was a long time ago and for you to still be this angry with me, well…it's…it's just childish." He regretted the words as soon as they left his mouth. Her eyes grew wide and fiery; her body tensed, and she clenched her fists at her sides. She opened her mouth as if to fire off some type of retort, only to close it. She closed her eyes tightly and rubbed her forehead. When she opened them, tears pooled in them, causing her green eyes to look glassy.

He opened his mouth, ready to apologize, but then stopped short. Why should he be the one apologizing for helping her son get home safely?

"You have no idea what I have been through since you left here." She took a step toward him, her eyes blazing, finger pointed at him, her voice eerily steady and quiet.

"You're ri—"

She interrupted him before he finished. "No idea, the problems that I have had to deal with." She continued to walk toward him until her finger poked him in the middle of his chest. "You have no idea what it's like to have a child with health issues. A child that you worry about every minute of every day. A child that you don't know from one minute to the next if he is going to make it. So If I get a little emotional when it comes to him and his well-being, that's my business. Not everything is all about you, Jake, not everything revolves around you and our breakup. I've had a life since you left here. I haven't just sat around pining for you. And if you think I have, well *that* is childish!" Her voice was an octave below yelling by the time she finished. She had raised up on her tiptoes and poked her finger in his chest to emphasize every word of her last sentence.

Jake was speechless as he stood there looking down at her. The tears that had once threatened to spill down her cheeks had been obliterated by the fire he saw in them now. As he stood there looking down into her flashing eyes, still feeling the tip of her finger as it jabbed into his chest, his ears ringing from her berating, he had the craziest desire to pull her into his arms. He briefly recalled the first time he had ever held her and how he had immediately thought that she was made just for him. Her head had easily rested under his chin, her body slid perfectly into his side, and for an ever so brief moment, he had an overwhelming desire to see if it still would. As soon as the thought came he pushed it aside and took a step back from her. He continued to back away from her, but held her fiery gaze.

"I'm sorry, Jules. Don't worry. You won't see me around your son again." His voice didn't hold a trace of anger or resentment; it was flat and resigned.

As he turned his back to her and slowly began walking back to the football stadium, he couldn't seem to shake the feeling that he was carrying a thousand pounds of weight. Meanwhile, Julie's stomach felt as if a brick had settled in the bottom of it and guilt hung around her like a heavy cloak. And neither of them could understand why they both felt an emptiness settle deep into their bones.

The short walk back to the stadium seemed to stretch on endlessly. He was determined to put Julie and her son out of his mind, and it angered him that he simply could not. Try as he might, he could not figure out Julie's reaction and he studied it from every angle. He didn't know what he had expected her to do, but he had thought it would be something a little less than jumping in his arms and a little more than the reception he received. He had never entertained the thought that he and Julie might be able to become friends, but the thought of her disliking him with the intensity she had just shown unsettled him. By the time he returned to the football field, practice was winding down. He absently walked to the sidelines and began packing up equipment.

Doug came by and slapped him on the shoulder. "Well, did you get Huck home safely?"

Confused, Jake looked up and asked, "Who?"

Doug stopped wrapping a cord from his hand to his elbow and looked at Jake as if he might be the densest person he had ever met. "Huck. Julie's son. Did you get him home okay?"

An uneasiness settled into the pit of his stomach. "His name is Huck?"

"Yeah," Doug chuckled. "You didn't even ask his name?"

"I guess not," Jake mumbled as he tried to identify the feeling that was slicing through his stomach.

****

Julie closed her office door behind her and sunk to the floor. Huck had been sulking in the corner booth when she had finally entered the diner, which had only been after she had watched Jake's back disappear around the corner. Looking through the diner bay window and seeing Huck laughing and talking with Jake had triggered a protective instinct in her that she hadn't known existed. Fear so strong it almost choked her took over and had directed her steps and her words. Only now, alone with tears streaming down her face in her office, did fear loosen its chokehold on her. Of course she was afraid of what Jake might do if he found out Huck was his son; she had lived with that fear for so long, it had become a familiar companion. But a new fear had emerged this afternoon, one that she didn't want to examine too deeply. The look of pure joy on Huck's face when he had been looking up at Jake with such admiration had incited a fear inside her that she had never felt before. Since the day Huck had been born, she had done whatever it took to take care of him and provide for him, never once thinking that she might not be enough for her son. Living in Bluff Creek had allowed Shep to fill the shoes of a male role model for Huck, but with Shep now gone, she realized she wasn't enough for him anymore. She took a deep breath and roughly wiped the tears from her cheeks. How could she continue to keep Huck all to herself, especially when his father was right here? A soft knock at the door brought Julie quickly to her feet, dashing tears away.

"Come in." She tried to make her voice sound light and cheerful as she busied herself straightening papers on her desk, refusing to make eye contact with whoever was at the door.

"Well, that looked pretty intense." Marti slipped inside the door and quietly shut it behind her.

Julie attempted a laugh but its fakeness made her cringe

inside. "Oh, that? It was fine, really nothing," she lied.

"Julie." Marti took a step toward her. "Julie." She repeated her name and waited for Julie to look up. When Julie still refused to meet her friend's gaze, Marti took her shoulders and gently turned her until they were standing face to face.

"It didn't look like nothing," Marti said gently. "And Huck isn't out there pouting over nothing."

Julie's chin began to tremble as she finally met her friend's concerned eyes. No longer able to hold herself together, she felt her entire body begin to shake. Her shoulders quaked violently, a sob wrenched from the deepest part of her being ripped from her lips and she fell into Marti's arms. Years of fears and doubts poured out of her body. Marti held her, rubbed her hand down her hair, and whispered promises that everything would be okay.

Julie finally pulled away from her friend, wiped her eyes, and whispered, "I'm sorry."

"Hey, you don't have to be sorry, Julie, that's what friends are for." Marti followed her across the room. As Julie fell into her desk chair with a thud, Marti leaned against the desk. "Now truthfully, tell me what happened out there."

Julie stared out into space for several long moments before she answered, her voice barely a whisper. "Marti I don't know, I just panicked. When I saw Huck with him…it was like my worst nightmares all came true in an instant. I lost it. I couldn't think, I couldn't reason. I just…reacted."

Marti grabbed a chair from the corner and dragged it over close to Julie. She sat down and reached for Julie's hand. "Sweetie, you can't keep this up. You know you have to tell him."

Julie bit her lower lip, her voice weak. "He'll be gone soon…"

Marti dropped Julie's hand and sat back in her chair as if shocked. She blurted out, "No he won't, honey. He's here to stay for the next six months."

Julie's eyes grew wide; her face paled and she gripped the arms of her chair until her knuckles turned white. "What?" She mouthed the word, her voice so weak Marti read her lips more than heard her.

"He's staying. He accepted the terms of Shep's will." Marti reached to hug her friend. "I thought you knew."

Julie stood and walked numbly to the small window in her office. "No, I didn't know," her voice small.

"Julie, you have to tell him the truth about Huck." Julie could feel Marti move close behind her. "Julie, do you hear me? You have to tell him. He deserves to know the truth. Coach and Mary deserve to know they have a grandson." She gently touched Julie's shoulder and turned her away from the window. She took Julie by both shoulders and looked into her eyes as she gently added, "Huck deserves to know that he has a dad and grandparents too."

Julie took a deep breath and closed her eyes, coming to terms with the fact that hiding the truth was coming to an end. "What if they try to take him from me?" Her voice broke as the words tumbled from her body on a sob.

"Julie" — Marti shook her slightly — "they can't take him from you. You are a good mother and you take good care of him. But you are keeping him from them. The thing you fear the most is exactly what you are doing to them. And how will Huck react one day if he finds out who his father was and you never told either of them?"

Julie turned her back to her friend and leaned her head against the windowpane. After several achingly long moments she cleared her throat. "I don't know if I can…I just don't know if I can tell them. I'm ashamed of what I did. When I first found out I was pregnant, I was so angry with Jake that I didn't tell him out of spite; I will admit that. After I found out about Huck's heart condition, I was just so scared. It was all I could do to make it through each day, I didn't think about telling Jake. By the time I could actually think about more than the next twenty-four hours at a time, Huck was two years old…by then I was just…ashamed. I told myself that I had done Huck and Jake both a favor. Jake was too immature, too self-centered to be a dad and would just have hurt Huck. But now…I just don't know…"

"Julie, we all make mistakes. You were under excruciating circumstances at that time. You just need to tell Jake the entire story. And yes, he's probably going to be really mad at you, but hopefully over time, you two can heal from all this and be the parents Huck needs."

"I just don't know Marti, the woman he's engaged to… I hear her dad is rich, they can hire the best lawyers and I can't…I'm just not sure I can take that chance."

"You are a good mom. No one in their right mind would take your son away from you." Marti chewed the inside of her lip, weighing her next words carefully. Clearing her throat she added, "You have to tell him, Julie. If you don't…then I will."

Chapter 12 *Surprises*

"Be sober, be vigilant; because your adversary the devil, as a roaring lion, walks about, seeking whom he may devour…" 1 Peter 5:8-9

    For the life of him, Jake could not shake the feeling of uneasiness that had settled into his bones after his altercation with Julie. He went through the motions of life for the rest of the week, and even after Bluff Creek won the game on Friday night, he couldn't seem to muster up the joy he thought he should feel. His mind wandered back to her and to her son. When he thought about the little boy and his deep green eyes framed in plastic glasses he couldn't stop the feeling of warmth that spread through him. The little guy had talked nonstop once they had begun the walk to the diner and Jake couldn't remember a time in the recent past when he had enjoyed someone's company more.

    He found himself searching the stands for them on Friday night. He internally called himself all the words for an idiot he could conjure up for looking for someone who had so clearly communicated she did not want to be around him. After the win and the final team meeting on the field, he began to help Doug clear the equipment from the sidelines. His sour mood must have been evident, because Doug picked up the final bag and slapped him in the shoulder. "You've acted like somebody licked all the red off your candy all week."

Jake forced a chuckle at the expression and mumbled, "Yeah, I'm sorry."

"Well, maybe that will cheer you up." Jake looked up to see Doug pointing to the end of the field. Jake turned quickly. His eyes searched the sidelines and landed on Whitney, reaching up on her tiptoes to wave at him. Jake's face momentarily fell as dread settled into the pit of his stomach. He quickly pushed aside the fact that he had briefly hoped it was Julie or Huck .

"You know, Jake, that's not the look I would have expected to see on a man's face when he sees his fiancée for the first time in what…a couple of weeks? Everything okay?"

Jake tried to smile as he busied himself rolling up headset cords. "It's fine. Whitney is just a bit much, Doug. She rubs some people the wrong way, specifically my dad."

"Son, take it from a man that has plenty of regrets about decisions from their past, you need to think long and hard before you go and tie yourself to someone who causes your face to look like that." Doug made a circling motion toward Jake's face.

"Thanks, Coach D, but it's not like that. Whitney and I are fine." Why did his throat get tight when he spoke that last sentence?

"Fine?" Doug spat the word as if it were the most distasteful thing he had ever spoken. "Young people in love shouldn't be just fine. A young man sees the woman he loves at the end of a game, he shouldn't still be here wrapping up cords; he should be running to greet her. If you feel this way about her now, it's not going to improve with marriage or with time. Life is tough, Jake, and a man and a woman have to truly love each other to withstand the storms that will come their way, and if not…well, the storms will destroy them. Trust me. I've been there and I don't want that for you."

Jake nodded to Doug but was unable to respond. He swallowed the lump in his throat and turned to see Whitney picking her away down the sidelines in stiletto heels. He jogged to her, determined to make Doug and anyone else watching realize that he was happy to see his fiancée. As he reached her, Whitney threw her arms around his neck and squealed his name.

"What are you doing here, Whitney?" He tried to make his voice sound light and happy.

Whitney, with her arms still around his neck, pulled back far enough to look him in the eyes, "Well, when I hadn't heard from you all week, I decided to drive up here and remind you how much you love me."

Jake forced himself to smile as he pulled her into his arms, unable to answer her. She pulled back and planted her lips firmly against his. Initially surprised, he deepened the kiss, trying to conjure up some type of happy emotions.

Julie stood at the end of the field and watched Jake pull his fiancée into his arms and kiss her passionately. After several days of turmoil and fear, she had come to the conclusion that Marti had left her no choice but to confess the truth of Huck's parentage to Jake. And while she had refused to speak to Marti since the woman's ultimatum, deep down she realized that her friend was more right than wrong.

After feeling nauseated for most of the week at the thought of uncovering all she had kept hidden, she had busied herself with inventory at the diner tonight while Huck had spent the evening at a friend's house. But try as she might, she could not get her mind to concentrate on anything other than Jake and Huck and the look of pure happiness on each of their faces as they walked toward the diner. She had decided less than an hour ago, after hours of counting and recounting inventory due to lack of focus that she had taken all she could. She would wait for Jake after his game, apologize for her behavior when he brought Huck home, and confess to him that he was the boy's father, ripping the proverbial Band-Aid off in one fell swoop. She knew it would be one of the most difficult things she had ever done, and she also knew that Jake would probably hate her after the truth came out, but the time had come to confess. The burden of carrying the secret, coupled with the fear of Marti getting to Jake before she did, had become too much for her to bear any longer.

As she stood and watched Jake and his fiancée gazing into each other's eyes lovingly, she began to second-guess her decision. Watching Whitney in her stiletto heels and designer clothes, she began to wonder how such an impeccably dressed woman would react to suddenly having a very messy, rambunctious five-year-old with health concerns thrust into their lives. Would she treat Huck like the innocent child he was in this situation, or would she treat him as an intrusion into their obviously charmed life?

She quickly wiped the lone tear that slipped from her eye and turned to leave, her eyes landing on Marti, watching her from a distance. She held her friend's gaze for several moments as if trying to determine if Marti was planning on finishing what Julie had attempted tonight. Julie clenched her jaw, raised her chin, and stalked back to her car. If Marti wanted to announce to Jake that he was a daddy with his high-maintenance fiancée hanging on his arm, then she was more than welcome to try.

****

Whitney had been less than excited to find out that Jake had been living with his parents and not at the farmhouse, which meant they wouldn't be enjoying any privacy during her visit. As soon as Jake had informed Whitney of his living arrangements, she had begun to pout and had stepped up the act to award-winning levels when she stomped and sighed up every step to his bedroom while he stretched out on the couch.

The smell of coffee brewing stirred him from his restless night sleep, his mind finding so many things to keep him up, instead of slipping into peace through sleep. He sat up, running his fingers through his hair, and shuffled into the kitchen. He found Coach sitting at the table, a steaming cup of coffee sitting in front of him. He nodded to his dad and fixed his own cup, taking the chair opposite him. They sipped their coffee in companionable silence for several moments.

"I was surprised to see Whitney last night." Coach raised his eyebrows as he looked at Jake over his mug.

"Yeah, me too." Jake's short laugh sounded bitter as the words rolled off his tongue and he immediately noticed his father's sleepy expression change to one of concern. Before he could offer an explanation to his dad, Whitney breezed through the kitchen door, her hair and makeup complete and in an outfit that looked like she had just stepped off the pages of a fashion blog.

"Good morning," she sang cheerfully as she bent, slipping her arms around Jake's neck and kissing him on the side of his mouth.

He and his father both mumbled a greeting and Jake watched his father study his coffee with intensity. As Whitney settled in the chair beside Jake, he tried to conceal his surprise at her early morning appearance. Whitney was not an early riser, preferring to sleep until noon if given the opportunity. She seemed downright giddy, even humming under her breath as she stirred her coffee, which made Jake uneasy.

"You seem chipper this morning." He hoped his strained smile wasn't too obviously forced.

"Well," her eyes shone brightly, "I guess I am!"

Jake nodded behind his cup and waited. He knew Whitney well enough to know she had more to say, and was acting suspicious. She perched on the edge of her chair, sipping her coffee, eyeing Jake with her eyes dancing, exuding excitement as she swung her crossed leg in a short, quick motions.

"What?" he finally asked, growing tired of her staring at him.

"I have a surprise for you!" She set her coffee down and reached for his hand. Dread sliced through Jake's stomach as his mind raced, trying to determine what her surprise might be.

"A surprise?" Jake slid his gaze from Whitney to his father to find Coach's brow furrowed, worry etched on his features.

"Yes!" she squealed excitedly. "And I just can't wait to show you!"

"What is it?" He untangled his hand from hers, straightening in his chair and leaning his forearms on the table.

She placed both her hands on his forearm and squeezed.

"Well, it wouldn't be a surprise if I told you, silly. Why don't you get dressed and we will go."

"Go?" Jake questioned.

"Yes, the surprise isn't here. I'll have to take you to it." Whitney stood and suddenly turned toward his father. "Coach, why don't you come with us? I think this surprise will be of particular interest to you."

Fear knotted in Jake's chest. He felt his heart begin pounding in his ears. What was she up to?

Coach set down his coffee cup. "I'm sure you and Jake would rather be alone and not have me tagging along."

"No. No, really, I insist that you join us, Coach." She winked and turned to leave the kitchen before turning back to them. "What about Mary? I think she might enjoy this too."

"Mom had to work this morning," Jake offered.

"Hmm, too bad. Maybe I'll video it and send to her." Whitney breezed through the kitchen door, throwing instructions over her shoulder that they would leave in fifteen minutes. Jake looked at his father's questioning gaze and shrugged his shoulders.

Less than fifteen minutes later, Jake scrunched into the backseat of Whitney's sports car, giving his father the front seat, and watched as she referred to a map on her phone to maneuver out of town. They twisted and turned down several roads before winding up on River Road, which led to Shep's farm. As they passed the last remote home on the road, knowing that the only property left was Shep's, a nervous, sickening feeling settled into Jake's stomach.

"Where are we going, Whitney?" he demanded.

"To the farm, silly." She smiled as she sped down the one-lane dirt road.

Jake chewed the inside of his lip and tried to calm his nerves. He had no idea what she was up to but a thousand scenarios played through his mind, all of which left him edgy. As Whitney pulled her car into the driveway, two SUVs along with several pickup trucks came into view.

"What's going on?" he demanded, not even attempting to

keep the anger out of his voice.

"You'll see." Her voice had a singsong quality.

When Jake finally extracted himself from the small backseat, his gaze followed Whitney, who was practically bouncing toward a group of about eight people standing just behind the barn, facing the expansive river bottom. Jake met Coach's hard, questioning gaze. Jake had no answers for his father, but he was determined to get them. He jogged to catch up with Whitney. As he approached the group of people, their faces came into focus and he recognized Mr. Peterson, Whitney's father.

Just as he was about to demand Whitney explain what was happening, she sang out to her father and the entire group turned to them.

"Whitney! Jake!" Mr. Peterson greeted them, closing the distance between them. He hugged his daughter and then placed his arm around Jake's shoulder and guided him to the group of onlookers.

"Gentlemen, this is the young man I was telling you about, this is Jake Rawlings," Mr. Peterson introduced Jake to the men standing in a semicircle facing him. Jake shook their hands and while Mr. Peterson told him each of the men's names, Jake could not have recalled any of them even if his life depended on it.

The man standing in the middle of the group raised an eyebrow and spoke first. "So you are the one who owns all this land?"

Jake's mind was racing, trying to decipher what was happening. Unable to speak, he nodded numbly.

"He doesn't own it yet," Coach spoke up from behind his son, having followed them quietly from the car. Mr. Peterson's eyes flashed as he turned toward Jake's father quickly.

"I'm sorry," Mr. Peterson addressed Coach, "I don't believe we've met. You must be Jake's father."

"Yes, Jim Rawlings." Coach offered his hand and Mr. Peterson grasped it, meeting Coach's steady gaze. Jake studied them and the silent exchange made him uneasy.

"Mike Peterson. Whitney's father."

"Nice to meet you, Mr. Peterson." Coach nodded to the other men standing around them. "Care to explain to us what you and your friends are doing here?"

"Oh of course." Mr. Peterson seemed to have momentarily forgotten the group of men standing close by. He returned his attention to Jake. "Jake, these men are the owners of Donaldson Development."

Jake nodded in their direction and looked back to Mr. Peterson and then to a beaming Whitney. "Sir, I'm not sure what's going on here."

"These men," Mr. Peterson gestured toward the group, "are responsible for some of the most successful all-inclusive residential complexes in the southeast. It's the new trend, not just to build subdivisions, but to build communities. Everyone wants to live in a small town, but still have all the conveniences of living in a city. When you told me about this place at first I thought just let it revert back to the estate, no need to give up six months of your life, but then when I saw the topography map, well…I got to thinking. Sure, you could let it revert to the other person mentioned in the will, or you could wait out the six-month stipulation and sell it and probably make a decent profit. But the real money comes in developing it. Just think about it, Jake." Mr. Peterson gestured across the expansive river bottom. "Houses, shopping centers, grocery stores, everything a person would need just right around the corner. That's what Donaldson Development specializes in; building communities. I've done some business with these fellas before and I reached out to them as a favor to you."

Coach blew a disgusted breath and Jake turned to see the dreaded look of disappointment on his father's face. "Mr. Peterson, I'm not sure if I'm going—"

Before he could finish, the tallest of the onlookers stepped forward. "Jake, we took the initiative and surveyed your property by drone. I think we are looking at upwards of four hundred rooftops, plus shopping center, gas station, a grocery store. We offer the finest in inclusive living. Like Mr. Peterson said, we build small communities really and since you inherited all this land, you stand to make quite a substantial amount from this. We've worked up a potential income forecast and I think you'll be quite pleased with your share of the profits."

Jake's bewildered look encouraged the man to continue. "We would want to be partners with you. We would put the money in up front and of course Mr. Peterson would be given a percentage of profits since he brought this project to us."

"We would also run all the home sales through our real estate group," Mr. Peterson added.

Jake stood still, his face ashen as he met the expectant gazes of those around him. When his eyes finally fell on his father's face, Coach turned to leave the group, throwing over his shoulder, "I've heard enough of this. I'll find my own ride back home."

"Dad," Jake began and took a step to follow Coach when Mr. Peterson's hand landed on his shoulder, stopping him.

"Jake, these men have driven a long way and are offering you their services. That's not something that just happens every day. I think you need to hear them out."

Jake looked back to the group of men watching him expectantly. He thought about his bookie and the debt he owed. He remembered the horrible financial shape of his bar and contemplated the lifeboat these men were offering him; a way out of every financial mistake he had made in the past few years. Jake studied Mr. Peterson's face and then Whitney's before turning to the men from Donaldson Development.

"Gentlemen," Jake began as he stepped toward them and offered his hand, "I think there has been some kind of misunderstanding. I don't technically own this land yet. I will inherit it if I live here in this town for six months. My grandfather was quite the character, as you can tell from the stipulations in his will, and honestly I'm not sure what I'm going to do with this property in six months."

The men looked at each other and then one spoke up. "Let us show you the mockup we have completed. I think if you could see our vision, you would see how amazing this community could be." Before he was finished talking, he had taken a roll of papers and spread them out on the hood of the closest SUV. Jake stood still as everyone gathered around the spread of papers. They looked back at him, but still he remained frozen in place. Whitney finally grabbed his arm and he allowed her to drag him over to view the mock-ups of the potential community. He looked at the sketches, the first being an overview of the farm dissected with streets and rows upon rows of houses. There was a central area that the developers had named the town square. They excitedly explained that the square would contain shops, a drugstore, and a hardware store, even a diner with a gas station and a grocery store in the outlying areas. The next sketches they showed him were a blur. His mind raced back in time to long afternoons spent with Shep on the farm. What would Shep think of him turning their peaceful sanctuary of a farm into a community of over four hundred houses?

"I'm sorry." He shook his head, taking a step back. "I think there has been some sort of mistake."

One of the developers looked at Mr. Peterson, his face flushed with anger. "Mike, you said this was a sure thing. We've done all this work" — he gestured to the papers slipping off the hood of the SUV — "and now he's going to back out."

Mr. Peterson raised his hand toward the men and gestured for them to calm down. He slipped his arm around Jake's shoulders and turned him away from the men. "Give us just a minute," he said to the group over this shoulder, but his eyes never left Jake's face. He waved his hand in front of them as if suggesting a walk. Jake's steps fell beside his as they walked as if out for a Sunday stroll toward the barn.

"Jake, Jake, Jake." Mr. Peterson continued to rest his arm around Jake's shoulders. "What we are offering you here is a game changer. You, me, all those men," he waved his hand toward the group of men, "we all stand to make a lot of money from this development."

"Mr. Peterson, I—" Before Jake could finish the older man interrupted him.

"Jake, maybe I should break this down in a way that you can

understand it." They stopped a few feet from the barn and Mr. Peterson turned to face him. "You are engaged to my daughter. She is accustomed to a certain lifestyle. You can't provide her with that lifestyle currently. This"—he made a sweeping motion with his arms—"this farm is your key to moving up in the world. To being able to provide for Whitney they way she should be provided for."

Jake ground his back molars as hot anger coursed through his body. "Mr. Peterson, if your daughter truly wants to marry me, maybe she should be willing to marry me for who I am and not what I can do for her."

Mr. Peterson narrowed his eyes and crossed his arms over his chest. "And just who are you, Jake?" On a bitter laugh, he continued, "You don't even know who you are and you would be more of a nothing than you are if it weren't for me and my daughter."

Jake stood wide-eyed, unable to respond to the man he had once aspired to be like.

Mr. Peterson began chuckling. "I can see I'm not getting through to you, so let's look at this another way." He glanced back over his shoulder and gave a quick wave to the group waiting for their return. "Do you honestly believe your bookie and his associates let you get out of town with your head still attached to your body because you promised to pay them later?"

Jake's face blanched and he quickly looked around and then back to Mr. Peterson, "What...how?"

Mr. Peterson guffawed as he slapped Jake on the back. "Oh, I can see that you did." Mr. Peterson continued to chuckle, then suddenly sniffed and all traces of humor left his face. Jake did not recognize the man in front of him as he spoke through clenched teeth. "The only reason your body isn't in a dumpster somewhere is because of me. The only reason your bookie doesn't drive to this Podunk town right now and take care of you is because of me. You want to know how I know about your gambling debt?" The man stepped closer until his chest was but a breath away from Jake's. "I make it my business to know about everything that might impact my daughter. I know about your gambling debt. I know that you couldn't manage your way out of a wet paper sack, much less a sports bar. I know you're broke. And I know that this is the only play you have left. You don't take this deal and I'll step aside and let you handle your bookie on your own. I'll also make sure that The End Zone closes its doors permanently."

Jake took a deep breath and raised his chin. He studied the farm around him and his mind raced quickly. The man he had thought would one day be his father-in-law had proven he was not a man to be trifled with. Jake weighed his options slowly, as a lone piece of loose tin slapped against the barn roof. What would Shep think about the predicament he had gotten himself in, and even more pressing was what would his father say to him? Suddenly Julie and Huck came to his mind and he briefly wondered what she would think of him too and then internally cursed himself for thinking about her at a time like this. He suddenly turned on his heel, never meeting Mr. Peterson's gaze, and returned to the men and Whitney, who had been watching from a distance.

As he approached he held out his hand and shook each man's hand. "Thank you, gentlemen, for coming out today, you've given me a lot to think about. As I said before, this land isn't mine for a few more months, but after that I will be in touch."

Chapter 13 Secrets Revealed

"Above all, love each other deeply because love covers over a multitude of sins." 1 Peter 4:8

"You're mad." Whitney glanced at Jake as she drove him back to his parents' home. Jake looked straight ahead, his mind turning over and over all that had transpired this morning. Before he had walked the developers and Mr. Peterson to their vehicles, he had seen Coach Doug's truck pull up to the end of the drive and his father get in.

"Jake, I said I know you're mad," Whitney repeated impatiently.

Jake studied the landscape outside the passenger's window and replied through gritted teeth, "You had no right to do that, Whitney."

"I thought I would be helping you." She reached over and touched his arm and he jerked it away as if her touched burned him.

"No, Whitney, you were trying to manage me," and then he added, "Just like you always do."

"Jake." Whitney's voice was whiny and Jake cringed at the sound of it. "We would be set for life with this one deal."

"Just take me to my parents' house, Whitney," and as he continued to stare straight ahead he continued, "And I think it would be best if you went home too."

They rode in silence until they reached his parents' home. Jake barely let the car stop before he jumped out and took the front steps two at a time. He strode purposefully through the house and was thankful when he found neither of his parents at home. He returned to the living room in time to see Whitney descending the stairs with her suitcase. She stopped when she saw him and they held each other's gaze for several long moments.

"I thought I was helping you, Jake. You know you would never make that decision without being nudged a little." Her voice was low when she added, "What does this mean for us, Jake?"

He put his hands on his hips and looked around the room, avoiding her gaze. "I don't know, Whitney. I need some time to think."

She took a step toward him as if to hug him and he stepped back out of her reach. She stooped to pick up her suitcase and tossed her hair over her shoulder. "This isn't the end of us, Jake. I refuse to accept that. Give it a few days and you'll see that Daddy and I were only doing what's best for you. I'll call you later."

Jake lifted his chin and glared at her as she let herself out the front door. He rubbed his eyes roughly and began to pace the length of the living room. He had thought that after six months all his problems would be solved, but now they seemed to multiplying at an alarming rate. Knowing that Mr. Peterson was the only thing keeping his gambling debts from being called was unnerving, especially since he was well aware that he had angered the older man by not jumping on the development deal. He hoped he had left the group of men with enough optimism that the deal would develop in six months that Mr. Peterson would continue to keep his bookie at bay.

And in six months, what would he do? At one time it had been so clear—sell the land and go back to his normal life—but the more time he spent around his hometown, the more a calming peace settled into his bones. It wasn't the glamorous life he had always dreamed of, but something about it was appealing to him. And he had found a satisfaction like none he had ever experienced while working with his father's football team. In the short time he had spent helping his dad coach, he had determined he was a much better coach than he ever would be a bar owner. If he could agree with Mr. Peterson on anything, it would have been that he wasn't suited to be a business owner. If he were honest with himself, he could admit he was tired; tired of pretending life was something that it wasn't, that he was something that he wasn't. But now that his father knew that Jake had entertained the thought of selling the farm, would he even want Jake to hang around anymore? As all of his worries tumbled through his brain, he sat on the edge of the couch and worked his bottom lip between his thumb and forefinger nervously.

The front door opened and Coach stepped into the living room. Jake jumped up to face his father. Their eyes met and Jake couldn't read the expression he saw there.

"Dad," he began and took a step toward Coach, but his father held up his hand for him to stop.

"Jake...I..." his father began and then stopped, releasing a sigh so deep his shoulders sagged.

"Dad, let me explain," Jake began.

"You don't have to explain anything to me," Coach answered, his voice soft. He cleared his throat and continued, "Jake, Shep left the farm to you and you can do whatever you want with it. I might not agree with your decisions, but I'm not going to let that put distance between us, not again. We've come too far, healed too much since you've been home for us to allow that to happen."

Jake stood, his mouth agape, trying hard to understand what his father was saying. Coach continued, "Jake, you're my son and I love you. You can't do anything that would make me stop loving you. Even if you sell the farm, even if you let those men put hundreds of houses on it, I'm still going to love you. I might not like what you are doing, but I will always want you in my life, son. I love you that much." He paused before adding, "All that I would ask of you is that before you do anything drastic or permanent, you pray about it."

Jake roughly ran his fingers through his hair. He knew Coach didn't want him to develop the farm, but here he was giving him the choice to do whatever he wanted with the land and to still be in his parents' lives. Jake couldn't imagine what drove Coach to that decision but he was relieved that his father wasn't asking him to leave and never come back. Coach stood just inside the living room and studied Jake. Jake opened his mouth, tempted to bare the deepest parts of his hidden secrets to his father, but something held him back. He had too much to think about and after several long, silent moments, Coach spoke up. "Where's Whitney?"

"Heading back to the condo." Jake couldn't be sure, but he was almost certain he saw relief flash over his father's face.

****

By the end of the week, Jake was no closer to figuring out his problems than he had been the day he decided to accept the conditions of Shep's will. His parents had acted as if the fateful encounter with the developers had never happened, and Jake wondered if his father had even shared the events of that morning with his mother. He had avoided Whitney's phone calls at every turn, and the only form of communication between them had been a terse text he sent her warning her not to show back up unexpectedly in his hometown.

By Friday he was exhausted. Sleep had eluded him most of the week, as he had lain in bed at night trying to find a solution to his mounting problems. If he allowed Mr. Peterson and his associates to develop the farm, his financial problems would be solved, but why did that option not seem so appealing anymore? And while his financial problems might be solved, his relationship problems would not be. He knew if he allowed the development to occur, he would have to face the ire of many of the citizens of Bluff Creek and for some reason that thought did not sit well with him. On the other hand, if he didn't allow the development to occur, his financial problems would be multiplied with the restraint on his bookie removed and Mr. Peterson bearing down on him. He spent most of his sleepless nights trying to figure out how he could come up with enough money to pay off his gambling debt without losing the farm and untangling himself from the sports bar and in doing so from both Whitney and her father.

So far he had come up with nothing. He felt hollowed out inside and try as he might, he didn't see a way out of his problems short of a miracle and he was confident he wouldn't receive one of those. He was desperate and thought about the advice of his father to pray about his problems. He knew that was what his father would tell him, that God could make a way when there seemed to be no way, but something in him held him back. God had never seemed to answer his prayers the way he needed them answered, so he would just leave God out of this decision.

As he opened the door to the indoor athletic facility that housed his father's office on Friday afternoon, he was met with a sea of boxes covering the floor of the open weight room. His father and Doug stood at the other end of the expansive room. While not close enough to hear what they were saying, they were both animatedly flipping through paper on a clipboard.

"What is going on here?" Jake questioned as he picked his way through the boxes and finally reached the two older men.

"Hey, Jake, can you believe all this?" Coach Jim's eyes were dancing in delight as he gestured around the crowded room.

"What is all this?" Jake looked around the room, which was filled with boxes upon boxes.

"You remember Lane McCay? He was a few years behind you in school, I think."

Jake jerked his head toward his father, immediately recognizing the name of a local boy who had become famous in recent years. "Yeah, I remember him; he's a big country music star now. I saw him in concert a year or so ago."

"Well, he reached out to us back in the summer. Wanted to know if we needed anything, anything he could help with; said he wanted to give back to the community. We told him about needing new uniforms and some new equipment. Never heard another word, until today and all this shows up."

Jake couldn't help but grin as he thought the two older men were happier than two kids on Christmas morning.

Jake opened the box closest to him to find a stack of new blue and gold jerseys. He thought about how excited the team would be when they received them. Then, out of nowhere, he was blindsided with jealousy. How nice would it be to just be able to outfit an entire high school football team and never blink at the costs? Jake had dreamed of executing such grand gestures that would cause people to look at him with such admiration, but instead he couldn't even afford to buy someone a cup of coffee at this point in his life. The despair he had felt all week seemed to double down on top of him with an intensity like never before.

As he began to sink into his own self-pity, Coach called his name and he turned his attention to his father.

"Jake, he sent some boxes of jerseys for the middle school team as well, will you drive them over there? We've got to get this stuff organized before the team shows up."

"Sure, Dad." Jake wished he could muster the enthusiasm that his father and Coach Doug had, but it just wasn't there for him. Instead, where excitement bubbled in them, bitterness took root and invaded his thoughts. He loaded the boxes into the back of his father's truck and the entire time he was slipping deeper into self-pity. Why, was the question he kept asking himself. Why did he have to get hurt and lose his dreams? Why did other people like Lane McCay get to achieve their dreams and he was stuck broken and trapped? Why were other people's lives so easy and his so hard?

He pulled into the Bluff Creek Elementary and Middle School parking lot still stewing over his problems. He was met with excitement as he explained the boxes he was delivering. He helped the coach unload the boxes and carry them through the school to the gym to be stored until he could hand them out to his players. As Jake stood in the gym of his former elementary school, nostalgia took hold of him. How many times had he run the length of this very gym? How many steps had he taken up and down these hallways? He glanced out the window of the gym door that overlooked the playground and saw the children playing. As he watched them he couldn't help but think about which ones were destined for greatness and which ones were destined for disappointment. He must have spent more time looking out the window than he thought as the coach slapped him on the back and gestured out the door. "I guess that's where it all started, right? Who knew that when you were playing football out there at recess, you would go as far as you did?"

"Yeah, who knew?" Jake mumbled and kept his eyes on a group of young boys playing football in the same spot on the playground where he had once played the game. His eyes followed a small figure as it left the group and took a seat on a nearby bench. His heart fell when he recognized Julie's son, Huck.

"You want to go out and throw the ball with them? I know they would love it. They might not have ever seen you play, but you are a legend around here." The coach opened the door and held it for Jake to step out onto the playground. As soon as he did, the group of boys playing football took notice of him and ran to surround him. He squatted down and spoke with them, as they all seemed to speak at once. He took the ball from one of them and threw passes with them, all the while casting glances toward Julie's son still sitting on the bench.

"Why is he not playing?" Jake nodded in Huck's direction, directing his question to the coach.

"Who, Huck? He plays, he just gets winded quicker than the other boys."

Jake could hear Julie's voice in his mind as she explained her son had some health concerns that caused her to worry about him. He tossed the ball to the coach and jogged over to the bench.

"Hey, Huck." He slowed as he approached the boy.

"Hey, Jake." The little boy grinned up at him and Jake couldn't help but return the smile.

"You mind if I join you?" Jake gestured to the bench.

Huck wiggled down the bench and pushed his plastic glasses back up his nose.

"You okay?" Jake questioned.

"Oh yeah, I'm fine, just catching my breath." Huck looked out over the playground and Jake's heart pinched. He wanted to question the boy about his health condition but decided against it.

"Hey." Huck looked up at him with surprise on his face. "How did you know my name?"

Jake nudged the boy with his own shoulder. "How could I not know the name of the most popular kid in Bluff Creek?"

Huck giggled and Jake continued, "You know, that is a really cool name, much better than say....Jake." Huck giggled again and Jake felt a warmth at making the youngster laugh.

"I used to not like it. Some kids made fun of my name but my momma told me a secret about why she gave it to me…" Huck whispered and looked around the playground as if to make sure no one could hear him.

"She did?" Jake watched the young boy move closer to him and he felt his stomach twist at the mention of Julie.

"Some kids were laughing at my name and it made me cry. My momma told me why she named me Huck, but she told me it was a secret. Want to hear it?" Huck's face was serious, as if he were sharing the world's greatest secret, and Jake had to smother a grin.

"Well, if your mom said you shouldn't tell anyone, maybe you shouldn't tell anyone," Jake advised.

Huck contemplated Jake's words but continued anyway. "I've only ever told one other person in my life and that was Shep. You said since Shep was living in heaven now, that me and you could be best friends. What good is having a best friend if you can't tell them your secrets?" Huck patted Jake's leg. Jake found it hard to argue with the child's logic, reasoning that the secret was probably something silly Julie had made up to comfort Huck.

"Well, since we are best friends, I guess you can tell me if you really want to."

Huck glanced around and scrambled up on his knees so that he could lean his mouth close to Jake's ear. He cupped his small hand around his mouth and whispered to Jake, "I'm named after my dad."

Jake was surprised at the feelings that statement caused in him. Why should it bother him that Julie's son was named after his father? Obviously she had loved the man enough to give her son his name and that shouldn't cause the stir of jealous emotions that it did in Jake.

"Was his name Huck, too?" Jake questioned. He thought he remembered hearing the boy's father had been a law student named Eric.

"No…I'm named after his favorite book…something called *Huck Finn*. Momma says when I'm older I can read it…"

Jake didn't hear the rest. He could see Huck's lips moving but the roaring in his head drowned out any words. He was immediately transported to the first time he had met Julie. He had been hiding, reading his favorite book, *The Adventures of Huckleberry Finn*. What was the likelihood that Julie had met another man who had the same love for that classic? He sat there unable to move, the roaring in his ears becoming overwhelming. His heart raced; he could feel it pounding in his chest. The activity on the playground fell away and all he could focus on was the little boy sitting beside him talking quickly.

"How old are you, Huck?" Jake's voice was barely a whisper.

"I'm five." Huck held up one hand with fingers spread wide for emphasis.

Jake tried to speak and couldn't seem to force the words out. He finally cleared his throat and pushed the words out. "W-When is your birthday?"

"August second," Huck announced proudly.

Jake mentally did the math and realization crashed over him as the time between Huck's birth and his night with Julie was approximately nine months. Bile rose up in his mouth and his stomach clenched. A teacher stood by the door and called for her class to line up. Huck jumped up and gave Jake a quick wave as he ran to join the rest of the kids. Jake sat, unable to move, and watched the little boy until he disappeared into the school building.

He wasn't sure how long he sat there, watching the door that Huck had disappeared behind, his mind reeling. The coach must have noticed something was amiss as he approached Jake and asked if he was okay. Jake didn't hear him the first time and he repeated his question, placing his hand on Jake's shoulder and shaking him gently. Jake mumbled to the coach and strode purposefully to the front of the school. Everything and everyone else faded into the background. His only focus was confronting the one person who would have the answers he needed.

****

When Jake charged through the door at Etta's Diner less than fifteen minutes later, he had a singular focus. He didn't notice any of the customers seated around the restaurant or at the counter; he ignored the workers eyeing him as his long legs ate the distance across the diner and he entered the kitchen. As soon as the swinging door slapped closed behind him he shouted Julie's name.

"Jake! What are you doing?" Marti hissed as she tried to grab his arm, planning to lead him outside. He jerked out of her reach.

"Where is she?" Jake's eyes were wide as they darted around the kitchen.

Hearing the commotion, Julie opened the door to her office and stepped into the kitchen, her eyes immediately locking with Jake's. Her stomach fell and she knew before he ever spoke that her secrets had been exposed.

As soon as their gazes collided, Jake stepped toward her, unconcerned with any of the onlookers, who had all stopped their work to watch the exchange, and he exploded. "Is he mine? Is Huck my son?"

Julie's face paled and she gripped the door frame as every nightmare she had imagined over the last few years played out before her eyes. She met Jake's angry gaze, but words refused to come; her mind became a jumbled web of phrases and plans she had practiced over the years if this moment ever arrived, but right now she couldn't get any of those tangled thoughts to form coherent words.

He took a step toward her, anger vibrating from his body, and repeated through gritted teeth, emphasizing every word, *"Is he my son?"*

She glanced around the kitchen, looking for anything or anyone that might give her strength right now. She leaned against the door, suddenly weak and tired.

"Julie, tell me the truth," Jake demanded.

Julie closed her eyes and leaned the back of her head against the door, then nodded ever so slightly. Silence surrounded them and Marti quietly ushered the kitchen staff out the back door to allow them a modicum of privacy.

Jake's mind reeled as he watched her ever so slightly nod her head. His body went numb and it seemed as if time stood still in that moment. He wasn't sure how long he stood there staring at her, a face so familiar to him, yet now she seemed like such a stranger. A treacherous, devious stranger. Her face was eerily pale and silent tears slipped down her cheeks. The magnitude of the realization that he was a father fell on him, a heaviness cloaked him, and suddenly he found it hard to breathe. He leaned over, resting his hands on his knees, and took deep, steadying breaths. When he finally felt as if he might not collapse, he straightened, swallowed hard, and finally found his voice. "How could you?" he seethed. "How could you not tell me?"

Julie opened her eyes and tears fell more rapidly. "Jake, let me explain." She stepped forward, reaching for him as if to grab his arm. Her voice was frantic, her body shaking.

"Explain?" he exploded, taking a step back out of her reach, "There is no explanation for what you've done." They stood there in silence, Jake's face flushed with rage and tears rapidly flowing down Julie's cheeks. Silence stretched before them, broken occasionally by Julie's sobs.

Jake finally spoke, his voice eerily calm. "I will never forgive you for this, Julie. Never."

    His words ripped her final resolve and she slid down the door as sobs racked her body. He watched her shoulders heave, heard her cries that seemed to have originated deep in her soul, and all he could feel was numbness. He turned, shoving the kitchen door with all his might, causing it to slap loudly against the counter. When he stepped into the diner, wide-eyed faces with mouths agape stared at him, the usual noisy clatter of the restaurant replaced with a deafening quiet. He raised his chin and strode purposefully toward the door, the sounds of Julie's sobs only muted when the heavy glass door fell shut behind him.

Chapter 14 *Unknowns*

"If it is possible, as far as it depends on you, live at peace with everyone." Romans 12:18

All sense of space and time left Jake. When he left the diner, all he could think of was getting away; if he got far enough away, maybe everything would make sense again. He drove for what seemed like hours, and his mind and body slipped into autopilot as he maneuvered roads that led to Shep's farm. He parked by the barn and walked down to the river. Without really thinking about it, he wound up at one his favorite fishing spots from childhood. He sat down on a large rock and studied the river flowing past him.

He absentmindedly tossed nearby leaves and twigs into the river and watched them float out of sight. He wished desperately that he could escape as easily. As if he didn't have enough problems, now to find out he had a child, and not just any child, but a child with Julie, a child who had some type of mysterious health problems. What did he know about being a father?

He thought about his own dad and how he had guided Jake through his childhood. He had always provided for Jake, given him sound advice and helped guide him into manhood. Not that Jake had always taken his father's advice, but it had been offered in wisdom nonetheless.

Jake examined his own life briefly and sank into an even deeper despair. He was broke, in debt, and if he was brutally honest with himself, in a relationship with a woman he didn't even like anymore, much less love. How could he be a father? He had no wisdom to share; he wasn't qualified to give anyone advice, and he was financially unable to provide for himself, much less a child.

From his innermost parts, fear gripped him and radiated throughout his body until he physically shook. He roughly grasped his hands together, trying to still them. Slowly the fear was replaced by anger as he thought about all he had endured since his football injury. Anger and jealousy stepped up to guide his emotions and he let them have free rein. What had he ever done to deserve such continued punishment? Why did everything in his life always have to be so difficult? Other people had easy paths, why not him?

He stood suddenly and threw his head back and roared, "What did I ever do to deserve this?" He waited, watching the heavens expectantly, as if he screamed loud enough the God of the universe would suddenly break through the clouds and answer him. "WHY? Why me?" he screamed through gritted teeth and when the silence of the evening sky was the only response he received, he let a guttural growl beginning deep down inside him rip through his body and echo through the river bottom.

"Jake?"

He turned quickly toward the sound of his name to find his father and Coach Doug warily approaching him. "Jake?" his father repeated. "Are you okay?"

Jake's eyes were wide and he stood there speechless as the two men approached. For the first time in what seemed like hours, Jake became conscious of the passing of time; the sun had been high in the sky when he had first sat down on the rock. He shivered and looked down to see that he was still in the shorts and T-shirt he had dressed in for practice. At some time, the sun had slipped from the sky and the darkness that had fallen brought a chill to the air.

"Son, what's going on? We've been worried about you." Coach Rawlings stepped closer to Jake and lifted his arm to squeeze his son's shoulder as if reassuring himself that Jake was really in front of him. Jake stared at his father, open-mouthed, unable to relate the events of the day that had led to his disappearance. Coach gripped both of Jake's shoulders and gently shook him. "Are you okay?"

Jake shook his head, hoping to clear his mind enough that he could form words that would satisfy the concerned look on his father's face. "I-I'm f-fine," he stuttered.

"Son, you don't seem fine." Coach smiled gently, still gripping his shoulders, worry etching his face.

Doug finally spoke up from behind Jim. "Fine don't take off in their daddy's truck and miss practice. We've been looking for you for hours, Jake."

"I'm sorry." He turned to face his father, the heaviness of the day weighing down on him, and tears rimmed his eyes. "I'm sorry, Dad."

Coach wasn't sure what had driven his son to miss practice and spend what appeared to be hours sitting on the riverbank, but he could tell from the emotion in Jake's voice and the tears in his eyes that whatever troubled his son was not trivial.

"Are you hurt? Has anyone hurt you?" Coach's protective instincts took over. Coach's mind jumped to the conversation he had overheard between Jake and Mr. Peterson. Coach had been waiting in the barn for Doug to pick him up after becoming utterly disgusted with the talk of developing Shep's farm during Whitney's staged surprise. He hadn't meant to eavesdrop, but eavesdrop he had and discovered his son was in quite the financial mess. He hadn't spoken to anyone about this information, but he had spent quite a bit of time since then trying to figure out what he should do about it, if anything.

"N-No, Dad. I'm not hurt." Jake gripped his father's hands as if they were a lifeline to him.

"Let's go home, Jake." His father guided him back toward the house. Only when his father's truck came into view did Jake realize he had not only taken his father's vehicle but also he had left the driver's side door standing ajar. He let Coach lead him to the passenger's side. Sliding in, he settled in the seat, his body suddenly overcome with exhaustion. As they drove back to his parents' house, he studied his father from the corner of his eye. What would Coach think about him if he knew he was not only a father, but had been for five years? Would he find his father's eyes filled with disappointment in him again? He closed his eyes and roughly rubbed his hands down his face. When they finally pulled into the driveway, he saw his mother step out onto the porch, her face hidden in the shadows, but he was sure it was full of worry.

He slipped quietly from the truck and made his way to his mother's outstretched arms. While her face was full of worry and questions, he was immensely grateful that she didn't pepper him with questions. She simply sat quietly while he ate and hugged him fiercely when he excused himself to go to bed.

Coach watched his son shuffle up the stairs appearing as though the weight of the world was on his shoulders. He wasn't sure what had happened to Jake today, but whatever it was, it had affected him greatly. He glanced over his shoulder to Doug, who had sat quietly in the living room, observing. When Jake disappeared at the top of the stairs, Coach turned and took the seat across from Doug.

"What do you think is going on?" Doug asked quietly.

"I'm not sure, but I think I have an idea." Coach pressed his lips into a thin line and then added, "Doug, I don't know how to help him. I guess a father never stops worrying about their kids even when they are grown."

Doug studied at this longtime friend thoughtfully before answering, "Jim, you know I haven't had Marley in my life since she was a little girl, but there is nothing I wouldn't do for her. I know you feel the same way. All you can do is make sure he knows you are there for him. He will come to you when the time is right." Doug rarely mentioned his estranged daughter, and Coach knew just to say her name brought his friend great pain. Coach nodded and glanced toward the kitchen to make sure Mary was out of earshot before asking, "If I needed your help — ?"

Doug interrupted, "Yep, sure can. I can do whatever you need, Jim."

"I just got him back, Doug, I'm not going to lose him again."

****

Julie stood in the middle of Huck's bedroom tossing items from the closet onto the bed. Once she had been able to gather herself off the office floor after Jake's confrontation, she had rushed to the school to pick up her son. The five-minute drive from school felt more like five hours as she planned her escape from Jake and any plan he might be plotting to take Huck from her. A soft knock on the door was the only thing that stopped her frantic packing. She stopped in midstride and stared in fear at the door. What awaited her on the other side? Were Jake and his parents on the other side of her door waiting to snatch Huck away? She chewed the inside of her jaw nervously, her body frozen in place.

Huck, in his childish innocence, bounced to the door and flung it open before she could stop him.

"Aunt Marti!" Huck sang out excitedly and surprised Marti by jumping into her arms. Julie glared at her friend over Huck's head, and stepped forward to remove Huck from the embrace. "Huck, why don't you go watch TV. Marti and I need to talk." Julie spoke to Huck but her eyes shot fiery darts toward their visitor. She turned away long enough to watch Huck skip back to the living room. As soon as she was satisfied that he was out of earshot, Julie turned back to the woman standing at her front door and spat, "What are you doing here?"

Marti jerked back as if she had been slapped. "I came to check on you."

"Check on me?" Julie stepped over the threshold and closed the door to leave just enough of a crack to hear Huck if he called out. "Why would you want to check on me? So you could see firsthand the destruction you've caused?"

"What? That I've caused?!" Marti placed her hands on her

hips.

"You told Jake about Huck, just like you told me you would. I would have told him, Marti, in my own time! Now look what you've done!" Angry tears streamed down Julie's face.

"Julie, I didn't tell him," Marti answered flatly. "It wasn't me."

Julie stared at the other woman, contemplating her claim. She had known Marti since they were teenagers. Since Etta's death she had been the one person Julie knew she could count on and her confidence in the other woman's guilt began to wane. "If you didn't, then who did?" Julie challenged.

"I don't know; all I know is that it wasn't me." Marti reached out to take her friend by the hands. "I know what I said, but Julie, you have to believe me; I didn't tell him."

Julie stood staring blankly at her friend. Moments ticked by and Julie tried to piece together what events might have occurred that would have revealed her secret to Jake. She searched Marti's face and saw nothing but sincerity there. Julie dropped her face in her hands and groaned, "I'm sorry, Marti. I'm so sorry. I just assumed…"

"It's okay, Julie, really it is." Marti gestured toward the door. "Let's go inside where we can talk."

As they stepped inside, Marti immediately noticed the suitcases lying open in the hallway and turned to Julie in shock. "What's this?" She gestured to the suitcases. "Are you running away? You know you can't do that."

"What choice do I have?" Julie began stuffing clothes strewn around the hallway into the nearest suitcase.

Marti reached around and grabbed her friend by the shoulders. "What choice do you have? How about letting Jake be a father and Huck have a dad? You can't run away from this. You have to stay. You have to face this once and for all."

They stared at each other, Marti's words diving deep inside Julie's consciousness. Suddenly sobs jerked through Julie's body as she fell in her friend's arms. "What if I can't?"

Marti let the other woman cry for a while and then gently gripped her friend's chin and raised her face to look in her eyes.

"What do you mean? Do you realize how strong you are? You've raised Huck by yourself since he was born. You took care of Etta while she was sick and managed Huck's health too. God brought you this far, He isn't going to abandon you now. He will see you through this too. You can't let fear make decisions for you right now."

Julie sniffed and roughly wiped her face on the back of her hands. "But the fear is so loud right now," she whispered.

Marti gave her a sympathetic grin. "Let your faith be louder." She let her words sink in before she added, "You need to talk to Jake."

"I can't do that." Julie replied quickly and stepped back from her friend.

"You have to." Marti took her hands and gently squeezed and repeated, "You have to."

****

For the next twenty-four hours, Julie conjured up and played out in her mind every worst-case scenario possible. Sleep eluded her. The sight of food made her nauseous. The nervousness that had settled into her stomach had now spread to every part of her body. Her hands and legs shook. Her stomach churned continually. She kept Huck home from school the following day, shutting every window and blind in her home. Every noise caused her to jump out of her skin. Fearing that if she stayed holed up in her house for one more minute, she would lose her mind, she took Huck to the diner. As she busied herself with mundane, routine tasks, she felt her stomach settle, only to have her nerves rattled again every time the bell on the diner door jangled. Each time she heard the bell, she jerked her head up expecting to see Jake barge through the door and demand custody of Huck.

The dinner crowd arrived early, decked out in blue and gold to attend the football game. By the time the rush was over with and darkness had fallen, Julie had decided she could take no more. Why was she worrying and waiting? She had spent the entire day studying her situation and something Marti had said yesterday kept replaying through her mind. It was time to stop worrying.

****

Jake watched the team celebrate their win in the middle of the field. He stood on the sidelines, arms crossed, legs spread, feeling detached from the situation. He had been useless tonight as an assistant coach to his father and he knew that. Their win had come, but with no help from him. His mind was stuck replaying the events of the previous day, like a movie on repeat. He went over every word; he could close his eyes and see Huck's innocent face as if the boy stood right in front of him. He studied the boy's features from memory, trying to determine if there was any likeness to his own.

The most problematic issue Jake faced at the moment was trying to determine his next move. He had never felt more lost or alone in his life, and he didn't think it was possible to feel worse than he had after his injury, but he did.

"Jake?"

He immediately recognized her voice, which caused an odd combination of stomach flutters and anger. He slowly turned to face her and the minute he saw her face his traitorous heart lurched in his chest. She looked as if she had been crying and the dark circles under her eyes led him to believe that he hadn't been the only one who had spent last night tossing and turning. He ground his back molars, angry with himself for feeling the least bit of sympathy for her.

"What do you want?" He put his hands on his hips and glared at her.

"We need to talk." Her voice was quiet and the tone of desperation tugged at his heart strings.

He screamed at himself internally to keep from softening toward her. "Talk?" he said on a bitter laugh. "Nothing but silence from you for five years and now you want to talk?"

"Jake, if you would just let me explain," she pleaded, her eyes searching his face.

"Explain?" he exploded and then quickly looked around to see if he had drawn attention to them. Stepping closer to her to try to keep their conversation quiet, he dropped his voice to a harsh whisper. "What is there to explain? You kept my son from me." Just saying the words "my son" caused his throat to tighten and then just to hurt her he added, "If he is my son."

Her eyes went wide with shock, and tears threatened to spill down her cheeks. She shook her head and reached out to grab his forearm. "I know you're angry, but *please*... Jake, we need to talk about this! I can't keep wondering if you're going to show up at my door and try to take him from me."

The touch of her hand on his skin caused an electric pulse to shoot up his arm and heat filled his body. He stepped back, unable to think clearly while her hand gripped his arm. His eyes searched her face, and the words that came out of his mouth shocked him as much as her. "I want a DNA test."

Julie's face blanched. Moments ticked by slowly and then she stammered, "Y-you t-think I was with someone else? You know me better than that, Jake."

He crossed his arms over his chest. "Do I? The Julie I knew wouldn't have kept my son from me. This person standing before me now, I don't think I know them at all." And just to make sure she was hurting like he was, he added, "I'm not sure I ever did."

She stood there staring at him, her mouth agape, unable to speak, tears pooling in the corner of her eyes. Again an overwhelming urge to reach out, wipe them away, and pull her into his arms welled up inside him. Willing himself not to feel anything other than anger for her, he added as he turned to follow the team to the locker room, "If you want to talk, you can talk to my lawyer."

****

Julie tried to hide her tears from Huck, but over the weekend he had caught her several times wiping her eyes. After his initial questions about what was bothering her went unanswered, he hadn't asked again, but simply hugged his mother often. In fact, when she dropped him off at school Monday morning, he hugged her fiercely and the tears threatened to spill down her cheeks again. She once again realized how blessed she was to have Huck as her son with his compassionate, loving heart. She had been on edge all weekend, expecting at any moment to hear from Jake or his lawyer, but Monday morning had dawned without any word from either. Work had taken her mind off her immediate troubles, but as soon as the breakfast crowd dispersed and Clay Phillips walked through the door with a concerned look on his face, she knew her troubles had resurfaced.

Clay set his lips in a grim line and nodded to her as he took a seat at the counter. She filled a coffee cup and set it in front of him. "Good morning, Clay. Can I get you something to eat?"

Clay tapped the counter and released a pent up breath. "Julie, I'm not here to eat."

She leaned on the counter wearily. "Somehow I knew that."

"Jake has asked me to represent him..." Clay searched her face, and she could tell from the painful look in his eyes that he was struggling to finish his sentence.

Julie reached over and placed her hand on top of his. "It's fine, Clay. I understand, you're just doing your job."

Clay looked relieved and his shoulders sagged. "He wants a DNA test."

Julie nodded, unable to speak, and Clay continued, "If you agree to the test, Dr. Carnahan can take the samples and send them off, shouldn't take more than a day or two to get the results."

"And if I don't agree?" Julie countered.

Clay's eyes looked bleak and Julie knew he didn't like the position he found himself in. "He can easily get a court order and force you to get the test."

Julie rubbed her temples and briefly thought how quickly her life had spun out of control. "Do I make the appointment or do you?"

"You can make it, Julie. I trust you."

"You might, but your client doesn't." Julie tried to make her voice sound light but failed miserably.

Clay stood, a pained look crossing his face. "I'm sorry. I truly am."

Huck didn't question the doctor's visit. He had endured so many visits in his life, it was simply routine. Julie, however, was a ball of nerves throughout the visit. Her face and neck flushed profusely as the nurse, whom Julie had known for most of her life, came in the exam room to swab Huck's cheek. She smiled brightly at Julie and announced, "That's it. You should have the results in a few days. I'm sure Doc will call you."

Julie felt the heat creep up her neck and face as she quickly gathered her things and ushered Huck out of the doctor's office. By the time she sat in her car, some of her embarrassment had channeled itself into anger. How dare Jake subject her to this humiliation?

****

"Earth to Jake." Coach waved his hand in front of Jake's line of vision. More than once in the past week he had caught Jake staring off into the distance or sitting by himself completely lost in his thoughts.

"Sorry, Dad, I guess I just drifted off there for a minute." Jake shook his head and tried to focus on the players practicing in front of him.

"You seem to be doing that quite a bit lately." Coach studied his son's profile as if something in his face would reveal what occupied his mind so much lately. "Something you want to talk about?"

Jake chewed the inside of his jaw. He doubted his parents hadn't heard about his confrontation in the diner, but they hadn't mentioned it to him. Did they know Huck was his son? He suspected that they had always been disappointed with him over the callous way he had ended his relationship with Julie. If they knew the details of how cold he had been to her the day after the Christmas parade, he knew they would not approve. But he also knew that they would be ecstatic about the idea of having Huck in their lives. But something kept him from being completely honest with his father; he had too much to work out internally and with Julie before he came clean with everyone. Dr. Carnahan had notified him two days ago that he indeed was Huck's father, he had immediately called Clay's office and made an appointment to discuss his next steps. In fact, when he glanced down at his watch he realized that exact appointment was only thirty minutes away.

With practice nowhere near ending he turned to his father, "Dad, I'm fine, please don't worry about me, but I do need to cut out a little early today if that's okay?"

Coach turned to face him and placed his hand on his shoulder. "Jake, if you are in trouble, let me help you. If it's the farm or…something else, just let me help you."

"Dad…" He searched his father's face. "It's nothing I can't handle, I promise."

Coach did not look convinced but nodded and gestured his head toward the field house. "Go on get out of here. I'll see you at home."

Jake pulled up in front of Clay Phillips's office as his secretary was leaving for the day. "He's waiting for you," she called out as she stepped off the bottom step and headed toward her car.

Jake took the steps two at a time, eager to speak with Clay. Apprehension filled his body as he thought about the prospect of getting to know his son. He had no idea what to expect or what would happen next, he just knew that something inside him felt all warm and fuzzy over spending time with Huck.

Clay jumped when Jake stepped inside his office; the nervous movement from the usually calm, cool lawyer seemed odd. Clay stood to shake Jake's hand, then laid his hand on Jake's shoulder to guide him back into the hall.

"Jake," Clay began gesturing down the hall, "let's go to the conference room."

Jake nodded and followed behind as Clay continued to talk. "I know you want to discuss your options regarding Huck's custody."

"I want to get to know my son, Clay." Jake spoke to the lawyer's back as he followed him and didn't even attempt to keep the bitterness out of his voice. "I have a lot of time to make up for."

Clay stopped at the end of the hall, and with his hand on the knob of the closed door he turned to face his client. "Jake, have you thought about how all of this will affect Huck?"

"What do you mean affect Huck?" Jake, not liking the tone of Clay's conversation, stood feet apart, hands on his hips as if ready to do battle, his voice angry. "Huck deserves to have his father in his life and I deserve to know my son."

Clay turned with his palms up. "Jake, I agree with you, I really do, but…"

Jake crossed his arms over his chest. "But what, Clay? You are supposed to be my lawyer—"

"I am your lawyer, Jake," Clay interrupted hurriedly, then paused took a deep breath and tried to reason with his client. "Jake, in my professional opinion, custody cases tend work out better when the parents talk to one another."

"Talk!?" Jake said forcefully. "She had five years to talk, and all she did was keep silent. The time for talking is over."

"There is more to this than you realize. You and Julie need to sit down and talk this out."

"I don't want to talk to her." Jake instantly hated how childish he sounded.

Clay put his hand back on the doorknob. "Julie has agreed to sit down and try to talk this out." He opened the door before Jake could respond, and revealed Julie seated at the table in the conference room, fidgeting nervously. Jake cut his eyes to Clay, unable to believe how he had been tricked. Clay gripped Jake's shoulder and pleaded with him, "Give it an hour, Jake. If y'all can't make the least bit of headway, I'll handle it from here on out at my cost."

Jake studied Clay's face, unwilling to look in Julie's direction.

"One hour, Jake." Clay looked hopeful as he pushed Jake toward the center of the room and quickly shut the door behind him.

Jake refused to look in Julie's direction. He stood in the middle of the room looking at everything except at the mother of his child. The only sound in the room was the ticking of the wall clock. He stepped toward the window, leaned one shoulder against the wall, and planned to wait out the next sixty minutes in total silence. Time seemed to drag by; he was confident that he had been in the room for an eternity when in fact he discovered when he looked at the clock he had only been there for a few moments. He returned his gaze to the scene outside, studying the shrubbery, parking lot, cars passing, without really seeing anything. The ever so slight sound of a sniffle caused an involuntary jerk of his head away from the window. He listened closely as he heard the distinct sound again and saw Julie's hand quickly wipe away a tear.

He turned back to the window, pressing his forehead against the pane. He closed his eyes, willing himself not to care that she was crying. He heard the sound again, and tried to conjure up all his anger to fight the urge to check on her. Admittedly he was not an overly sympathetic person; spending most of his energy feeling sorry for himself, he had little time to share in anyone else's pain. Plus the years he had spent with Whitney had hardened his heart; she had viewed sympathy as a weakness and had pounced on Jake if he ever showed any sign of weakness.

But try as he might he could not help feeling the slightest bit concerned over Julie's tears. He turned his head to study her. He could see her profile and witnessed a tear roll down her cheek. He gripped his hand as he fought an overwhelming urge to cross the room and wipe her eyes. He tried to think about the five years she had lied to him; had lied to his family. He thought about how she had lived in this town, seeing his parents regularly, and keeping their grandson from them. The anger that never seemed far from the surface began to boil in him.

But as soon as he thought he had stirred his anger enough to get him through the next hour, he glanced in her direction in time to see her shoulders shake from a silent sob. He huffed bitterly and thought to himself that some things never changed. The sun came up in the east and set in the west, rivers ran toward the ocean, time passed whether you wanted it to or not, and he never could stand to see Julie cry.

He turned his head toward her, still leaning on the windowsill. "Are you crying?" His voice sounded harsh and bitter.

"N-no." She straightened in her chair and turned her face away from him to wipe the tears in secret.

He pushed himself off the windowsill and was across the room within a few long strides, standing on the other side of the table, facing her. "Looks like you're crying to me." His voice was a touch softer as he gripped the back of the chair opposite of her with two large hands.

She folded her hands together as if praying and pressed her mouth against them, tightly closing her eyes. Twin tears escaped from the corner of either eye and they were Jake's undoing. He sighed deeply as he pulled the chair out and sat across from her. He studied her for a moment, her head bowed, unwilling to meet his eyes. In his mind he could see them as teenagers, inseparable, laughing and loving each other. He remembered the way she would gaze at him with love in her eyes. In those moments he had felt as if nothing were impossible for him if she just continued to look at him that way. A small ache bloomed inside him as he wished his confidence could be found so easily again, just from a loving look. He thought about how much he had loved her and how he had sacrificed that love in his all-consuming quest to become a football star. His father's words echoed in his head as he roughly rubbed his chin: *"Son, if I have ever been disappointed in you, it was never, ever over football, but in the man you've turned into since your injury. We didn't raise you to treat people the way you do..."*

He leaned back in his chair, letting his arms fall between his long legs. "Why are you crying?"

The question hung between them for so long Jake began to doubt she would answer. But finally Julie sniffed and roughly wiped her cheeks. She straightened in her chair, leveling him with her tear-filled eyes. "I'm scared, Jake."

Her voice was small and her words dove to a place deep inside him, stirring an arcane urge to protect and care for what was his. He straightened his spine and leaned his arms on the table, mentally reminding himself that she definitely was not his to protect and that this woman, whom his mind and body were suddenly betraying him over, had hidden his son from him for five years. He licked his lips and tried to keep any emotion he might be feeling out of his voice. "What are you scared of?"

His question seemed to open a dam inside her as she began talking hurriedly. "I'm scared of you, Jake, and your parents! I'm scared of your fiancée and all her money and her daddy's big fancy lawyers. I'm scared you are going to take my son from me! I'm scared that everyone in this town is going to hate me when they find out what I did and no one will come to the diner anymore and I'll lose my business. I'm scared that Huck is going to hate me when he finds out about you. I'm afraid that your parents will hate me…" Her voice trailed off and she stood suddenly, turning away from the table.

Jake, shocked by her outburst, mouth agape, was unable to move out of his chair or take his eyes off of her. Finally she turned to face him and, tears now freely streaming down her cheeks, she took a deep breath and finished, "I'm afraid that Shep died hating me because he somehow found out the truth…and…" She dropped her face in her hands, her voice broke and tortured as she continued, "And as mad as I have been at you for the last six years, I guess I'm scared that you hate me too." Sighing deeply, she fell heavily back into her chair.

Jake took a breath to steady himself and slowly released it. He rested his elbow on the table and gripped his mouth in his palm, studying her face. She raised her head and returned his steady gaze, seemingly stronger now that she had voiced all her fears. He tried to speak several times and stopped himself.

Finally swallowing, clearing his throat, he responded, his voice soft and low, "I'm not going to try and take Huck from you, Julie; I wouldn't do that to him. I just want to know my son."

She nodded slowly and he continued, "And for him to know me...to know that I am his father."

She twisted her fingers together in her lap. "I'm just worried how Huck is going to handle all this. This is lot for him to process."

"No, you're worried about how you're going to handle it," he snapped.

Julie rubbed her temples and let out a shaky breath, feeling the walls closing in on her. She debated walking out of the room, but knew that Jake wouldn't stop. She knew him well enough to know the determined look in his eye meant he wouldn't stop until he got what he wanted. If she continued to keep Huck away from him, would he change his mind about not talking Huck away from her? Backed into a corner, she considered her options and could only see one way out. "Okay..." She closed her eyes and bit her lower lip. "Why don't you come over sometime and he can get to know you? I've been thinking and maybe this would be easier for Huck if he got to know you first, before we tell him."

Jake nodded. "That seems fair, Julie, and that is all I ask from this point forward is for fair treatment. I'm angry with you and I'm not sure I'll ever get past that, but I promise I won't use that against you when it comes to Huck."

"I know you're angry." Her voice was small as she dusted imaginary lint from her lap, not meeting his eyes.

"Wouldn't you be?" he challenged.

Her eyes cut to his quickly. "I'd be livid if you had kept him from me."

"Then why did you do it?" Jake cried, his anger rising again.

Julie stood quickly, causing the chair she had been sitting in to roll back and thud against the wall. She paced for a few moments before stopping in front of the window Jake had recently vacated and looked out. Time passed slowly until he was sure she was done speaking to him. He stood and turned toward the door but stopped in his tracks when she began, her voice so low that he had to step toward her to hear her.

"I was so mad at you after that morning. You know I wouldn't….do *that* with just anyone. I wouldn't have done it with anyone but you. And I know it was wrong. I've begged God to forgive me for being so weak…but I just…" She rubbed her forehead and her shoulders slumped forward. "I…I had missed you so much. Since that day in your driveway when you broke up with me, something had been missing, something in my life was just….gone. I went through the motions, but I was never truly happy…I never felt happiness…and then there you were and I felt so much joy at being with you again…at having you look at me like you cared again."

Jake stood motionless as she continued, still staring out the window. "But that next morning…it was like having my heart ripped out all over again. I was mad at you, mad at myself for letting you hurt me again. When I found out I was pregnant, you were the last person I wanted to talk to. I kept putting it off. I knew I should tell you, but honestly at that point I didn't know this person you had become and I worried that you wouldn't want us, or that you would hate me for being pregnant, but I did plan on telling you before the baby was born. I did plan that. But during an ultrasound they t-told m-me…" She began to cry. "…that the baby had something wrong with his h-heart… I was terrified, I didn't know what to do. I hadn't even told Etta I was pregnant, I was too ashamed. But when I called her, she came to me, s-she never hesitated. She stayed with me from then on, dropped everything just to take care of me. When Huck was born, he stayed in the NICU for months."

She turned to him at this point, tears freely streaming down her cheeks. "He's had three open heart surgeries. The first one when he was just two weeks old. I was so scared. All I could think about was Huck and maybe it was wrong and maybe it was the most selfish thing I've ever done, but I just couldn't deal with you and our sick son at the same time. All my focus was on Huck and I just put you out of my mind."

Jake stood there staring at her as she bared her heart to him.

He tried to speak but his mouth was too dry so he swallowed and began slowly. "But he did get better? I've seen him playing at his school, he is better?"

"Yes, he is, for all intents and purposes, just like every other five-year-old little boy as long as he takes his medication and follows his cardiologist's directions."

"And in all those years, during all those surgeries, during all those doctor's visits, you never once thought that I should know? That I had a right to know?" He stepped toward her as he spoke, anger rising in his voice again.

She began to wring her hands as she spoke. "Once Huck was to the point that I knew he was going to be okay, Etta started to get sick. And I just...I just kept telling myself I didn't have time to deal with telling you about Huck."

"Didn't have time?" he exploded, his voice harsh and loud. "One phone call, Julie, one phone call was all it would have taken! It's not about having time, you were punishing me for the way I treated you!"

"Maybe I was!" she screamed back at him and as soon as the words were out she clapped her mouth over her hand in shock.

"And you lived in this town, right under my parents' nose, with their grandson and never even thought about telling me or them." His voice was low as he spoke between gritted teeth.

She crossed her arms tightly over her chest and spoke, refusing to meet his steely gaze. "I'm not proud of what I've done, Jake. I'm truly not...but...but it was as if I just got into the lie so far, I couldn't find my way out of it."

Jake felt as if she had punched him in the stomach. Wasn't he in just as deep in his own lies? Lying to his parents, his best friend, his fiancée, and even himself to keep up the façade of a successful, powerful life, when in reality if his father hadn't given him a part-time coaching job he wouldn't have a dime to his name. He stood with his feet apart, hands resting on his hips, unable to speak.

"I'm sorry, Jake. I know that the words will probably never be enough, but I truly am sorry."

He nodded his head and swallowed hard, trying to find his

voice. "We can't change the past, Julie, we just have to promise each other that no matter what or how we feel about each other, Huck comes first." She nodded her agreement and he continued, "When can I come over and spend some time with him?"

Chapter 15 *Hellos*

"Love is patient, love is kind…" 1 Corinthians 13:4

Jake stood nervously in front of Julie's front door, wiping his hands down his pants. He shifted his weight from one foot to the other and lifted his hand to knock; much to his surprise the door flew open, revealing Huck excitedly jumping up and down.

"Jake Rawlings, Jake Rawlings," he repeated excitedly. "What are you doing at my house?"

Jake squatted down until he was face to face with Huck. "Well, your mom invited me over for dinner." Suddenly Jake felt his throat tighten as he studied the excitement dancing in his son's eyes. Emotions welled in his chest and he felt moisture fill his eyes.

Julie had been a jumble of nerves all afternoon at the prospect of Jake having dinner with her and Huck. Marti had finally ordered her to leave the diner after the lunch rush to try and gather herself. She found herself sitting on the bench under the towering trees in the churchyard trying to find some peace. She prayed that God would forgive her for her role in all of this deception. She also prayed that Jake and his parents would forgive her. Despite the fear of how Huck, along with Coach and Mary would react when they found out the truth, Julie felt a burden had been lifted now that Jake knew the truth. Some of the fear she had lived with for so long had dissipated after their meeting in Clay's office. She wasn't sure if Jake would ever forgive her, but she was surprised that she felt some modicum of relief that she no longer had to lie awake at night wondering what would happen if Jake found out about Huck.

She was in the kitchen putting the finishing touches on dinner when she heard Huck race toward the front door. Her stomach plummeted as she knew Jake stood on the other side. She rounded the corner in time to see Jake squatted down in front of Huck. As she stepped closer, she noticed the tears welling in his eyes.

Stepping forward, she placed her hands on Huck's shoulders and turned him toward the kitchen. "Huck, why don't you go clean up your schoolbooks so we can eat dinner." Jake took the brief moment to wipe his eyes, nodding gratefully at Julie when she looked over her shoulder to check on him.

Jake followed Julie and Huck into the kitchen, feeling a familiarity at being back in the home Julie had grown up in. Huck scrambled onto a barstool and began frantically finishing his homework.

"Slow down there, buddy," Julie admonished. Jake slid into the barstool beside Huck and peeped over his shoulder.

"It's math," Huck offered with a disgusted tone.

"Do you like math?" Jake asked.

"It's okay...I'm learning to read. I could read a book to you."

Jake nodded as he found his throat tight with emotion once again. "Sure, Huck, I would love that."

"Let's eat first, and you can read to Jake after dinner."

As they took seats around the kitchen table, Julie turned to Huck. "Why don't you say the blessing."

Huck nodded and waited for everyone to sit down and bow their heads before he began. "God is great, God is good, let us thank him for our food. And thank you, God, that Jake is with us too."

Jake felt the now familiar lump of emotion well in his throat once again. Huck kept up a steady stream of conversation during dinner, which Jake and Julie were both grateful for. As they cleared the table, Jake found himself agreeing to watch Huck ride his bike.

"If that's okay with your mom?" Jake ventured as he met Julie's eyes over the top of Huck's head.

"Of course." Her voice was soft as she nodded.

Jake helped Huck ride his bike, shoot some basketball, and competed in a foot race down the driveway. Jake couldn't help but think it was one of the best nights of his life. Finally Julie announced it was time for a bath.

"Mom!" Huck face turned red and his voice was strained. "Not in front of Jake."

Jake chuckled. "It's okay, buddy. I need to be going anyway."

"But we didn't even get to play football!" Huck turned to him, disappointment on his face.

Jake bent down so that he could look Huck in the eye. "We will play football some other time, I promise."

"Tomorrow?" Huck asked brightly. "You could come back tomorrow night."

Jake wanted to immediately accept, wanting nothing more than to spend time with this amazing little boy, but instead he looked up to find Julie's eyes. "Well if it's okay with your mom?"

"Sure. Why not?" She nodded, a slight trace of sarcasm in her tone, and Jake couldn't quite read the emotions that played across her face.

"What if I bring pizza?" Jake offered, and Huck began to jump up and down shouting his excitement, then abruptly wrapped his arms around Jake's neck. Jake hesitated only a moment before tightly wrapping Huck's little body up tightly in his arms. Huck wiggled out of his embrace and yelled over his shoulder as he raced toward the house. "See ya tomorrow, Jake. I like cheese pizza!"

Jake felt awkward standing in the driveway alone with Julie. He absently kicked a rock across the driveway, and briefly wondered whether his nerves were about meeting his son, or being alone with his son's mother. "Thanks for dinner and for letting me come back tomorrow night."

"Well, I didn't really feel like I had a choice, but it's fine. Huck's excited…" Her voice trailed off.

"He's an amazing kid, Julie," Jake whispered as he met her gaze.

She nodded in agreement and Jake continued, "When can we tell him that he's my son?"

Julie bit her lower lip and glanced over her shoulder to the house before looking back to Jake's questioning gaze. "Soon, Jake, soon."

****

Not only did Jake eat dinner with Julie and Huck the next night, but every night for the following week. His parents didn't question where he was spending his evenings, but just smothered grins and exchanged looks as he announced once again that he wasn't going to be around for dinner. They fell into an easy routine which included dinner, helping Huck with homework, and playing games. Jake had even begun staying late enough to help read Huck a story before bed. As long as Huck was present, Jake and Julie were cordial to one another, but as soon as Huck was asleep, Jake hurriedly said goodbye. Seeing Jake and Huck interact heaped guilt on Julie's already burdened conscience.

Tonight had been no different. To anyone who didn't know better, they would appear to be a perfect little family, but as soon as Huck went to sleep, the walls came back up between Julie and Jake. He paused as he was walking out the front door, meeting Julie's gaze over his shoulder, his voice low. "He asked me tonight why I keep coming around. He asked me if you and I were dating."

Julie covered her mouth with her hand and lowered her eyes. Clearing her throat, she stepped toward him. "We'll tell him tomorrow night…if that is okay with you."

Jake nodded and took a step out the door, but before he could close it, Julie stepped forward and grabbed the handle. "Jake." She paused for him to turn around. "Jake…I'm sorry. I know that doesn't make up for the years...but I truly am sorry. Seeing the two of you together..." She nervously bit her lower lip, holding her hands tightly together. "You are a good father, Jake. I guess I always thought you would hurt him...the way you hurt me. But now I know I used my anger and fear to justify keeping him from you. I know if I said I was sorry every minute of every day for the rest of my life, it would never be enough...but I truly am sorry, Jake."

Jake cleared his throat and thought about the words he wanted to say. "That night at Shep's...I wasn't in a good place, mentally or emotionally. I haven't been in a good place mentally or emotionally for a really long time. I've spent a lot of time being bitter about not getting what I thought I deserved out of life." He cleared his throat and chose his next words carefully. "I'm not saying what you did was right, but I can't say that I would have always put Huck first, or have been a very good father to him. I've been pretty selfish."

Julie nodded and it was all he needed to continue. "That night at Shep's and the first time I broke up with you, I didn't treat you very well; in fact, I treated you pretty poorly. All I cared about was myself and...and I'm sorry that I hurt you."

Tears pooled in the corners of Julie's eyes and as one tear slipped out, Jake's hand voluntarily cupped her cheek and wiped the tear away with the pad of his thumb. Their eyes locked and he took a step toward her and, slipping his arms around her, he pulled her body next to his and buried his face in her hair, breathing deeply. They held each other tightly, trying to convey all the emotions they were feeling through their embrace. He pressed her body tightly against his and then released her, taking a step back but never breaking the connection of their eyes.

"Do you think Shep somehow knew about you being Huck's dad? Do you think that's why he wrote his will the way he did?"

Jake chuckled, thinking back to the day Huck had shared his secret, "I'm pretty sure he figured it out." Then he added softly as she nodded, unable to speak, "I'll see you tomorrow night."

He turned his back to her and his steps felt lighter than they had in a very long time.

****

"My, my, Jake, you sure look nice." Mary grinned as her handsome son stepped into the kitchen. Coach turned from the pot on the stove he was stirring and let out a whistle. "What would Whitney say about all this going out you've been doing?"

Jake looked down at his jeans, pressed button-down white shirt, and sport coat and felt the nerves he thought he had under control flirt dangerously close to a full-blown panic attack. The time had come to share his news with not only Huck but also his parents. He sat down at the kitchen table and wiped his palms down his thighs. "I'm not sure, Dad, we haven't spoken too much lately."

Mary asked, her eyes dancing merrily, "Well, where have you been spending all your time lately?"

Jake licked his lips and glanced from his mother to his father's expectant eyes. He took a deep breath and as he exhaled, he decided the best way to break the news was to just put it out there. "With my son."

Mary dropped the bowl she had been carrying her eyes widened, her face blanched. Coach stepped forward, raising his eyebrows. "Your son, huh?" he repeated and then glanced to his wife.

Jake nodded, his mouth suddenly so dry he couldn't form words. He tried to speak, but nothing would come out. He coughed and tried to continue, nodding his head. "Yes…my son."

Coach turned to his wife, frozen in the middle of the kitchen, the ruined bowl of mashed potatoes still at her feet. He went to her and guided her to the table, helping her into a chair. Mary's face was still pale, her eyes glued to her son's face. Coach took a seat as well and turned his gaze to Jake, his eyes softened along with his voice. "So the story going around town is true, huh?"

Jake's eyes dropped to his lap. He gathered his strength and looked from his father to his mother before he spoke. "Julie's son, Huck…he's…he's mine. Huck is my son."

Moments ticked by as his parents studied him. Mary reached out and took her husband's hand as they exchanged a look. Jake's stomach churned as he waited for his parents' response. Coach finally turned his eyes to Jake.

"Jake, I'm no mathematician here, but Huck's about five or six, right? I mean, you and Julie haven't dated nine or ten years. This just doesn't add up."

Jake rubbed his hand down his mouth and leaned his arms on the kitchen table. "Do you remember the Christmas right after my accident when I came home for the Christmas parade?"

Mary gasped and quickly covered her mouth. Coach squared his shoulders and drew in a fortifying breath. "And you just now found out that Huck is yours?"

"Yes, about than two weeks, I began to figure it out…" He watched his parents as they absorbed the news before he continued, "Julie never told me about him…but I don't want you to be angry with her. It's …it's really complicated and we are working it out, but the main thing I want to do is… I want us all to do what is best for Huck and being angry with his mother is not what is best for him."

His parents exchanged a look and he was unable to read their expressions. He swallowed and continued, "I'm not saying I'm not upset with her. I am, but I'm not completely innocent in all this either. I didn't exactly treat her the way she should have been treated and I don't think that justifies her keeping Huck from me or from you, but being angry and holding a grudge just makes a tough situation even tougher. I just want to do what's best for Huck."

Mary reached across the table and squeezed her son's hand. "I don't know if I have ever heard you be more mature."

Jake nodded. "I've been going over there every night this past week and we've decided that tonight is the night. We are going to tell Huck the truth tonight." Jake looked down at his attire and added, "I'm not sure how to dress for telling someone you are their father. I think I might be overdressed." Jake laughed nervously and hesitated before glancing over at his father, expecting to find the look of disappointment having returned. Instead, when he met his father's gaze he was surprised to see Coach's eyes watery. Coach reached over and clapped his hand on Jake's shoulder. "Well, son, when do we get to meet our grandson?"

****

"Do you think he's okay?" Jake asked as he and Julie stood shoulder to shoulder staring at Huck out the kitchen window.

Julie chewed her lip nervously. "Just give him some time. We gave him a lot to deal with."

They had waited until after dinner to sit Huck down on the couch and gently explain to him that Jake was in fact his father. Huck had taken the news quietly, nodding his head, looking from his mother to Jake before asking to be excused. He had slowly walked out to the back deck and sat down on the top step where he still remained. They had tried to follow him, but he had asked to be left alone, leaving them to stare out the window and conjure up the worst-case scenarios that might follow. When Huck stood and turned toward the house, they practically tripped over each other trying to get to the door. As Huck silently entered the back door, Julie slipped her arm around his shoulder. "Are you okay, buddy?"

Jake looked at the boy expectantly and held his breath. Huck stepped toward him. "I just have one question."

Jake dropped to one knee in front of Huck and nodded for him to continue. "Of course, Huck. You can ask anything."

"Where have you been all my life?"

Jake looked over Huck's head and met Julie's horrified gaze. She quickly knelt down beside him to face Huck, smoothing her hand over her son's head. "Oh, buddy... I didn't....Jake didn't know about you." Her voice broke over a sob.

"Huck." Jake placed his hands on the boy's shoulders. "Listen to me, okay? It's true that I didn't know about you, but I wasn't in a good place when you were born either. I wouldn't have been...I don't know if I could have been a very good dad to you. But now... now I want that more than anything in the world, just to be a good dad to you. We can't change the past, all we can do is try from this point forward to do the right thing."

Huck looked from Jake to Julie as they both held their breath waiting for him to respond. A grin broke across Huck's face as he said excitedly, "No one at school is going to believe this! Jake Rawlings is my dad!"

Laughter rumbled through Jake's chest as he wrapped his son up in his arms. Standing up, he swung boy around. "How would you like to play some football?"

"Sure...Dad? Is that what I'm supposed to call you?"

Jake struggled to find his voice. "You can call me anything you want, Huck. Anything at all."

Chapter 16 *Trials*

"Have I not commanded you? Be strong and courageous. Do not be afraid, do not be discouraged, for the LORD your God will be with you wherever you go." Joshua 1:9

Jake stretched to his full height, unfolding his long frame from his sports car, and it wasn't the first time that he had thought the car just didn't suit him anymore. He took a step toward Julie's house and felt his phone buzz in the back pocket of his jeans. He took it out and glanced at the screen. He scrubbed a hand down his face when Whitney's name appeared. He stopped in midstride and thumbed the ignore call button. He hadn't seen his fiancée — if he could even still call her that — since her surprise visit to reveal her even more surprising plans for the farm. They had exchanged texts, hers long, flowing texts full of apologies and I love yous; his short and terse. He had put the entire situation with Whitney and her father on the back burner while he dealt with suddenly becoming a father. But it had been three weeks since Whitney's surprise visit and it was time to deal with the situation.

He slipped the phone into his back pocket once again and reaffirmed that he would have to do something about her sooner rather than later. He knew ignoring her wasn't right and he also knew that the more time he spent in Julie's house the harder it was to tamp down the old feelings that he had for her that seemed to resurface. Part of him wanted to hold on to his anger with her, but another part of him desperately wanted to throw that anger aside and pull her into his arms.

As they spent time together in the evenings, Jake found himself watching her. In the years that he had spent away from Bluff Creek he had convinced himself that what they had shared as teenagers wasn't anything special. That she hadn't been anything special, just a high school girlfriend, but sitting across from her at dinner, watching her laugh, watching her take care of their son, he knew he had lied to himself. She was special. The way she made him feel, the way she laughed, the way his pulse raced when she accidentally touched him. She was special and becoming more special in his eyes as each day passed. He spent most of his days looking forward to his evenings spent not only with Huck, but also with her. Deep down, he knew he couldn't continue to nurse the anger he had toward her, and he also knew that no one had ever gotten to him more than she did. He found himself daydreaming about spending time with her, holding her hand, pulling her close, kissing her lips. But he knew he had to get his life straightened out; he had some wrongs to right before he could explore these emotions any further.

****

Julie peeked out the window for the millionth time before Jake arrived. She felt a sliver of excitement race up her spine as she thought about him. She shook her head and tried to focus on preparing dinner, telling herself for not the first time in the past few weeks that she would be best served to keep her emotions in check when it came to Jake Rawlings. Try as she might to nurse the anger she had for him in the past, she couldn't deny that his presence caused emotions she thought she had long since buried to resurface. He had become a fixture at her house in the evenings, and even though she still felt somewhat of a distance between them, she couldn't stop her heart from beating double time when he stepped through the door. She couldn't stop herself from occasionally pretending the evenings were real and he was there for more than just time with Huck, but there for her too. She told herself she was being silly and setting herself up for a broken heart again. She reminded herself that he was still upset with her for keeping Huck a secret and that while he didn't mention Whitney, she also had not heard that they had broken up either.

Occasionally her mind would drift to what would happen if Jake appeared at her door one night with Whitney on his arm, wanting his fiancée to meet his son. The thought caused her chest to ache and her breath to become labored so when it tried to invade her mind she pushed it away. She also kept telling herself that he very well might leave Bluff Creek after the terms of Shep's will were met. She had to be prepared for the worst, even if that meant putting some distance between her and Jake. She wasn't sure her heart could survive him leaving her again.

****

"Sidelines passes?! Like actually on the field?!" Huck's high-pitched voice echoed the excitement on his face.

"Yep, on the actual field." Jake chuckled as he watched his little boy clutch the passes to his chest.

"And this is where you played?" Huck hopped up and down, his little body unable to contain its exuberance anymore.

Jake nodded his head and caught the concerned expression on Julie's face. He had been so excited when his college coach had sent him the sideline passes, knowing Huck would be thrilled, that he had immediately given them to Huck when he came over for dinner. But now he tried to rein in his excitement as he caught the fleeting look on Julie's face.

"And we get to go!" Huck squealed excitedly.

"As long as it's all right with your mom." Jake raised his eyebrows and met Julie's gaze over Huck's head.

Julie's smile seemed a little too forced and her eyes a little too bright as she responded, "Well, who am I to ruin all the fun?" She turned her back and headed back into the kitchen. Jake quickly followed.

"Julie, are you okay with me taking him?"

Julie tossed the dishrag she had been twisting in her hands on the counter and turned to face him, prepared to give him a reality check, but when she saw Huck following quickly on his heels, excitement still dancing in his eyes, she stopped short. Huck took the brief moment of silence to throw his arms around Jake's waist and squeeze as hard as his little arms allowed, "Thank you so much, Dad, I love you."

Julie saw the emotions in Jake's eyes before he quickly turned and caught the little boy up in his arms and whispered, "I love you, too."

Julie turned back to the stove, trying to hold her own emotions in check. She busied herself putting the finishing touches on dinner. After dinner, Huck kept up a steady stream of conversation even as he and Jake went out to the back yard to toss the football. Darkness finally chased them inside and after Julie announced it was time for Huck to take a bath, she and Jake found themselves alone for the first time tonight.

He absently picked up the dishtowel and began drying the dishes she had washed. She knew he had something on his mind but she waited for him to speak first.

"Do you not want me to take him to the ball game?" he asked quietly, not meeting her eyes.

"Jake, it's not that I don't want you to take him, it's just that Huck is special. He has special medical concerns and there is more to being a parent than just always having a good time."

He furrowed his brow and bracketed his hips with his hands. "I know he has medical concerns, Julie."

"Yes, but you don't understand them! You don't know his medical history."

He took a step toward her, his voice eerily calm. "And whose fault is that?"

"Dad!" Huck's voice called from the bathroom down the hall, interrupting them. They glared at each other for several seconds before he brushed past her and headed down the hall. She heard water splashing and muted giggles as she finished cleaning up the kitchen. Indignation warred with guilt inside her; part of her wanted to be angry with him, another part of her felt that he might be right. Huck ran quickly into the kitchen announcing that Jake was going to read him a bedtime story; he hugged his mom tightly and ran back to his bedroom. Julie finished wiping down the counter and headed to the bathroom to clean up after Huck's bath.

As she picked up the wet towels, she heard a buzzing sound. She picked up towels and Huck's dirty clothes to find a phone face down on the counter underneath a dirty T-shirt. She picked it up and turned it over to see a picture of Whitney's smiling face looking back at her. She stared at the phone until it went black, indicating that Whitney must have hung up. She could see from the screen that Jake had missed several calls from his fiancée tonight. She was surprised by the hurt and anger the missed calls stirred in her. She tossed the towels in the hamper and went back to the kitchen, anger building in her body.

"He's asleep." Jake's soft voice behind her caused to jump. "Went out like a light."

Julie pressed her lips and nodded, and he continued, "I'm sorry. I was a jerk earlier. I should have never said that and I'm sorry about not asking you about the game before I told Huck." He shrugged his shoulders and lifted his hands palm up. "I'm new to all this and I guess I got a little excited about taking him to the game."

Julie remained silent, still gripping his phone in her hand. He took a step toward her and continued, "And I'm sorry if it seems that all I want to do is have fun with him. I know there is more to parenting than that…I guess I'm just still trying to find my way." He shoved his hands into his jeans pockets and leaned against the kitchen bar. "Sometimes I worry that he is going to resent me or something for not being around, so yeah, I guess I am trying to make up for that by being fun."

The silence stretched between them as they held each other's gaze. She could see the remorse in his eyes, but something internal kept her from letting go of her anger. She knew that she had no rational reason to be upset that his fiancée had been calling him. He had never made her any promises, he had never acted like he wanted more than to just be Huck's father. So why did the calls from Whitney cause such an ache in her chest?

He reached out, grasping her fingers and pulling her closer to him. "Don't be mad at me, Julie. You know I always hated you being mad at me."

Being close enough to him to smell his cologne was more than Julie could handle. His nearness caused a firestorm of emotions inside, and fear took over. She quickly shoved his phone into his chest.

"Your fiancée called." She stepped away from and could see the look of shock play across his face and it emboldened her. "In fact, she has called several times."

He slipped the phone into the back pocket of his jeans and looked at Julie with tortured eyes, and a quiet voice. "What do you want me to say?"

"Does she know you're here every night? Does she know that you spend all your free time with me and Huck?"

Jake dropped his gaze to the floor, heat rising up his neck.

Julie's anger swelled in her chest. "Does she even know about Huck?"

Jake scrubbed his hand down his face, his gaze bouncing around the room, looking at everything except Julie.

Julie took a step toward him and spat between gritted teeth, "Does she know about Huck?"

"No." he answered solemnly. "I haven't told her about Huck."

Julie turned her back to him, not wanting him to see the tears that she was desperately trying to keep from falling. "Get out," she whispered.

"Let me explain." He touched her shoulder to try and turn her to face him. She wrenched her shoulder out of his grasp, keeping her back to him.

"Julie...it's complicated." Part of him wanted to tell her every detail. How he was being blackmailed by Whitney's father and that until he could figure out how to pay off his gambling debt and avoid bodily harm from his bookie, he wasn't sure of the next move to make. Now that Huck and Julie were in his life, he also feared that anything that he might do that defied Mr. Peterson's wishes might bring harm to them as well. The people he had placed his bets with weren't exactly choir boys; they wouldn't hesitate to hurt his family to send a warning to him.

But in that instant, with her back turned to him, he felt more afraid than he ever had in his life. His injury, the loss of his dream, the debt he was in, the threats from Mr. Peterson and his bookie, none of that instilled fear in him like the sudden thought of not having Huck and Julie in his life. He couldn't exactly pinpoint when he had begun considering them his family, but he did and he would fight for them. Whatever it took, no matter what he had to face, he would protect and fight for his family.

Feeling suddenly confident, he placed his hands on her shoulders and gently turned her to face him. "Julie, I need you to believe me, it's over with Whitney. It's been over for a very long time and I've been too scared…too much of a coward to admit that or to do anything about it. But I'm done with that. There is a lot involved here that you don't know about, but you have to trust me that I'm going to handle this. And it's true, I haven't told her about Huck, but it's not that I don't want her to know, it's just that in my mind, it's been over between Whitney and I since I came back here for Shep's funeral. It's not that I'm keeping Huck from her intentionally, I just…I just don't share anything in my life with her anymore."

Julie studied the toes of her shoes and sniffed. "You need to tell *her* this, not me. Obviously she still thinks something is going on because she's called you ten times tonight." She raised her eyes to meet his. "And until you do, I think it would be best if you didn't spend so much time here. We've become too comfortable with each other, fallen back into old habits, and I can't do that right now. You're engaged, for goodness' sake, and yet if someone didn't know better they would think that we were…well, that we were, you know. You can still spend time with Huck; we can work that out, but I think it would be best if it were somewhere else."

Jake's face fell and she quickly continued, "You can still take him to the game on Saturday, but for now I think it would be best if you left and don't come back tomorrow night for dinner."

"Julie, please don't do this..." he began but she quickly interrupted him.

"What are we doing here, Jake? I mean honestly, the more time you spend here it's just going to be confusing to Huck. He's going to start thinking we are a real family." She threw hers arms up and fought the emotion tightening in her throat.

"We are a family!" The words slipped out before he could stop them.

"No." Her voice was small and she wouldn't meet his eyes. "No we aren't. Not really."

He reached to grab her elbow. "Julie, don't—"

"Can you let yourself out?" She stepped out of his reach and he could see the tears shining in her eyes. "I'll have Huck ready to go to the game Saturday morning."

****

Huck kept up a steady stream of conversation all the way to the football game. Jake tried to concentrate and answer when appropriate, but his mind kept wandering back to Julie and her behavior. Huck had been waiting for him at the front door and the moment he pulled into her driveway and parked this morning, Huck had run to the car, excitement shining in his eyes. Julie had waved from behind the front door and shut it quickly as if to let Jake know he wasn't welcome inside.

He hit the drive-thru at a fast food restaurant and told Huck he could have anything he wanted. Huck ordered a breakfast that Jake was sure he wouldn't be able to eat and a soda that was so large it wouldn't fit in the cup holder. He doubled down on his efforts to push Julie out of his mind and focus on Huck. They took in all the festivities and Jake indulged the young boy's every whim. He began to wonder where the boy was storing all the food, candy, and sodas he was consuming. The bright afternoon sun beat down on them as they watched the team walk to the stadium. Jake noticed that Huck stood quietly watching the team walk by; he guessed the little boy was awestruck by being so close to them. After the team had filed past them, Jake led Huck over to the center of campus to watch the school band play. He also took him by the bookstore and let him pick out a sweatshirt before they headed back across campus to the stadium. Jake led them down onto the sidelines and turned to Huck. "What do ya think, Huck? Pretty cool, huh?"

"Yeah, it's really cool." Huck's voice didn't quite hold the same excitement as it had this morning.

Jake furrowed his brow and squatted down to Huck's level. "You okay, buddy?"

Huck wiped the sweat off his brow. "Yeah...I'm just really thirsty."

"I can't believe you'd want anything else to drink after that bucket of Coke you drank earlier." But Jake stood and flagged down a vendor to get Huck another soda.

The sun was high in the sky as the team began coming onto the field to warm up. He spoke with several of the coaches and took pride in introducing Huck as his son. Huck had become increasingly quiet and Jake decided he must be awestruck at being on the sideline. The game began and Jake began pointing out aspects of the game to Huck. He thought about how lucky he was to be able to share this moment with his son. Right before halftime, Jake turned to shake hands with an equipment manager who remembered him from his playing time, when he felt Huck touch his hand. Jake turned to his son and was instantly alarmed. Huck had suddenly turned extremely pale and was sweating profusely. "Dad," his voice small and weak, "I don't feel so good."

Before Jake could question him, Huck's eyes rolled into the back of his head and he collapsed, his small body lying prostate on the ground. Jake yelled his name and fell to his knees beside him. Time seemed to move in slow motion. He wasn't sure how it happened, but suddenly he was surrounded by paramedics. His mind couldn't process the questions they asked him concerning Huck. They strapped the small boy to a stretcher, his body limp, eyes still closed, his face much too pale. Someone urged Jake to follow them and he ran alongside the stretcher, clutching Huck's limp hand. The paramedics told him he would not be allowed to ride in the ambulance, and he stood dumbfounded, his feet rooted to the ground, as he watched his son being loaded into the emergency vehicle, sirens blaring as it pulled away. Someone touched his elbow and he recognized the equipment manager he had been talking to earlier. He led Jake to a car and they followed the ambulance with flashers blinking.

"Jake," the man reached over and shook Jake's shoulder, "is there someone you need to call?"

Jake nodded numbly and fumbled for his phone. His fingers were clumsy and he finally found Julie's number and pushed the button to call. She spoke as soon as she answered, not giving Jake a chance to speak. "I saw it on TV. What hospital are they taking him to?"

Jake couldn't find his voice. Swallowing hard, he looked desperately over to the man who seemed so familiar to him. He nodded, gently taking the phone from Jake, and calmly gave Julie directions to the hospital. Jake felt like he was walking through a nightmare; nothing seemed real. He had no concept of time or space as he waited to hear any news of Huck's condition. He sat with his head in his hands, waiting impatiently to hear any news about his son. Nurses came and asked him numerous questions about Huck's medical history, none of which he could answer, and whenever he asked if he could see his son, he was met with a sympathetic smile and a "not yet" response.

Time seemed to stretch into infinity as he waited, going over and over in his mind every event of the day that might have led to Huck's collapse. Ultimately he decided whatever the cause, a better father would have been able to keep Huck safe. His thoughts spiraled out of control as he internally berated himself. His thoughts slipped into a dark hole which seemed to have no end. If he hadn't taken Huck to this game, the boy would be safe at home with his mother. What other calamities would he bring to Huck's life? It was obvious that anything he touched turned to ashes. What other harm might befall Huck and Julie or even his parents now that he was back in their lives?

He faintly heard his name being called. He struggled to pull his thoughts out of the bleak abyss and focus on the present. Again he heard his name; he looked up and swung his gaze in the direction of the voice. Julie walked hurriedly down the hall toward him, calling his name again. Relief swept over him, immediately followed by gut-wrenching guilt. She would hate him forever now, of that he was certain, but for a brief moment his worry and concern for their child overrode his crushing guilt and shame and he immediately pushed himself from his seat and ran to her. He swept her into his arms, crushing her to his chest. She briefly returned his embrace, before pushing back and looking deep into his eyes.

"Where is he?" She searched his face and immediately knew he was struggling keep himself together. "Jake, listen to me. Where is he?" She placed her hands on either side of his face and repeated her question.

Jake nodded to a set of double doors. "Back there. They won't let me see him, Julie." Tears slipped from his eyes and Julie instinctively wiped one away before releasing him and disappearing behind the doors. He stood, rooted to the ground, staring after her. He finally returned to his seat, his eyes widening when he saw his parents practically running down the hall toward him, worry and concern etched on their faces.

"We came as soon as we heard." Mary slipped her arms around her son's waist.

"How is he?" His father gripped his shoulder as if trying to give him strength.

Tears again clouded Jake's vision. "I don't know… they won't tell me anything."

"He's going to be fine," his mother stated confidently. "We've been praying since we saw it happen. God is going to take care of him, Jake. I know He is."

Jake nodded, unable to even conjure up the least bit of cynicism about God's providence. He was willing to try anything and if God made Huck better, Jake would spend the rest of his life thanking Him.

Mary led him back to his seat and took his hand as she sat beside him. His father took the other seat, bracketing him, and Jake could not help but feel protected by them. Minutes ticked by at an agonizing pace. He glanced at his mother, who clenched his hand in hers as she bowed her head. He knew she was praying not only for Huck but for him too. A fleeting thought screamed through his mind that maybe he should pray too. In recent years, he had spent more time shaking his fist at God than praying. A nervousness slipped inside his belly. What if God were so mad at him that He would take Huck away? What if Jake's ultimate punishment was losing his son? An emotion so strong welled inside him that his chest constricted and his breath became labored. He jumped up and began pacing in front of the chairs.

"Jake?" His father scooted to the end of his seat, his voice heavy with concern.

"I can't take this." Jake ran his fingers through his hair roughly. "I can't take this anymore!"

He briefly contemplated charging through the doors and demanding information about his son, but before he could, Coach slipped his arms around his shoulders, guiding him in the other direction. "Let's go for a walk?"

"I can't. I can't leave, Dad." Desperation dripped from Jake's voice.

"You aren't leaving. We are going to take a walk. If anyone comes out with news, your mom will find us." Coach could tell Jake was about to refuse when he added, "You aren't any good to Huck if you spin out of control here, Jake. They are taking good care of him. Come on." Coach gently turned Jake's shoulder away from the doors and guided him down the hall. They walked in silence, Jake letting his father lead him.

"You know, Jake, when I am feeling the worst, I always find comfort in taking my problems to God." Jake stopped when he realized his father had stopped walking. He turned to find his father gazing at a sign that said Chapel. "Do you want to go in?" Coach gestured toward the door.

Jake took a deep breath, suddenly feeling as if he were on the edge of a cliff with nowhere to turn. A small alcove directly across from the chapel door, only big enough to hold two chairs, appeared to be his only escape. He sat heavily in the chair, followed closely by his father. They sat in silence for a long time. Jake finally leaned over, resting his forearms on his thighs, hands dangling between his knees.

"This is all my fault," he whispered, scrubbing a hand roughly down his face.

"How do you figure that?" his dad questioned with no judgment in his voice. He leaned forward, mimicking Jake's stance.

"Because, Dad, everything I do turns out wrong. My football career crashed and burned. I worked so hard, I conditioned relentlessly, I watched game films, and I studied other teams… just to crash and burn. My bar is a joke. I look at those financial books over and over and I can't make heads or tails of them. I can't even cover payroll most weeks." The tightness in his chest lessened and a dam seemed to break inside him as he continued, words tumbling from him, "I thought I could fix everything, so I placed a bet with a bookie, only of course with my luck, I eventually failed at that too. I owe a man a lot of money and he is not going to let me forget it. Whitney's dad is blackmailing me to try and force me to develop the farm…I coasted into town for Shep's funeral on fumes because I couldn't even afford a tank of gas. I've lied to Whitney about the whole thing and the bad thing is…I don't even care if she gets mad at me…I don't even think I love her… Dad, I am a joke. And now…now the first time I take my son by myself to a football game, we wind up in the hospital. Everything I do turns out wrong. Julie and Huck would be better off without me."

Coach sat up, tapping his forefinger against his lips, contemplating Jake's emotional confessions. He cleared his throat and responded, "That's a lot to deal with, Jake, and while I will agree with you that life has not always been easy for you, there is one thing I notice here."

Jake leaned back and away from his father, resting his cheek in his hand. "Yeah what's that?"

"Jake, you know the word you used the most just now was 'I.' Every other word out of your mouth was 'I.'"

"Well, like I said, Dad, I'm a failure."

"No. No you're not, but you are going about life all wrong."

Jake turned his head quickly to meet his father's gaze. "What do you mean?"

"Jake, you're trying to do everything in your life through your own power, so of course you're falling on your face. I would be too—everyone in the world would be—if they were trying to go through this life on their own. You need God's guidance; you need to ask Him to show you how to handle the ups and downs of life."

"Dad—" Jake began.

"No, listen to me," Coach interrupted. "I know that getting hurt and losing the dream of going pro was a powerful blow to you. It knocked you down and you've just stayed down. You didn't seek God's guidance and quite honestly, Jake, you've been pouting all these years over it and you've let it make you bitter."

Jake bit his lip and let his father's words tumble through his mind. When he didn't respond, Coach continued, "The Bible warns us not to let bitterness take hold in us. When we do, then we see the entire world through the lenses of bitterness." Coach paused only briefly before continuing, "Look at all the good things that happened to you—you can't see them because all you can focus on is the bad. That's because you've let bitterness shade your vision."

Jake stood and walked to the window across the hall. He studied the scene below him without seeing anything and contemplated his father's words. He knew he couldn't argue with him. He had let his bitterness over the loss of his football dreams drive him. Not only bitterness, but pride had blinded him and dictated his path for the last several years. He slipped his hands in his pockets and turned to face his father.

"I don't know how to fix this…I don't know how to change." Jake's voice was small and his father had to strain to hear him.

Coach quickly crossed the hall, grabbing Jake by the

shoulders. "You don't have to know, all you have to do is let God lead. Ask Him and He will guide you. All you have to do is ask and listen."

Tears pooled in Jake's eyes. "I've been pretty mad at Him for a long time. I don't know if He'll forgive me for that."

"Jake," Coach's eyes softened, "is there anything Huck could do that would make you stop loving him? Stop being there for him?"

"No," Jake said forcefully.

"There is nothing you can do to make God stop loving you either. The Bible tells us that as bad and imperfect as we are and we still know how to give good things to our children, how much more will God give to us? Just ask Him, Jake. Just ask Him. He is waiting. He wants to show you how to walk through all of this heartache."

Jake caught movement coming toward them out of the corner of his eyes. He looked up to see Julie rushing toward them, his mother following close behind. Fear swelled in his chest and held him immobile. Thousands of horrible scenarios flitted through his mind, and while he wanted to hear what she had to say more than anything, he also wanted to keep her from confirming any of the million horrible what-if scenarios concerning Huck running through his head.

"He's okay...he's going to be okay," she called out before she reached them, a smile splitting her face.

Relief coursed through Jake causing his knees to buckle. He steadied himself against the wall, unable to speak.

"He got dehydrated mostly due to the heat and a lack of water. It happens quicker with him because of his heart, and it caused his heart rate to get too high, but he's going to be fine." Julie stopped in front of him and Mary quickly wrapped her arms around him. Jake dropped his head, unable to express the emotions he was feeling. His shoulders shook as he wept with relief.

"He's asking for you." Julie gently touched his hand.

Jake's head shot up, eyes wide, his voice no more than a whisper. "He wants to see me?"

"Of course, Jake." Tears rimmed Julie's eyes as she added, "He loves you."

Jake shook his head. "I just...It's all my fault. You tried to talk to me about his health and I just didn't listen. I didn't know, Julie. I wouldn't hurt him for anything and I—"

"Jake," she interrupted, "I know you wouldn't hurt him. It was an accident and thankfully he is going to be just fine." She squeezed his hand before she added, "Let's go see him."

As they turned to walk back down the hall toward their son, Jake slipped his arm around her thin shoulders and she leaned into his body, each drawing comfort from the other, as they went to Huck's bedside. Late that night as he watched Julie sleeping peacefully in a chair beside Huck's hospital bed, he released a pent up breath. His parents had finally left after spending time with Huck. Jake had known the moment he introduced Huck to his parents last Sunday afternoon that they were instantly wrapped around the boy's little finger, and he had been proven right today. His parents had doted on Huck until they had left the hospital, promising gifts when he arrived home. Huck seemed to be back to his old self, but was being kept overnight for observation.

The room was quiet and for the first time since Huck had collapsed, Jake felt as if his mind had stopped spinning. He looked from Julie to their son and something in his chest tightened. He loved them. Not just Huck and not just Julie because she was the mother of his son. He loved them both with a love so deep and genuine in that moment it almost overpowered him. He studied her face and the love he felt toward her soared and filled his entire body to the point he felt he might burst open from it. As he examined the emotion, he realized it had always been a part of him, from the time he first met her as a child to this exact moment; the love he had for her had always been there. For years he had shoved it aside and fought it because he was so singularly focused on his dream life. Now he could say without any uncertainty, she and Huck were his dream life.

His mind drifted to the conversation he'd had with his father this afternoon. He didn't know how he was going to do it, but somehow, someway, he was going to start looking to God for help. After all, he vaguely remembered making a promise to God that if He would heal Huck, Jake would spend the rest of his life thanking Him. No time like the present to get started, he supposed.

He heard his phone buzz and he glanced to the bedside where he had placed it hours ago. Whitney's face lit up the screen. His stomach sank as he reached for the phone; it was time to put an end to this farce of an engagement and focus on winning back his family. He stepped outside the hospital room and swiped his thumb across the screen to answer the call.

"I saw you on TV today," she spoke before he could say anything, her voice even and unemotional.

"Whitney—" he began.

"You have a son?" she interrupted. "They were showing you on the sidelines and they kept saying there was a medical emergency with your son. What is going on, Jake?"

He took a deep breath and looked up to the ceiling. "Yes, Whitney, I have a son. His name is Huck and he is five years old. I didn't know about him until a few weeks ago." He could hear her soft sobs through the phone and while he knew he had never truly loved her, she had helped him through one of the hardest events of his life and he hated to make her cry.

"Why didn't you tell me?" she cried.

"Whitney…don't cry, okay? Let's meet somewhere and talk this out."

****

Julie stood with her back against the hospital room wall and let the silent tears fall down her face. Had she imagined what they had shared not only today, but in the last few weeks? She had heard the hospital room door shut and had gotten up to check on Jake. He had been overwhelmed with guilt and fear and she wanted to make sure that he was okay. Instead she had heard him making arrangements to meet Whitney. Hadn't he told her just the other night that his relationship with Whitney was over? Not for the first time, Jake Rawlings had made her feel like a fool. She quietly slipped back to her chair, turning her back to the room so that when Jake returned, he wouldn't see her tears.

Chapter 17 *Endings and Beginnings*

"My grace is sufficient for you, for my power is made perfect in weakness." 2 Corinthians 12:9

"Look who made the *Southeastern Coaches Journal*." Doug dropped a magazine on the desk in the coach's office. Jake glanced over from the game film he was watching on his computer to see an animated picture of him coaching from the sidelines of their last game. Jake glanced up at Doug and continued watching the game film. Doug picked up the magazine, flipped to the article, and quoted the story.

"Rookie Assistant Coach Jake Rawlings is making a name for himself among Division 4A coaching ranks with his quarterbacks leading not only their division, but also their region in passing and rushing yards along with touchdowns."

Jake threw a pen at the older man and grumbled for him to be quiet. He found it odd that at one time he had sought fame and now all he wanted was to help his dad coach this team without any distractions.

"I think we got a celebrity in the making on our hands, Jim." Doug sat down while tossing the magazine to Jake's dad. Coach Rawlings only nodded but Jake could see the pride in his eyes.

Doug continued, "Article says they think you might be named not only Division 4A rookie coach of the year, but the State Rookie Coach of the Year. What about that?"

Jake looked back to the film playing on his screen as heat crept up his neck, and mumbled, "I just want to get ready for the game against Morristown next week."

"Still, it's a big deal just be mentioned in a magazine like this." Doug gestured to the magazine Jake's dad was now reading. "I think we should celebrate after the game tonight."

Jake glanced over at Coach and cleared his throat. "I can't tonight. I have to leave right after the game."

"Jake's got some personal business to take care of tonight, but we'll celebrate another time," Coach offered.

It had been almost a week since Huck's collapse. The hospital had finally released him late Sunday evening. Julie agreed that he could miss school on Monday to rest. Jake had stayed with him that day and the boy seemed to have bounced back to his usual self. Jake had ignored Julie's previous statement about his spending time with Huck away from her house and had shown up every night. Julie had been cordial to him when he arrived in the evenings but she also kept her distance. She stayed in the kitchen or in her bedroom while he spent time with Huck. It pained Jake to his core to feel her avoidance, but until he settled things with Whitney he knew he didn't have any right to expect anything from Julie. He had made arrangements to meet Whitney at their condo after tonight's football game. He knew it would be the wee hours of the morning before he made it back to the beachfront building, but she had agreed to not only the meeting but also the time. As much as he knew this conversation had to happen, he wanted to get it over with and get back to Bluff Creek as soon as possible. As soon as he settled things with Whitney, his pursuit of his family could and would be his sole focus.

****

It was almost dawn when Jake finally pulled into the parking garage at the condo he had once called home. He had drunk more coffee on this trip than ever before in his life. He wasn't sure if it was the coffee or the anticipation of the impending conversation that had him so jumpy. The elevator quickly took him to the sixth floor and Whitney opened the door before he could even knock, causing him to jump nervously. He wondered if she were still tracking his phone and made a mental note to double-check his phone for her app.

"Jake," she said softly and slipped her arms around his torso. He immediately tensed at her touch and untangled himself from her and nodded his greeting. Not for the first time, he regretted that he had stayed in this relationship much longer than he should have.

"It's so good to have you home!" Sweetness dripped off her words as she again tried to slip her arms around his waist. He caught her arms and set her away from him.

She pouted and crossed her arms over her chest.

"Whitney, I've been awake more hours than I care to think about," he began and her face quickly brightened.

"Well, why don't you go to bed? We can talk after you've slept."

"No. No, Whitney, we need to talk now." He gestured for her to sit down, his fatigue and sense of urgency leaving no room for small talk at this point.

She sat down, wrapping her silk robe around her, the look of disappointment evident when Jake chose the seat opposite of her. "Jake, I—"

He held his hands palms up to stop her. "Whitney, just let me get this all out, okay?"

She nodded and he continued. He told the story of his and Julie's relationship, confessing the night he had spent with Julie while he and Whitney were together. He told her about Huck, finishing up with his collapse one week ago.

He let her absorb the details of his story before continuing. "Whitney, I'm not the same person I was three months ago when we left here to attend Shep's funeral. So much has changed; I've changed."

"Don't be silly, Jake. You are still the same person I fell in love with. We can make this work. I mean lots of people have kids from previous relationships and they make it work."

He leaned forward, releasing a breath. "Whitney, I want to live in Bluff Creek. I want to spend every moment I can with my son." He paused, searching for the right words. "I don't want the same things out of life that I used to. Whitney, you were there for me through one of the worst times in my life and I will always be grateful for that…but now…but now I just don't think we want the same things anymore. I just don't think continuing this relationship is good for either of us."

"Are you breaking up with me?" Whitney mouth fell open, her hand flying to her chest.

He dropped his head, took a breath, released it, and raised his gaze to meet hers. "We don't want the same things anymore, and if we were both really honest with ourselves, this," he waved his hand between them, "hasn't been in a good place for a while—long before we went to Bluff Creek for Shep's funeral."

Whitney cleared her throat and shifted uncomfortably on the couch, looking at everything in the room but Jake. Knowing he had hit a nerve he continued, "And if we were really truthful, I was a project for you, someone you could mold into the exact husband you wanted, and for me you were a link to a life a thought I wanted, thought I deserved."

Whitney sniffed and rearranged her robe. "So what now? Are you going to marry this old high school girlfriend?" She refused to say Julie's name, as if the name itself left a horrible taste in her mouth.

"I don't know. I don't know how she feels about me, but I am tired of the lies and living a life of deception. I love her, Whitney, I guess I always have and if she will have me and forgive me, yes, someday I want to marry her." He was surprised at the joy he felt when he made the admission out loud for the first time.

She finally met his gaze and studied him for a moment. "If you can be happy in that little town with that woman, then you didn't have what it would take to be married to me anyway. I guess you're right, we don't want the same things."

He studied the woman across from him and wondered how he had ever tolerated her spoiled behavior. He breathed deeply and began the second conversation he needed to have with her. "I've been looking into the bar, how it was legally set up."

"Yes, I guess we do need to settle that."

"It's a partnership between you and I but the way your father has set it up, we can't sell it unless we both agree to the sell."

"Is that what you want? To sell the bar?" Whitney questioned.

"Whitney, I assume you know that the bar is in horrible financial shape. And I am also assuming that your father has told you about the gambling debt I am in." He waited to see her response and he could tell she wasn't surprised by either admission so he continued, "I want to sell the bar and try to pay off my gambling debt. You've never had any interest in it."

"Up until this point that is true. I haven't been involved with the bar, but it's a good investment if managed correctly."

"Whitney, you and I both know the bar was something for me to do that was socially acceptable to you and your father, it was never anything more."

She stood quickly and turned her back to him. "I've always viewed it as a sound investment, Jake, and if you didn't maybe that's why it's failing."

Jake rolled his eyes, exhaustion overtaking the adrenaline he had felt when he started this conversation. "Okay, if it's such a sound investment, you buy me out, my half of this partnership is useless. The way I read this contract, I can't do anything without your approval."

She turned to him then. "Why would I buy you out when you've run it into financial distress? No, I won't do that. Until you get the bar back onto sound financial footing, I'm afraid I can't buy your half."

Anger rose inside him. "Whitney, come on, I need this money."

"I'm sorry, Jake, looks like you're stuck with me…at least when it comes to the bar." She walked to the door and opened it, indicating it was time for him to leave. "And I'm sure Daddy will continue to keep your bookie at bay as long as you still plan on developing the farm; of course he would require a substantial manager's fee for that development, but that's a small price to pay for keeping your limbs intact." She smiled at him sweetly. With his mouth set in a grim line, he left the condo, determined to find a way to cut all ties with his now ex-fiancée.

****

By the time Jake reached Bluff Creek it was afternoon; exhaustion had given way to delirium hours ago. He had only one thing on his mind and that drove him. He extracted his tired body from his car and with an energy he didn't have, jogged up the steps to Clay Phillips's front door. He knocked and waited only a second to knock again; fatigue and urgency drove his impatience.

Clay opened the door and studied him for a moment before stating on a sigh, "Well, I guess I should have expected this visit."

Jake was briefly confused but too tired to press the issue. "Clay, I need your help." He thrust the contract agreement for the End Zone partnership into the man's hands. "Can you look over this? I have to find a way out of this."

Clay seemed bewildered as he took the papers, flipping through them quickly before glancing back up at Jake. "Jake, I'm not sure I can do this for you."

Jake stood with his hands on his hips and demanded, "Why?"

Clay sighed and looked away. Moments ticked by before he answered, "I've got a friend I went to law school with that specializes in business law. I can send it to him and let him look at it."

Jake clasped the man's shoulder. "Thanks call me when you hear something."

****

Jake only made it as far as his parents' couch before collapsing. He slept fitfully, worries crowding his mind. He awoke after a few hours and took a quick shower, eager to see Julie and Huck. He hadn't spoken with Julie since Thursday night and he hoped she wouldn't be too upset with him for just dropping in. With his relationship with Whitney clearly over, he was eager to confess his feelings to Julie and begin to win her heart back.

He pulled in behind Marti's car and felt a brief stab of disappointment that they wouldn't be alone. He rapped on the door sharply, almost giddy with excitement over seeing both Julie and Huck. Marti opened the door, her smile immediately falling, eyes widening when she saw Jake.

"Jake," she said her face white, obviously surprised by his presence. She quickly turned and called loudly behind her, "Julie, Jake is here."

With her announcement, Huck came bounding out of the living room chanting "Daddy" and launched himself into Jake's outstretched arms. The little boy wound his arms tightly around Jake's neck. "Daddy, did you have a good trip? I'm so glad you're back. Did you just get back?"

Before Jake could answer, Julie emerged from hallway, hair and makeup perfectly done. She was wearing skinny jeans that encased her long slender legs and a white sweater that revealed one bare shoulder, its color causing her complexion to glow. She was breathtaking and for a moment Jake couldn't perform a coherent thought. He set Huck down and took a step toward her.

"What are you doing here, Jake?" she asked before he could tell her how beautiful she was. "Huck said you were taking a trip."

"Uh, i-it was a quick trip," Jake stammered.

"But what are you doing here?" she asked again and Jake realized the tension in voice.

"I wanted to see Huck and you. I wanted to see you." His voice no more than a whisper; he stepped toward her and involuntarily reached to tuck a wayward strand of hair behind her ear. Before he could touch her, she stepped out of reach.

"You should have called, Jake, this is not a good time." She shifted nervously and glanced from Huck to Marti.

Jake glanced around the room, lack of sleep dulling his ability to reason at this point, but aware that everyone in the room knew something that he didn't. "I'm sorry. I just thought—"

"No you didn't think," Julie interrupted. "At least not about anyone but yourself and what you wanted."

"Julie," he began, his voice full of emotion.

"Don't be mad at Daddy," Huck cried angrily from behind him, wrapping his arms around Jake's legs.

Jake turned to his son quickly but before he could say anything Julie stepped forward. "Huck, go to your room, now."

"I don't want to go to my room." Huck released Jake and crossed his arms over his chest. Jake was speechless at this son's unexpected behavior. "And I don't want to stay with Aunt Marti while you go on a date. I want to stay with Daddy."

The word "date" buzzed through Jake's brain like a saw. Surely he had heard Huck incorrectly. He turned to face Julie and breathed the question, "Date?"

She inhaled deeply and faced Jake. "Yes, a date. I am going on a date."

Jake felt like he had been sucker punched in the stomach. He fought to draw air into his lungs and steady himself. "A date?" he repeated, his entire world spinning.

"Yes, Jake, a date," she repeated angrily before turning to Huck and imploring her son to go into the back yard with Marti while she and Jake spoke.

Jake watched the back door shut and from the smirk on her face, he could tell Marti was enjoying his predicament a little too much.

"Look, let's don't make a big deal of this in front of Huck." Julie stepped toward him, dropping her voice.

"Not make a big deal of it? It is a big deal, Julie. Why didn't you tell me?" he asked, his hands on his hips.

She studied him for a long moment, the silence stretching between them broken only by the sound of the doorbell. She glanced to the door and then back to Jake. "Where did you go last night, Jake? I don't expect you to tell me about your trips to visit your fiancée; you can't expect me to tell you about my love life either."

He opened his mouth and quickly closed it, trying find the words to explain to her why he had gone to Whitney, but before he could she continued, "We share a son. That doesn't mean we have to just pick up where we left off years ago."

She stepped around him and opened the door. He heard her invite the person in and he turned just in time to see Clay Phillips step inside. Their eyes met and Clay nodded a greeting. Julie grabbed her purse from the foyer table and turned to Jake, stepping closer and lowering her voice. "You can stay with Huck for a few hours, but you don't need to be here when I get home."

Jake ground his molars together and nodded his agreement, feeling his heart shatter as she turned, slipped her hand inside Clay's arm, and gently closed the door behind them. A sickening feeling settled in the pit of Jake's stomach. He was too late; he had missed his chance to unite his family. He stood staring at the closed door; the only thing breaking his reverie was Huck grabbing him from behind. He tried to turn his focus to his son. He tried to be present in the moment with him, but no matter what he tried, no matter how hard he attempted to focus, he couldn't fight the knot of despair that had settled into his stomach. He had never thought it would be easy to reconcile his family, but he had believed that Julie felt the same way about him that he felt about her. But now he wasn't so sure.

He also wasn't sure what to do with his unrequited feelings that he seemed to be drowning in. He doubled down on his efforts to get through evening and focus on his son. He put one foot in front of the other, always aware that Marti seemed to be smirking in the corner. He read as many books as Huck requested at bedtime until finally the little boy drifted off to sleep. He sat staring at him, feeling as if he had not only failed himself but also his son.

Love for the boy surged through his body, overwhelming his emotions and causing tears to slip from his eyes. How could he just give up? His son needed him and he wasn't going to lie to himself anymore; he needed not only his son, but also his beautiful mother. When Jake set his mind to something, he could endure a lot to see it through. He decided in that moment, there was nothing he wouldn't endure to unite his family. He bent over and kissed Huck on the forehead. "Don't worry little buddy," he whispered. "Daddy won't stop until we are all together...a family." He turned and quietly slipped down the hall; his hand was on the front doorknob when Marti stepped behind him.

"Did you really expect to just waltz right back into her life and pick up where you left off years ago?"

Jake inhaled deeply. Dropping his head back, he studied the ceiling for several long moments before turning to face Marti. "I don't know what I expected. The past three months have been a whirlwind. My grandfather dies; I find out I'm a father..." He shrugged his shoulders and slipped his hands into his jeans pockets.

"I haven't been a big fan of yours since you broke up with her in college, but I want you to know..." she paused and searched for words, "I didn't know that Huck was your son. I might not like you very much, but you deserved to know. And for what it's worth, it's obvious how much you love him and how much he loves you."

He nodded and she continued, crossing her arms over her chest, "But you really hurt her. More than you can ever know, you hurt her. She hit rock bottom, you know, back then. She still loved you and you didn't love her back. You can't expect her just to forget that."

Jake sighed heavily. "I know I hurt her. I'd take it back if I could, but I can't. I was in a really bad place mentally and I took it out on her. I guess I can never apologize enough, but she isn't exactly innocent in all this. She kept Huck from me. But what I want is for us both to let everything in the past go and start over."

"Just let her go, okay?"

"What?"

"I see the way you look at her, I see that look in your eyes.

Your life is falling apart so you think you'll fall back on good reliable Julie."

"That's not what I think at all." Jake shook his head vehemently.

"Look, she deserves to be happy, she deserves to be with someone who isn't going to abandon her the minute something better comes along."

"I'm not going to do that." He took a step toward her.

"If you think that you care about her at all, just let her have this with Clay. He can treat her better than you ever could. There is too much hurt between you two. You can be Huck's father and not completely destroy Julie's heart all over again."

He stood with his hands on his hips. "She tell you all this?"

"She didn't have to. I'm her best friend. I've been here for her when you weren't. I know that she's always been weak when it comes to you." She lifted her chin and stepped toward him, closing the distance between them to mere inches. "I don't want to have to pick up the pieces again when you leave and we all know that you will leave as soon as something better comes along. And it's not just Julie you'll hurt this time, but Huck too."

He took a step back, never breaking eye contact with her. "Marti, I'm not going anywhere, I'm here to stay. And I'm not going to give up until I have my family together. I'm going to enjoy proving you wrong."

She laughed bitterly. "And you just keep proving me right, because all you care about is winning."

Chapter 18 *Betrayal*

"For whosoever shall call upon the name of the Lord shall be saved." Romans 10:13

Jake stood on the sidelines of the football field, hands on his hips, watching his team practice. He tried to focus on the players in front of him, but his mind continually wandered to Julie and Huck. It had been almost two weeks since he had discovered Julie's relationship with Clay Phillips. Since then he had spent time with Huck every day but never at Julie's house. In fact, Jake had never felt more avoided in his entire life. No matter how hard he tried to manufacture a moment to see Julie, she always seemed to be unavailable.

Jake glanced down the sidelines and felt his stomach drop as his eyes fell on Clay Phillips walking in his direction. Jake blew his whistle and ended practice by sending his team to the locker room. He stood still, watching Clay as he approached, anger and resentment burning inside, trying to keep his face neutral. Clay stopped a few feet from him; both stared at each other for a few moments.

"Jake." Clay broke the silence.

Jake nodded and tried to keep the disgust out of his voice. "Clay."

Clay reached into his back pocket, drew out a folded packet of papers, and extended them to Jake. "My friend looked over your contract for The End Zone."

Jake studied the lawyer for a few moments, before taking a step closer and taking the papers.

"He says it's pretty ironclad, Jake. I'm not sure exactly what you want to do, but it would seem you can't do anything without approval from Whitney."

Jake blew out a breath and glanced around the stadium. "That's what I was afraid of."

"You have the authority to make day-to-day decisions without her, employment decisions, menu options, vendor choices, you know, things like that, but selling the bar has to be approved by you both."

Jake bit his lower lip in frustration and nodded his understanding. "Thanks, Clay." He slapped the papers against his open palm and attempted to step around the other man.

"And Jake, considering the situation we find ourselves in, I think it would be best for me to resign as your lawyer. I've attached a couple of business cards of lawyers that I know that would be happy to take you on as a client."

Jake nodded and turned his attention back to the field.

"Uh, Jake, one more thing."

Jake stopped and looked over his shoulder, raising his eyebrows as Clay produced another packet of papers.

"What's this?" Jake knit his eyebrows together as he turned to take the papers.

Clay let Jake open the papers before answering. "It's a custody agreement that Julie had written up."

Jake skimmed the papers, then cut his eyes up and said bitterly, "Well, isn't that convenient."

"Jake, listen—"

Before he could finish, Jake interrupted, taking a step toward him, his voice eerily calm and even. "No, Clay, you listen. I will never stop fighting for my family and whether you like it or not, Julie and I have a connection that you will never understand. I love her; I've always loved her, and given enough time she will realize she still loves me too. I won't stop until we are together." Jake didn't know who was more surprised at his admission, him or Clay, but once the words were out it solidified his resolve to unite his family.

"Jake, you can't seriously expect her to believe that you want to have a relationship with her?" Clay tossed his hands up in the air. "And do I need to remind you that you are engaged?"

"No. No, I'm not engaged, not anymore, and why would it be so hard to believe I want a relationship with her? She's the mother of *my* son."

"You don't really want to be with her, you just don't want anyone else to be with her."

"That's not true!" Jake exploded.

The two men stood staring at each other for a long time until Clay dropped his shoulders. "Jake, you hurt her. For years you have avoided her and this town and now you expect her to believe that she's always been your one true love? Just let her go, I can make her happy and she wouldn't feel as if someone just settled for her because all his other options were gone. I'll treat her like she deserves to be treated. I'll devote my life to her and to Huck, and I'll never regret making them a priority in my life. Can you say the same things?"

Jake studied the other man, allowing his words to penetrate his heart and mind.

Clay added, "I would never try to keep you away from Huck."

An anger and a possessiveness burst through Jake's chest with an unexpected intensity. He pinched the bridge of his nose and tried to formulate a coherent thought. He cleared his throat and began, "Clay, I'm going to real honest with you right now. Wild horses couldn't keep me from my son so I don't need your promises. And I know I haven't always treated Julie like she deserved, but I'll spend the rest of my life making that up to her if I get the chance. And I will never give up on getting that chance. You might have her heart or a piece of it right now, but she is my heart, and I'm hers, and it's been that way since we were kids. Yeah, I've messed that up right now, but I'm not going to let her ever forget the history that we have, and every time she looks at our son, she thinks of me and all that we've shared."

Clay nodded slowly and added before he turned to leave, "Good to know where we stand with each other. The contact information for the layer Julie hired to handle this is listed on the papers. Have whatever lawyer you hire contact them about the arrangements."

Jake glared as the other man stalked past him, continuing to watch him until he got into his car and left. Jake slapped the custody papers against his leg. He was tired of this game Julie was playing. He needed to speak to her face to face and he wasn't going to be avoided this time.

****

Jake pushed through the diner's swinging door, his eyes zeroing in on Julie as she stood behind the counter. His long legs covered the distance between them and he slapped the custody papers on the counter.

"Your boyfriend delivered these for you," Jake spat between his gritted teeth.

Julie closed her eyes, trying to gather herself, and spoke quietly, "Jake, please…"

"Please what?" Jake's voice shook with anger. "Please don't be upset? Please don't make a scene? Why didn't *you* talk to me about this, Julie? Why did you send him?"

Taking a deep breath, she gestured toward the back of the restaurant. "Let's go into my office and talk."

He raised his eyebrows. "You sure you want to talk without your lawyer present?"

She rolled her eyes and turned to lead the way to her office.

Before the office door closed behind them, Jake began again. "You didn't need to get your boyfriend involved. We could have worked this out."

Julie sat heavily in her desk chair and rubbed her hands down her thighs. "I just thought it would be best to have something legal between us concerning Huck."

"You thought that or your boyfriend told you that?" Jake

quipped sarcastically.

She folded her hands in her lap, gripping them so tightly her knuckles turned white. "We just need something legal and permanent between us. It's the right thing for Huck. He needs to know that there are rules and a schedule for visitation. The way we are handling things now will just make him think that there is something more between us than there is. You playing pretend family with us is just going to hurt him."

"Who's playing?" he exploded. Her eyes grew wide and her face paled. He ran his fingers through his hair roughly and slowly kneeled before her. "I'm not playing with you, Julie. The time we spent together…it means everything to me. We are a family—"

"You're engaged, remember?" She jumped from her chair, sending it rolling back into the wall. The room was suddenly too small and she dragged a deep breath, in trying to steady herself.

"Not anymore. I'm not engaged anymore, Julie," he spoke quietly to her back. When she didn't respond he continued, "That's why I went to Whitney's after the game. I ended it. I've been wanting to tell you that, but it seems like you've been going out of your way to avoid me lately." He reached out and gently tugged on her arm to turn her around to face him. When their eyes met, he could see the tears pooling in the corners of hers and his heart plummeted. He drew her close and was thankful she didn't protest.

"Julie, I've always loved you. I never loved Whitney the way I loved you." He held her away from him so he could see her face. Unable to gauge her reaction, he continued, "I was messed up for a long time after I got hurt, but coming back here, it's changed so many things for me. Hitting rock bottom—"

"Oh, so when there is no other option, you love me!" Julie shoved against his chest, breaking free from his embrace, tears freely flowing down her face now.

"No, Julie, let me finish." He stepped toward her just to have her move out of his grasp.

"Since being back here is rock bottom, you might as well try to patch things up with the old girlfriend that was never enough for you? What really happened, Jake? Did your fiancée dump you so now that you've got no other options left, you want me and Huck?"

"No! That's not what happened, Julie, I love you, I've always loved you." And before he could stop himself he added, "And you love me too, Julie. I know you do."

He stepped toward her again and she put her hand, palm up to stop him. "You don't love me, Jake. When you love someone, truly love someone, you are willing to make sacrifices and…and you'll do anything to be with them. You suddenly professing your love for me because you've lost all your other options…that's not love." She dashed the tears away and straightened her spine, meeting his gaze. "That's desperation because your world is falling apart, and as soon as something better or a more glamorous opportunity comes along away from Bluff Creek, you'll be gone again."

He shook his head vehemently. "That's not true, Julie. I realize now how special what we had was; what we can still have."

"When you left me crying in your driveway all those years ago you sure didn't think it was too special." She crossed her arms over her chest.

"I'm sorry I treated you that way. I was young and dumb. I think we've both made some mistakes that we wish we had handled differently, but that's in the past. I'm willing to let all that go, why can't you?"

He placed his hands on his hips, emphasizing his tapered waist giving way to long muscular legs, and Julie's traitorous mind and body couldn't help but feel a sliver of attraction. Her heart pounded in her chest, and she frantically fought the attraction by seizing the old anger she had nursed for him for years. "And just what are you letting go, Jake? You talk as if I treated you just as poorly as you did me. I was always there for you, Jake—"

"You kept my son from me!" he exploded. He quickly turned his back to her and paced the length of the small office, placing both hands on the top of his head, taking and releasing a deep breath before turning to face her, his voice calm and quiet. "You kept my son from me, Julie. I missed years that I can never get back. I missed seeing him when he was first born, taking his first steps, saying his first words, his first day of kindergarten. I missed it all and my brain tells me I should hate you for doing that, but my heart can't help it, it loves you…it always has…ever since that day you found me behind that dugout, you took my heart and I've never gotten it back. And I'm tired of playing games. I want you and me and Huck to be a real family."

She stood quietly, returning his gaze, silenced stretching between them for several long seconds before she responded quietly, "I don't believe you, Jake. You want me now, because you think that's your only option and I …I can't handle you leaving again, because this time it won't be just me you hurt, it will be Huck too and I can't risk that."

He began shaking his head before she finished. "I'm not going to hurt Huck; I would never hurt him. Any pain that he has experienced by not having a father around is squarely your fault, Julie." He pierced her with his steady gaze.

"I did you a favor by not telling you. You would have never picked us over life with your rich fiancée. I kept you from showing everyone your true colors; now you still get to be Jake Rawlings, hometown hero." Her voice was laced with bitterness.

He stepped toward her, his voice calm and steady. "You don't know what I would have done, because you never gave me that choice. You made all the decisions, Julie, now you want to make me out to be the bad guy. I'll admit I've not always treated you the way I should have, but don't you dare, for one minute, tell me you did me a favor by hiding my son from me. You know me, Jules, better than anyone else in this world you know me." The sound of her old nickname rolling off his tongue in his low deep timbre caused shivers to run down her spine. "And if you were honest with yourself, you know deep down, I would have been here if I would have known about Huck."

She raised her chin and returned his gaze, hoping she appeared more confident than she felt. She reached around him and picked up the custody papers that had set this entire confrontation into motion and handed them to him.

"Have your lawyer contact my lawyer if you have any questions. If not, you can pick Huck up after school on Thursday."

He returned her gaze, an array of emotions playing through his eyes. Finally, after several long, tense moments, he took the papers from her hand and turned to leave without saying a word. Julie stared through the empty doorway, lost in her thoughts, finally dragging herself across the room. She gently closed the door and turned the knob until she heard the click of the lock sliding into place. She turned to lean her back against the door and slid to the floor, tears flowing freely. Everything she had ever dreamed or hoped to hear from Jake, he had said to her today, but she couldn't bring herself to believe him. She had barely survived when he had first abandoned her, and she knew that a second chance with him would cost her more than she could ever withstand. She had Huck now, she had to play it safe, and taking a gamble with her heart on Jake Rawlings was more of a risk than she was willing to take.

****

Jake nailed loose boards back to the barn, praying the peace of Shep's farm would seep into his own troubled heart and mind. He had gotten up early this morning, long before his parents, and escaped to the farm to be alone. Troubled thoughts bombarded him and he had planned on spending his entire Saturday in solitude at the farm trying to figure out his next step. He found himself sitting on an overturned bucket, staring out into the fields, thoughts tumbling through his mind. How could he get out of his contract with Whitney concerning The End Zone? How could he satisfy his gambling debt without sacrificing Shep's inheritance? Most importantly, how could he ever convince Julie that she was his first choice, not his last? As much as he worried over these thoughts, the answers never came. By midmorning he had done very little repair work to the barn and had spent most of his time sitting and staring into space.

The crunch of gravel in the driveway sent him off the bucket and to the barn door. He stepped out into the sunlight just in time to see his father step down from his truck. When their eyes met, Coach gave him an affectionate grin and began walking toward the barn.

"You must have left the house early this morning," Coach called out as he strolled toward him.

"Couldn't sleep." Jake leaned against the barn door and crossed one leg over the other at this ankles. "I thought I would come out here and work on the barn."

Coach nodded, his gaze taking in the aging structure and finally settling back on his son. Instinct told him that something troubled Jake, but fatherly wisdom also told him confronting Jake wouldn't get him the results he wanted. He crossed his arms over his chest and studied his son. "You coached a great game last night, Jake. You see things out on that field…things that I don't see. I'm not sure if I've ever been able to see the field the way that you do."

Jake nodded and kicked at a pebble, mumbling his thanks.

"It's a gift, Jake. You have a gift." Coach placed his hands on his hips.

Jake's felt heat creeping up his cheeks. Humility and embarrassment were not emotions he was familiar with.

"And you love it, don't you?" A smile broke across Coach's face.

Jake couldn't stop himself from grinning. He swallowed hard and tried to put his feelings into words. "My whole life I thought I was destined for greatness, to have a life that other people envied…that I deserved to have something greater than this, this town… Honestly, I guess I thought I was too good for this town. For so long, I thought my ticket out was to play professional ball and when that didn't happen, I thought I would never be happy, never find anything I would be good at. I was not good at running The End Zone, obviously, but I kept at it because I liked the image, I liked people thinking I was successful, even when I wasn't. But when I'm out there on that field, I don't care what people think about me. It's like that field is exactly where I'm supposed to be; I was made to be there. And when I'm out there, I...I don't care about money or status or anything... I just love being out there."

"And that is exactly what it takes to be a good coach. Those kids look up to you. You have a chance to help them, guide them. It's a heavy burden, but it can also be one of the most rewarding thing you've ever done."

Jake shook his head. "I'm not sure I need to be guiding anyone."

Coach studied his son thoughtfully. "Why do you say that?"

Jake pushed off from the barn door he had been leaning on, settled his hands on his hips, and looked out over the farm without really seeing anything. Long silent moments ticked by before Jake began, his voice low, "Dad, I've messed up everything."

Coach stepped forward and placed his hand on Jake's shoulder. "You've not messed anything up so bad that God can't fix it. You've just got to let go and give God control."

Jake's mouth twisted as he continued to gaze out into nothing. "I don't know how to do that."

"It's like I told you when Huck was in the hospital, ask God. He will show you."

Jake kicked at the ground before turning to face his father. "I'm not sure what God could do to help me. My life is in shambles, Dad. Whitney refuses to let me sell my half of the bar; her father is basically blackmailing me to develop this farm, I owe money that there is no possible way I can ever pay back on an assistant coach stipend, and Julie served me with custody papers."

"Custody papers?" Coach's eyes widened.

"Yep, her boyfriend, Clay Phillips, hand delivered them to me the other day." Jake didn't even try to keep the bitterness out of his voice.

Coach pondered the information before responding,

"Boyfriend, huh?"

"Yeah." Jake's voice was laced with bitterness. "I thought we were... I thought we were finding our way back to each other, and then boom, she's dating someone else."

"Well, to be fair, Jake, up until a few weeks ago, you were engaged to another woman."

"I never felt for Whitney what I feel for Julie." Jake's voice was tortured.

"Have you told Julie that?" Coach studied his son's profile.

Jake laughed bitterly. "How can I? She avoids me at all cost and the one time I did get to speak to her, she wouldn't believe me!" He scrubbed his hand down his face roughly. "I've really screwed everything up"

Coach let the silence stretch between them and collected his thoughts before he spoke "Jake, during the years that you were distant from us there was one Bible verse that I kept praying; one verse that kept me going. It's in Joel and it tells us that God will restore to us the years that the locusts have eaten."

"Dad, locusts aren't my problem!" Jake cried.

"It's a metaphor, Jake. God promises he will restore the years that we lost if we will return to Him. I prayed that promise from God for many years and look where we are now. You are back in my life, just like I believed and prayed for."

Jake looked up and met his father's eyes. "You think that would work for me?"

Coach stepped forward and gripped Jake's shoulder. "Here is what I do know. God has a good plan for you, Jake, and no matter who or what that plan includes, it is what you should pursue for your life. Apart from God's plan, your life will always be in shambles. I know right now there seems to be no way out of all this mess, but God can make a way when there seems to be no way."

"I don't know, Dad." Jake shrugged his shoulders.

"Well, Jake, the way I see it, you've tried it your way and look where you are. Why not try it God's way for a while?"

Jake rubbed the back of his neck and continued to gaze out into the field, avoiding his father's watchful gaze.

"You've got a lot to think about, Jake. I'm going to give you some time. When you are ready, you let me know." Coach patted Jake's back, walked steadily to his truck, and left Jake alone with his thoughts. Jake turned back inside the barn, his thoughts tumbling around his mind at a frantic pace. He sat down heavily and dropped his head. Could God show him a way out of the mess he had created? His parents had raised him in church, but he had never depended on God the way his father did. He couldn't even remember the last time he had prayed. He pulled his phone out of his back pocket, launched the internet, and typed in the phrase his father had quoted. It didn't take him long to find the verse from Joel. *"And I will restore to you the years the locust hath eaten…"*

Jake thought about all the years he had wasted chasing dreams that turned out to be nothing but a disappointment. He couldn't help but think that all these years he had been chasing something to fill up an empty place inside him, but nothing had ever seemed to be enough. He chewed his bottom lip and thought about the choices he had made since high school and where they had led him. He took a deep breath and a heaviness settled inside him. He was tired; tired of trying to maneuver and manipulate life's situations to procure an outcome that might make him happy. He kicked absently at the dirt at his feet and decided it was time to stop.

"God," he whispered, "I don't know what I'm supposed to say, but I've pretty much messed up everything. I've done so much wrong, I don't even know which way is the right way anymore. But I'm ready to stop making my own decisions and just let You show me what to do." He glanced up at the ceiling. "Would you do that…would you just show me what to do?"

****

Coach sat on the front porch of his home, his Bible open in his lap, and prayed for his son. It had been hours since he had left Jake in the barn, sensing that if he had pushed any further, Jake would have resisted surrendering to God. He closed his eyes and reminded himself of God's promise that if he planted the seed of faith, God would see it through. He stopped rocking his chair when Jake pulled into the driveway. Coach watched as Jake exited his car and slowly walked up the front steps. Coach waited with bated breath as Jake stopped at the top of the steps and leaned on the porch post.

Jake dragged in a deep breath, looked up the street and then back to his father. "I want God to lead my life. I've messed it up enough on my own. I'm ready to let Him have control."

A slow grin spread across Coach's face as joy spread through his chest. He nodded to the rocking chair beside him. "Let's see what Jesus has to say about how to do that."

Chapter 19 *Full Circle*

"Behold, I am doing a new thing; now it springs forth, do you not perceive it?" Isaiah 43:19

Jake leaned back in his chair and rubbed his eyes. He had spent hours watching game films preparing for tomorrow night's playoff game. He glanced at the clock. 10 a.m. He had just enough time to pick up Huck and make it back to his parents' house for their first annual Thanksgiving meal. He had to admit he couldn't remember a holiday he had been more excited about in years. He stepped out of the coach's office into the warm fall morning and chuckled as he spied his ten-year-old pickup truck sitting in the parking lot. He couldn't help but be reminded how much things had changed. The truck was old with a dented fender and a sputter when it started that tested Jake's faith in the vehicle every time he turned the key. A year ago, he wouldn't have been caught dead in such a ride, but now, appearances didn't mean as much to him. The truck got him around town and unloading the expensive sports car had been a step in getting his finances under control.

He slipped into the driver's seat and had to slam the door twice to make sure it shut. The truck's engine rumbled to life and he silently thanked God. He drove slowly through town, waving at people he knew, and for the first time in a long time he felt content. His situation hadn't changed that much. He was still partners with his ex-fiancée in a failing bar, he still owed debt he couldn't pay, and Whitney's father still expected him to develop the farm. He prayed about his situation every day and he believed God would show him how to handle it all. He couldn't help but give God credit for the change in his life. He still had problems facing him on all sides, but he still felt a peace and contentment that he had never been able to achieve by playing football, being financially sound, or associating with the fabulously wealthy.

Only when he pulled into Julie's driveway did he feel a pang of disappointment. He had stopped praying that God would make Julie love him again and instead prayed that God would just lead Julie to the happiness she deserved. He also prayed that God would take the pain away that he felt every time he saw her and was reminded of what might have been.

He swung his long legs out of the truck and studied her house for a moment. He thought of the times he had spent here with her as a teenager, and then the nights he had spent here with her and Huck just a short while ago. His longing to be with her seemed to intensify as the memories played through his mind like a highlight reel. Would he ever be able to pick Huck up without the pain of losing her piercing through his chest? He prayed every day that he would.

He plastered a smile on his face, even if it didn't quite reach his eyes, and took the steps two at a time to the front door. Before he could even knock, Huck was throwing open the door and jumping into his arms. Huck immediately began asking questions about what they were eating and did Grandma make chocolate pie. Jake chuckled and hugged his son tightly to his chest. He looked up to see Julie standing in the door and he nodded a greeting. In the weeks since she had served him with custody papers, he had strived to make peace with her and she seemed to be willing for them to at least be cordial to each other. Letting Huck slip from his arms, he reached into his back pocket and extended a folded check in her direction.

"It's your child support." He tried to keep any emotion out of his voice.

Julie hesitated before taking the check; not for the first time she regretted the custody agreement. "Thanks," she mumbled.

"I'll have him back by three o'clock tomorrow afternoon?" Jake raised his eyebrows.

Julie's stomach dropped and tears threatened at the thought of missing the first holiday ever with Huck. She bit the inside of her jaw and willed herself not to cry in front of Jake. She nodded her head in agreement and called for Huck, who had already run to put his overnight bag in the truck, to come back and give her a good-bye hug. Jake watched them hug and his chest burned with regret.

The burning question that Jake hadn't been able to get off of his mind suddenly came tumbling out of his mouth, surprising him as much as her. "So are you spending the day with Clay?"

She jerked her head up suddenly and Jake could see the surprise in her eyes. "I'm sorry I asked that." He waved his hands. "It's none of my business."

She licked her lips nervously and she looked so fragile, Jake fought the urge to reach out and touch her.

"I-It's fine," she stammered and then quickly blurted out, "Clay went to his sister's house up in Nashville, so I'll be by myself today."

Jake's head jerked up and he frowned. "By yourself?"

She smiled as she nodded, but Jake could see the despair in her eyes and his heart twisted. He couldn't leave her here alone on Thanksgiving, could he?

"I'll be fine." She hoped she sounded more carefree than she felt. "I'm going to watch the parade and then I brought home some leftovers from the diner...." Emotion caught in her throat and she forced a smile.

Jake looked off in the distance as if he was internally debating his dilemma before turning his gaze back to her. "Come with us."

"No, Jake, I couldn't," she protested.

"Why not? It's not like you haven't spent holidays with my family before," he reasoned.

"That was different," Julie mumbled and dropped her eyes to

the ground.

"How was that different? Look, you will always be a part of our family; Huck guarantees that, and you will always be welcome at our table."

She looked up and they held each other's gaze, each of them wondering if they could make it through a holiday dinner with the other one present. His face split into a grin as he jerked his head toward his truck. "Come on. I know you've just been dying to take a ride in my truck."

"Let me get my purse," she whispered, realizing that resistance at this point would be futile, and she wondered if she would ever be able to resist his smile. Her initial nervousness about attending his family's Thanksgiving meal was soon put to rest as Coach and Mary welcomed her with open arms. In fact, she felt so relaxed during the meal and the thought of being alone on a holiday was so depressing to her that she agreed to spend the afternoon with them. She and Mary swung lazily on the front porch while Coach, Jake, and Huck tossed a football around in the yard. An unwanted thought of how much they appeared to be one happy family screamed through her mind. She sat up straighter and chided herself internally for not even thinking about Clay throughout the day. Coach flopped down on the steps and held up his hands, signaling to Huck he was giving up.

"Mary, did we eat all that pie?" Coach asked over his shoulder. "Coffee and pie sure would be good."

"I'll go start a pot. Julie, you want to help me?" Mary turned to her as she stood up from the swing.

Julie looked across the yard to meet Jake's steady gaze. "Oh, I guess I better be going."

"Why? No! Stay with us and enjoy pie," Mary encouraged. Julie looked back to Jake as if silently asking if it were okay that she stay. Jake gave an almost imperceptible nod, grinned at her, and turned his attention back to showing Huck how to throw the perfect spiral. She helped Mary serve up pie as Coach found a Christmas movie playing on the television and called Jake and Huck inside to join him. By the end of the movie, all the pie had been eaten, the coffee drunk, and Huck had passed out on the couch, his head in Julie's lap, his legs thrown across Jake's, connecting them in a way.

As the movie credits rolled, Jake gathered Huck up in his arms and whispered, "I'll put him to bed, then I will take you home." She nodded and again expressed her thanks to Coach and Mary for having her join them. She watched Jake carry their son up the stairs, Huck's small body encased in secure muscular arms. She hated the fact that she noticed his chiseled legs and the loose-hipped way he descended the steps.

He found her waiting for him at the bottom of the steps and raised his eyebrows. "Ready?" She nodded, unable to speak. The passenger's door of his old truck squeaked its protest when he held it open for her and the engine refused to crank to life. After several attempts, Jake turned to her, a flush creeping up his face. "Umm…sometimes it has a mind of its own. We can take my dad's truck."

They made small talk about Huck and laughed about how much he had eaten throughout the day. Julie expected him to simply drop her off, but instead when they pulled into her driveway, he came around and opened the truck door for her and then proceeded to walk her to the front door.

"Thanks, Jake." She turned to face him when they reached the top of the steps.

"You know Shep would kill me if I didn't walk a lady to the door," he chuckled.

"No, I mean for inviting me to join you today."

"Oh,…well, no problem. It was a good day. I think Huck had fun."

"Yeah, it was a good day." She bit her lower lip and looked up at him through her lashes. "To be honest, I was really dreading spending today without him."

He slipped his hands into the front pocket of his jeans and shrugged. "It worked out then, I guess." Their eyes met and they held each other's gaze. Jake was mesmerized by her and without thinking he reached out and skimmed his palm over her shoulder and down her slender arm. She stiffened and he immediately stepped back.

"S-Sorry," he stammered.

She dug in her purse for her keys and unlocked the door. "I'll see you tomorrow," she called over her shoulder.

He nodded and watched her until she closed the door behind him. He walked slowly to the truck, the longing for her that he fought every day surging through his body and settling into his bones. Would it ever not hurt to see her and to know how close he had been to having everything, just to ruin it all? He closed his eyes as he slipped behind the wheel and breathed a familiar prayer for God to help him get over her.

****

Julie told herself that the reason she had repeatedly peered out the front window to the driveway was because she was eager to see Huck and had nothing to do with catching a glimpse of Jake. She had closed the front door last night before she had done something she would end up regretting. But she had watched Jake through the blinds as he stood on her front porch in the dark, staring at the house. Since their confrontation after Clay had given Jake the custody papers they had developed a tenuous understanding when it came to co-parenting Huck. They were cordial to each other, but stayed at arm's length.

But she knew if she had given him any encouragement last night, they would have kissed. And even though she had never made Clay any promises, she couldn't do that to him. She reminded herself of all of Clay's wonderful attributes. She then went through the long list of all the times Jake had disappointed her and that he might be content in this town for now, but when the bright lights of the big city came calling, he would go running. Her heart couldn't take that again.

The bucket of rust Jake drove these days pulled into her driveway, and Julie suppressed a smile. He had actually blushed last night when the truck wouldn't start. Embarrassment was not an emotion she was accustomed to seeing in Jake Rawlings and it had been endearing. She watched through the blinds as he slid from the driver's side, stretching to his full height, his long legs giving way to his tapered waist. He was dressed in khakis and a Bluff Creek High School coaching staff golf shirt and she momentarily thought that it should be a crime to look so good in such a bland ensemble. The shirt stretched over broad shoulders which rippled underneath as he swung Huck's overnight bag out of the back of the truck.

"Is Huck home?" Clay's voice behind her caused her to jump and let out a small cry. He had appeared at her door this morning unannounced, as he had a habit of doing. She knew he wanted their relationship to be more than what it was. She had a fondness for him, but something inside her wouldn't let him get too close. That, however, did not keep him from trying.

"Yep, he's home." She hurried to the front door, hoping that Clay didn't see the flush creeping up her cheeks. He followed and stood behind her as she opened the door to a chattering Huck. She met Jake's gaze over their son's head; he slid his gaze over to Clay and then back to her. Julie couldn't quite read the emotions that clouded his eyes. He nodded his greeting to Clay and extended his hand to the other man. He handed Huck's bag to Julie and asked, "Y'all coming to the game tonight?"

Before she could answer, Clay slipped his arm around her shoulders and pulled her closer. "We wouldn't miss it."

Julie noticed the clench in Jake's jaw, but his voice held no emotion as he answered, "Good, I know Huck's excited."

"Winwood is pretty good, right?" Clay asked about the impending opponent.

"They are, but I think we are ready for them." Jake nodded and then glanced to Julie. Embarrassment burned inside her; what must he think of her? After they had been so familiar with each other yesterday and now she stood with another man's arm around her. "Well...I gotta go. Tell Huck to find me after the game." And with that he turned and left them. She would have stood and stared after him if not for Clay's gentle nudge to turn back inside the house.

****

Jake stood at the end of the sideline, away from the all the action, and watched as his team celebrated their win. Five minutes ago, he had been in the middle of the celebration, shouting for joy and returning rough hugs and slaps on the back from his players. Fans had taken to the field and the scene before him was one of joyous chaos. He stepped back, wanting to take the moment in. As a sense of joy and accomplishment, the likes of which he had never felt as a player, enveloped him, a sense of missing hit him as well.

He glanced over the stadium, looking for Huck and Julie. While the win brought him joy, he wanted nothing more than to share the moment with them. He looked up to see Huck, running toward him down the sidelines as fast as his short legs would carry him. He began walking toward Huck and when the boy was close enough he launched himself into his father's arms. Jake laughed at his son's excitement and held him close. He looked into the stadium and his eyes immediately collided with Julie's. The desire to run to her, to grab her up in his other arm and hold both her and their son tight, was so overwhelming he actually took a step toward her. Clay's body stepping between them and breaking the connection of their gaze stopped him. She wasn't his to catch up in his arms. She wasn't his to share this moment with. He hugged his son tighter and turned back into the crowd on the field. The joyous celebration was now tinged with disappointment for him. He was stopped by a strong arm on his shoulder; turning, he came face to face with Scott Kilzner.

"Scott!" He grabbed the other man about the shoulders with his free arm. "What are you doing here?"

"Man, I couldn't miss seeing you coach in the big game, could I? Congrats, man, that was awesome!" He grinned at the young boy in Jake's arms and added, "This must be Huck."

"The one and only." Jake's smile widened with pride. They embraced again and Jake jerked his chin toward the celebration still going strong at center field. "Come on, man. There are some more people I want you to meet."

****

Jake rubbed his hand down his face as he sat on the edge of his bed and squinted to make out the time on his phone. 8:00 a.m. He rested his forearms on his bare legs, contemplating why he was awake so early. The adrenaline rush from the team's win the night before had kept him awake until the early hours of the morning. Even after the fans and players had left the stadium, Jake had sat with his friend Scott, his father, and Coach Doug in the locker room laughing and talking. He could tell that Scott immediately liked the two older men and it felt as if they had all four been together their entire lives. Around 1:00 a.m. they had reluctantly left the field, with Scott following Jake home to crash at the Rawlings' house.

Jake heard a noise from downstairs, realizing that the commotion from the lower level must have been what had woken him up. Now awake with no hope of going back to sleep, he grabbed a pair of sweats and started down the stairs. Much to his surprise, when he reached the living room, he heard Huck's voice in the kitchen. But what stopped him in his tracks was the sweet sound of Julie's voice wafting through the room. Without thinking, he hurried across the living room and through the kitchen door.

"Daddy!" Huck cried and once again launched himself into Jake's arms.

Jake caught his son and hugged him tightly. He set him down and squatted so that he was face to face with the young boy. "This is a nice surprise. What are you doing here, Huck?" He cocked an eyebrow and gazed from his parents to Julie, expecting one of them to answer.

"We are going to get new shoes!" Huck bounced up and down. "Me and Grandpa and Grandma."

"New shoes?" He looked back at Huck's excited face and couldn't help but smile.

"He told me last night at the game that he needed some new shoes, so your father and I are going to take him over to that new shopping center in Lancaster," Mary explained.

"And we are going to the movies!" Huck interjected.

"And the movies?" Jake looked over at his parents, realizing they were both fully dressed and ready to leave. His gaze settled on his father. "Don't you usually watch game film on Saturdays, Dad?" Jake couldn't keep from smiling as he teased his father. He knew his father's post-game routine better than most, but also knew that Coach Jim Rawlings was enamored with his grandson and would likely do anything the boy asked of him.

"Uh, well, yes I do, but you know what, Jake? Sometimes change is good, and the boy says he needs shoes."

"He doesn't need shoes, he wants shoes," Jake said softly, his heart full with love for his family. He thought about how different things might have been if his parents hadn't welcomed Huck into their lives with open arms. He knew his parents might not approve of the way Huck had been conceived, but they would never hold that against their grandson. He straightened his tall frame and looked at Julie, who had been particularly quiet since he had entered the kitchen.

"Hey, Julie." He nodded his head as he greeted her, resting his hands on Huck's shoulders.

She stared at him for the span of several heartbeats before she began babbling, "Well, I better go. Gotta work the morning shift at the diner, had a waitress call in sick. Huck, come give momma a hug and be good today. Thank you all so much for taking him. I didn't think I would ever get him to bed last night, it was all he talked about." She hugged Huck fiercely and quickly turned and began walking out the door. "Well, call me when you get back and I will come pick him up or you can drop him off, whatever works, just call me."

She shut the door behind her, straightened her shoulders, and walked to her car. Only when she was safely stopped at the stop sign at the end of the street did she let her forehead fall onto the steering wheel and groaned. The moment Jake had entered the kitchen without a shirt on to cover his muscular chest, she had become embarrassed and flustered. She tried to recall what she had even said as she tried to hurriedly make her escape and she prayed she hadn't embarrassed herself. She tried to reason with herself; Jake was an attractive man, no one could argue that. It was a normal response. Guilt crept in as she thought about Clay. Even if Jake had worn a shirt this morning, being in close proximity to him always flustered her and scattered her thoughts. If she were truly honest with herself, she could admit she never had that kind of pulse-pumping reaction to Clay.

She began listing all of Clay's admirable traits. He was dependable, loyal, and trustworthy, and even though she couldn't say Jake had been those things in the past, she had to admit that he had changed. He seemed more at peace, not quite so restless these days; dare she say he almost seemed content?

She shook her head as if to refute that thought. There was no way that Jake Rawlings would be content in this little town, being an assistant coach and driving a beat-up old truck to boot. Clay was solid as a rock and that was exactly what she needed in her life. So he didn't make her heart race or give her stomach butterflies whenever he was near; following those feelings had caused her years of heartache and she refused to allow that to ever happen again.

****

"I'm starving; is there someplace around here we could get a decent meal?" Scott got up to pour himself another cup of coffee. When he had awoken, Scott had found Jake sitting in silence in kitchen. They had shared a pot of coffee while Scott filled him in on all the happenings with The End Zone. He had informed Jake that Whitney had been making regular appearances at the bar, trying to impose her will.

"I can fix us something." Jake stood and walked toward the refrigerator.

"Man, I'll pass, I've had your cooking before." Scott grinned. "What about that little diner I saw when I drove in last night?"

Jake shrugged and mumbled under his breath that he could cook.

"What's the matter with you?" Scott leveled his gaze on Jake.

"What? Nothing," Jake scoffed, hoping he was believable.

"Then let's go." Scott stood and gestured to the door.

Jake rubbed the back of his neck and tried to come up with a plausible reason for not going to the diner. He finally sighed and decided to try the truth. "Huck's mother owns that diner—"

"All the more reason we should go," Scott interrupted. "I want to meet this lady."

"Fine," Jake grumbled and grabbed the keys to his truck.

Jake and Scott slipped into a corner booth in the busy diner. Scott immediately craned his neck toward the kitchen before turning back to face Jake. "Is that her?" He jerked his head toward the counter and Jake looked to see Marti pouring coffee into a customer's cup.

"No," Jake said emphatically. "Definitely not." He took a menu from its place behind the napkin holder and handed one to Scott, hoping to momentarily distract his friend from searching for Julie.

As they studied the menu, several customers stopped by their booth to congratulate Jake on the team's win last night. He focused on each person, smiling and responding accordingly, but his senses knew the minute Julie entered the room. From the corner of his eye, he saw her glide through the kitchen door into the dining area. He felt his pulse pump and a nervous shiver slide through his belly. He took a breath to steady himself and prayed the all too familiar prayer that God would take those feelings from him. He clenched his jaw and forced his mind to focus on the older gentleman who had come by to discuss last night's game and was recounting a story from his own glory days in high school. When the older man finally left their table, Jake's gaze slid to the back of the diner and collided with Julie's.

Julie felt as though the entire restaurant quaked when her eyes met Jake's. Why was he here? She had just made a complete fool of herself in his kitchen and now he was here giving her that half smile that didn't quite reach his eyes, which made him look like he had a secret that no one else knew or that he carried a hurt so deep he couldn't share it. She never could decide which it was, but either way, it annoyed her.

She glanced around to see Marti taking orders on the other

side of the diner. With her other scheduled waitress calling in sick this morning, she was short-staffed and had been waiting tables herself. Her stomach fell when she realized she would have to take Jake and his friend's order. She cleared her throat, squared her shoulders, grabbed a coffee pot, and plastered a fake smile on her face.

"Good morning again, I guess." She cringed inwardly at the high-pitched tone of her voice.

"Hey, Julie." Jake widened his grin and gestured across the table. "This is my friend Scott. Scott, this is Julie…Huck's mother."

Scott's eyes brightened. "Well, it is so nice to meet you." Jake didn't like the gleam he saw in Scott's eyes and tried to communicate that by kicking him under the table. Scott ignored him and continued, "I met Huck last night; he's an amazing kid."

Julie ducked her gaze and began filling up their coffee mugs. "Yes, he's very special."

"He seems to have the entire town wrapped around his little finger," Scott commented as he sipped his coffee and nodded toward Jake. "Reminds me of his ol' man here."

Julie wasn't sure why heat flushed up her neck. While there were still some whispers, most of the town had accepted that Huck was Jake's son and had moved on to the next tidbit of juicy small-town gossip. But hearing Scott refer to similarities between Huck and Jake unnerved her. She got the feeling that Scott's comments were not spoken offhandedly; he was searching for some type of reaction from her. She glanced at Jake, who seemed unaffected by the comment. His arm rest casually on the back of the booth and he appeared to be lost in his coffee.

Jake finally found Scott's foot underneath the table and squarely ground the heel of his shoe into it. He wasn't sure where Scott was heading with his comments, but by the gleam in his eye, he knew his friend was up to something. He was relieved when Julie finally asked if she could take their order and he hurriedly asked for the breakfast special.

Scott tapped the menu. "Gosh, I haven't even had a chance to look at the menu. What would you suggest, Julie?"

"Get the special." Jake hoped his voice sounded light to Julie but that Scott got the message to stop whatever it was he was up to.

"What is the special, Julie?" Scott directed his question to her, but his gaze was pointed squarely at Jake.

"A western omelet, hash browns, and toast." Julie offered, while writing on her order pad.

Jake applied more pressure to Scott's foot under the table. Scott turned a megawatt smile to Julie. "That sounds wonderful. Make it two."

When she had finally walked away, Scott deepened his grin. "What's up with you? Why were you trying to crush my foot under the table?"

Jake shrugged and looked out the window, trying to sound nonchalant. "She's busy. I didn't want you messing with her and wasting her time."

Scott raised his chin and acted as if he wanted to continue that line of conversation, but dropped it and offered, "So what do you want me to do about Whitney making regular appearances at the bar?"

"Well, she owns half of it so I guess she can," Jake quipped.

"She's trying to make some pretty drastic changes." Scott's voice was serious. Jake turned from his window gazing to meet his friend's concerned eyes.

"Really? She never even darkened the door of the place and now she wants to be involved?"

"I have a theory if you want to hear it," Scott offered and didn't wait for Jake to acknowledge him before he continued, "I think she's trying to draw you out. The more drastic the changes she makes, fundamentally changing The End Zone, she thinks you will come back and get involved."

"She's wrong," Jake answered quickly. He had no intention of ever returning.

"Any luck on finding a way out of owning the bar with her?"

"Nope," Jake sighed. "I had a lawyer look it over.

Apparently, I can't sell my half unless she agrees and we both know that isn't going to happen. I can't believe I ever thought I could marry her. I wouldn't care if I never saw them again." Jake rubbed the back of his neck and shook his head.

"Them?" Scott questioned.

"Mr. Peterson is keeping my bookie at bay as long as I agree to develop Shep's farm into some shopping center subdivision, of course with him getting a big cut of the profits." Jake cut his gaze up to his friend to gauge his reaction. He could see the shock spread over Scott's face.

"What?" Scott's voice was an octave too loud and heads turned toward their booth.

"Shhh." Jake tried to quiet him and then continued, lowering his own voice, "Whitney and her dad brought a group of developers to the farm and totally blindsided me. He told me that if I didn't develop it, cutting him in on the profits, that he would unleash my bookie on me. I don't know what to do and the six months will be over in a few more months and I'm no closer to an answer than I've ever been."

Before Scott could respond, Julie appeared at their table holding two steaming plates piled high with food. She set the plates in front of them and then said, "I told them no onions in your omelet, Jake."

He grinned at her and said softly, "Thanks, Jules."

As she turned back to the kitchen he followed her with his eyes. When she disappeared behind the kitchen door, he looked over to find Scott studying him. Several moments ticked by before Scott said, "We've got to find you a way out of this mess."

Scott studied his friend throughout breakfast; how he smiled at his son's mother when she came back to fill up their coffee, the way he ever so slightly tensed when their hands touched as he handed her his empty plate. Things he had always wondered about concerning Jake were becoming clearer to him. Scott insisted on paying for both their meals and they strolled out onto the sidewalk, the sun shining brightly on their shoulders, a cool fall nip in the air.

A man about their age crossed the street in front of them, heading to the diner. Scott noticed Jake's demeanor change and he watched the man as he approached.

"Morning, Jake," Clay Phillips called as he stepped up onto the sidewalk in front of the diner.

"Clay." Jake nodded. Clay glanced over to Scott and Jake took the moment to reluctantly introduce them. "Clay, this is my friend Scott Kilzner. He's running the bar for me."

The two men shook hands and exchanged pleasantries before Jake continued, trying to sound light, "I was going to try and sell my half of the bar to this guy."

Clay thought for moment and looked at him quizzically. "Wait a minute; you only want to sell your half?"

"Yeah, I just want out of it," Jake said.

Clay was silent for a moment before asking, "Jake, do you still have that contract?"

"Yeah, it's at the house." Jake stood, his hands on his hips, studying Clay.

"Bring it by the office. Let me look at this time," Clay said as he reached for the diner's door.

"Thanks, man. I'll drop it by on Monday." Hope sprung anew in Jake's chest.

He spent the rest of the day showing Scott around Bluff Creek, eventually ending up at Shep's farm. They hiked trails on the farm for most of the day, ending up by the river as the sun slipped down into the western sky, casting shadows over the farm.

They had been sitting quietly for several minutes when Scott offered thoughtfully, "You've changed, man."

Jake chuckled as he tossed a rock into the river. "Oh yeah?"

"Yeah, you have."

"Yeah, I don't drive a fancy sports car any more or date a millionaire's daughter."

"No…it's more than that," Scott began slowly but then quickly added, "You're different. Not just the material stuff like the car, but… I don't know… you seem content, not quite so restless…dare I say happy?"

Jake nodded his head and stared across the river, gathering his thoughts before he spoke. "I've been going to church, Scott. I've been praying and reading the Bible. I don't claim that I understand it all, but..." He shrugged before adding, "I've been trying to let God lead my life."

Scott studied his friend as if seeing him for the first time before saying, "That's great, Jake. I'm happy for you." And then because he couldn't resist, he added, "And just so you know, it's as apparent as the nose on your face that you still love Huck's mom."

Jake jerked his gaze over to Scott, and wished he could wipe the smirk off his friend's face. He thought about Scott's observation and wondered if his feelings were that obvious to everyone. He looked back across the river, decided he was tired of living in denial about his feelings, so he shrugged and said, "It doesn't matter; she's with someone else."

"Married?" Scott asked.

"No!" Jake answered quickly. "But still...she's with someone else. In fact, she's seeing the lawyer we met outside the diner this morning."

Scott kicked at a rock on the riverbank before answering, "Jake, she may be with someone else, but there is something there. I could tell it this morning at the diner. It's easy for anyone to see that both of you still have feelings for each other."

Jake picked up another rock and tossed it into the river. "Well, even if that's true, I'm in no position to be professing love for anyone. I mean look at my life, I'm tied to a failing business with my ex-fiancée whose father is blackmailing me, I'm broke, and I'm a part-time assistant football coach who is currently living with his parents. I don't have a lot to offer her, and Clay...well, he's successful, has his own practice, a really nice house. He can give them things that I can't."

"Jake, you of all people should know when it comes to true love it's not about the material things you can give the other person. Whitney could have given you everything you wanted, but you never looked at her the way I saw you look at Julie this morning."

Jake rolled his shoulders, trying to relieve some of the tightness that had settled there before he spoke, his voice low. "I keep praying God will take the feelings I have for her away. Every time I see her and I know she's with someone else, it's like a knife straight to my heart."

Scott stepped toward his friend and gripped his shoulder. "Maybe there is a reason God hasn't taken those feelings from you. Come on, it's almost dark and we need to start figuring out a plan to get you out of all this mess because unless I've totally misread this situation, you have no intention of letting Whitney and her dad develop this farm."

Jake met his friend's gaze, verbalizing for the first time the conclusion he couldn't exactly pinpoint the moment he had come to. "I don't want to and I want to stay here, Scott. I never thought I would want to live here, I was always chasing the next big thing that I thought would make me happy. But being here, with Huck and…and my family, being a coach, having a relationship with God…I've never felt anything like it."

"That's great, Jake, I'm really happy for you. Come on, I think we need to visit Julie's lawyer boyfriend. He seemed to have an idea this morning. Why wait until Monday?"

****

A week later, Jake waited nervously in the Clay Phillips's office, hoping the lawyer had good news for him.

"Sorry you had to wait." Clay breezed in the door dressed in an expensive suit. "I had to be in court over in Rockwood today and it ran a little late."

Jake tamped down the shot of jealousy that sluiced through his veins. Clay had expensive clothes and a nice car; both of those things had once been very important in Jake's life. Not to mention he had a relationship with Julie. Try as he might to prevent it, sometimes the temptation to envy Clay welled up in him.

"I hope you've got good news for me." Jake laughed nervously and wiped his palms down his thighs.

Clay sat down behind his desk and rifled through a stack of

file folders. "Well, I think so. I guess that really depends on what your plans are."

Jake slid to the edge of his seat, his heart thumping wildly in his chest.

Clay flipped open the folder, licked his finger, and thumbed through the pages until he found the one he was looking for. "Okay, here we go." He handed Jake a page out of The End Zone contract in which a paragraph had been circled. Jake studied it, laid it back down on the desk, and looked back up at Clay. "Honestly, Clay, you're going to have to explain this, I have no idea what I just read."

"You and Whitney are both fifty percent shareholders in The End Zone. The bar can't be sold unless you both agree to the sale."

"Tell me something I don't know," Jake grumbled.

"But," Clay continued, "there is nothing in this contract that states you can't sell a portion of your shares without Whitney's consent."

Jake pinched his lower lip between his forefinger and thumb and looked back at the contract. "So you're saying I could sell part of my half?"

"You could sell as much of your half as you wanted. You could sell ninety-nine percent of your half, leaving you with just a small piece of ownership." Clay leaned back in his chair, a triumphant look on his face. "Not only that, but whatever ownership you retain, you can appoint someone else to be your proxy."

"What does that mean?" Jake cut his eyes to the other man.

"They would act in your interest. In essence, your ownership would be on paper only. You would not have any interaction in the daily business, nor would you have any say in decisions made. You would simply collect a check for your piece of the profits."

Jake gave a short humorless laugh at the idea of The End Zone turning a profit and asked, "And you think this will work? Mr. Peterson has a team of lawyers, Clay. Will this stand up in court if it comes to that?"

Clay cleared his throat and leaned forward. "Jake, despite what you might believe, there are lots of gray areas when practicing law. While your right to sell a portion of your ownership isn't explicitly spelled out in the contract, it isn't explicitly forbidden either. If they wanted to press the issue, we could tie if up in court for a while." Clay paused for a moment before adding, "I did a little research on Mr. Peterson. I can't imagine someone with such diverse assets wanting to waste a bunch of money in court cost over this."

"You might be surprised," Jake mumbled.

"It's either make this play or keep on the way you are. It's up to you, Jake."

Jake leaned back in his chair and studied Clay thoughtfully before he spoke. "I appreciate your looking over this for me, Clay, but I guess I have to ask you something."

"Sure, go ahead."

"Why on earth are you helping me?"

Clay sighed heavily and leaned his forearms on the desk, returning Jake's steady gaze. Several long moments passed before he spoke. "Jake, whether you mean to or not, whether you even know it or not, your life and what goes on in it bleeds over into mine." Clay paused and when Jake didn't respond he continued, "You cast a big shadow. It seems no matter what Julie and I do, you are always there…casting your shadow."

Jake cleared his throat and straightened in his chair. "I've told you before that Julie and I have a connection that you will never have and I also warned you that I would never stop fighting for my family to be together."

"She's not your family," Clay said forcefully. He straightened his tie and tried to rein in his emotions before he continued by repeating calmly, "She's not your family, Jake. You share a child and that is where your connection begins and ends."

"That's where you're wrong." Jake took the contract and stood abruptly, turning on his heel to leave. Before he could get out the office door, Clay spoke to his back.

"I'm asking her to move to Nashville with me." Clay's words caused Jake to stop in his tracks. He slowly turned back into the office and Clay continued, "My sister lives in Nashville and I've been offered a partnership in a firm there. I want Julie and Huck to go with me; to start over in a new place. She holds back from me; won't let me completely in and I think if we moved it would help that."

Jake glanced up at the ceiling as his mind reeled. Emotions he couldn't even name began to spin and swirl through his body. Anger and fear fought to take over his thoughts and speech. He took a deep breath to steady himself before he spoke. "So this," he held up The End Zone contract, "was what? You were going to help me because you're planning on taking my family from me? Finding a way out of that contract help you ease your conscience?"

Clay stood and met his angry gaze. "No, Jake, I was hoping that by helping you get out of that contract it would free you up to move on to your next big thing. We all know that's what you want. All you care about is winning, that's all you've ever cared about. You don't care about Julie; she isn't your long-lost true love. All this is to you is about winning. You want to win and you want to see me lose. Something with that bar is holding you back, keeping you in town, and we all know this town isn't big enough or good enough for Jake Rawlings. But when you go this time, don't worry, I'll be here to pick up the pieces for Julie and Huck."

Unable to speak, Jake turned and left the office, the only thought in his mind escaping the room before he said or did anything that he would later regret. He slid into his old pickup truck, his hands shaking so bad, he closed his eyes and drew in several deep breaths to steady himself. He replayed the conversation in his mind. The thought of Julie and Huck moving to Nashville caused a chasm of despair to open inside his chest.

"God, help me, please." He rested his forehead on the steering wheel and tried to calm himself. He thought about the accusations that Clay had hurled at him. Did everyone in this town, including Julie, still believe he was just passing off time here? He had been very clear about his feelings for her but nothing he did or said seemed to change her mind. Had he completely missed his opportunity to bring his family together? He felt physically sick at the thought that he had permanently lost any chance with her. He opened his eyes, his gaze falling on a torn piece of paper stuck in the dash of his truck. He studied the words on the paper, a verse he had jotted down and placed on his dash as a reminder. Isaiah 43:2: *When thou passest through the waters, I will be with thee, and through the rivers, they shall not overflow thee, when thou walkest through the fire, thou shalt not be burned; neither shall the flame kindle upon thee.*

"God, I feel like I'm drowning here," Jake whispered. Fear crowded in his mind. How could he get through this? Suddenly spurred into action, he cranked his old truck and threw it into gear. He would go to Julie, confess everything from his gambling debt to Mr. Peterson's blackmail, then he would throw himself at her feet and beg her not to move to Nashville with Clay.

As he turned out of the parking lot of Clay's office a portion of a verse he had read days earlier screamed through his mind. *"Peace, be still."* He ignored it and continued to drive, his only thought on getting to Julie. Again he heard the verse, *"Peace, be still."* In fact, the words seemed to be on repeat in his mind, so much so that he pulled over before turning down the street that led to Julie's house.

"God, how can I be still when so much is at stake?" he whispered. He reread the verse from Isaiah sticking in his dash and prayed, "God, what should I do?" He waited; the silence in the truck was deafening. Again *"Peace, be still"* reverberated in his heart and mind. Releasing a pent up breath, he put the truck in gear and turned it around, heading away from Julie's house while whispering, "All right, God. I'm going to follow you on this one."

He drove slowly through town, the sense of fear and anger slowly dissipating in the light of faith. He drove aimlessly, sometimes praying quietly, sometimes pleading loudly for God to intervene, sometimes sobbing uncontrollably as he thought of losing Julie for good. Without realizing his whereabouts he found himself in front of his parents' house. He wasn't sure how long he had been sitting in his truck when the silence was shattered by the ringing of his phone.

Scott had gone home a few days before, but Jake knew he was eagerly awaiting word about the future of The End Zone. He slid his finger across the screen. "Hey, Scott." He tried to make his voice sound light.

"Hey, man, any word on the contract?" Scott's words brought him back to the sliver of hope he had felt about the information Clay had shared concerning The End Zone contract.

"Yeah, I think I may have something we can use."

****

Jake had been at The End Zone for less than an hour when Whitney and her father burst through the back door.

"Right on time," Scott murmured as he moved to stand shoulder to shoulder with his best friend.

"Jake!" Whitney screamed when she saw him standing behind the bar. "What is the meaning of this?" She shook a handful of papers gripped tightly in her fist at him.

Jake let them storm into the room, the four of them sizing each other up. Jake prayed silently for patience and wisdom to prevail before he began, "I see you got the package we had sent over."

"Is this some kind of joke?" she spat at him, slapping the papers onto the bar.

"No." He hoped his voice sounded calmer than he felt inside. "No, it's not a joke. I have sold part of my ownership of The End Zone to Scott. He's done a much better job managing it than I ever did."

"You can't sell anything without my permission! It's part of our contract." She stepped toward him, hands on her hips. Jake glanced across her shoulder to meet her father's penetrating gaze.

"Now that's where you're wrong, Whitney." Jake leaned his palms on the bar, arms ramrod straight. "We couldn't sell The End Zone without both of us agreeing on that, but there is nothing in our original contract that prevents me from selling part of my ownership and I don't need your permission."

Jake glanced back to Whitney's father; he could see the anger in his eyes and he knew that if the man had any way to combat Jake's claims he would already be voicing them. The fact that they were here trying to intimidate him was more proof that he was onto something. The thought gave him confidence and he continued, "Of my fifty percent of The End Zone, I sold ninety-five percent of that to Scott. He will also be acting as my proxy in all matters concerning The End Zone."

"Your proxy?" Whitney scoffed.

"Yes, my proxy." Jake kept his voice even and calm. "He will make all decisions on my behalf. I will in essence only be a silent partner and in the event I am asked to weigh in on any decisions, you should know I will *always* side with Scott."

Whitney whirled around to face her father. "Daddy! Do something!"

Mr. Peterson, who seemed to be internally weighing his options, didn't react immediately. Instead he quietly studied the two younger men, and Jake, who never flinched under his heavy glare, seemed to possess a confidence he hadn't had the entire time he had dated Whitney. Mr. Peterson stepped forward, crossed his arms over his chest, and directed his words to Jake. "You seem to be changing your mind on a lot of things lately; marrying my daughter, and the future of The End Zone...I hope you are smart enough to not change your mind on the development of your farm."

Jake didn't hesitate before he responded, "And if I have?"

Mr. Peterson chuckled as he pulled a bar stool out and perched on the edge. "Jake, Jake, Jake...you think I care about this little bar? I don't. This," he waved his arms around the room, "this was nothing more than to give you something respectable to do when you were involved with my daughter. So you found some minuscule loophole to sell part of it? You think that makes you smart? You think that you can outsmart me now? I don't care about this bar and I don't really care if you want out of it. You should have told me that, we could have worked something out. Sell it outright and shut it down for all I care."

"Daddy!" Whitney cried, but immediately fell silent when Mr. Peterson held his hand, palm up, in her direction.

"But what I am interested in is your decision on developing your farm. We both stand to make a substantial amount of money off that deal." Mr. Peterson leaned back in his chair and crossed his arms over his chest. "And as you know, in return for your promise to develop the farm, I have been keeping your bookie at bay…I would hate to have to tell him that I no longer had any interest in your body staying intact…or even alive for that matter."

Jake looked from Mr. Peterson over to Whitney, who wore a smug expression on her face, and he briefly wondered how he had ever brought himself to love her, much less propose to her. Gratitude flooded his chest as he realized how God had delivered him from a miserable life. He turned his eyes back to Mr. Peterson and announced calmly, "I paid my bookie off this morning. All the money I had promised to pay him plus interest. Luckily for me, he was a big fan of mine back in my playing days and when I told him I could ensure he could get season passes to all games, he assured me that he and I were square and that any threat you might try to deliver using his name was nothing but empty words."

"Where did you get that kind of money?" Whitney exploded. "You didn't make that much money off this joke of a sale."

"Don't worry about it, Whitney," Jake snapped and then closed his eyes to bring his emotions back under control. He took a deep breath and looked at his former fiancée. "Whitney, you don't want me; I never really fit into your world and we both knew it from the beginning. I was a project for you and you were an escape for me. You deserve someone who will love you for who you are and so do I. Let's not try to tear each other apart over hurt pride."

Silence stretched before them and hope of an end to this nightmare welled in Jake's chest. Mr. Peterson finally picked up the papers Whitney had slapped down on the bar, "You know

I'm going to have my lawyers look at this."

"Go ahead. The lawyer who helped me is the same one who wrote my grandfather's will, and if I remember correctly, you were so impressed with his work, you wanted to hire him."

Mr. Peterson stood and gestured to Whitney that they were leaving. Jake held his breath until he saw them disappear behind the closing back door. When he finally heard the door latch, he collapsed on the bar and with Scott slapping him on the back, he quietly thanked God.

****

The December sun offered a small amount of warmth as it beat down on Jake's back. It had been a week since his showdown with the Petersons and to his knowledge if they had found a mistake in his agreement with Scott, they hadn't vocalized it. Scott had in fact called him earlier to explain some of the changes he was making to The End Zone. He assured Scott again that he truly was just a silent partner and had no interest in the daily happenings. In fact, nothing of his former life seemed to hold much interest for him lately. Instead, he found his happiness in the small things of life like watching his son in the Christmas play at school, or helping his parents decorate the Christmas tree in their living room, or puttering around Shep's farm like he was this morning.

The only tinge of regret that shaded his life occurred when his mind slipped to thoughts of Julie. At first he had prayed that God would remove the feelings he had for her, but now his prayer had changed. He prayed that she would be happy and if that was with Clay living in Nashville, he would have to accept that. Gone was the possessive need to have her, and in its place was a true desire to see her happy, even if that meant she spent her life with someone else. He had decided that no matter what happened to him, or how far away Julie moved, God was good and His plans were perfect. He would follow God, even when he didn't understand and even when it hurt to surrender his life and his desires to Him.

He continued to rip rotten boards from the front porch of

Shep's house. It was probably a job that should have waited until spring and warmer weather, but he had been restless sitting in his parents' house, unwanted thoughts tumbling through his mind. As usual, on Friday afternoon he had driven over to Julie's house to pick up Huck for the weekend. Clay's car had been in the driveway along with a brand new SUV. Huck had bounded out of the house, his usual excitement amped up even more.

"Daddy, Daddy!" He had run toward Jake excitedly. "Look at our new car!"

Jake had squatted down and extended his arms just in time for Huck to run into them. He picked him up and studied the SUV as Huck rattled on about all the buttons on the inside. Jake let out a low whistle. "Man, that sure is nice."

"Clay bought it for us and it has a TV, Dad. A TV! I can watch anything I want on it." Huck continued to ramble as Jake turned his head just in time to see Clay and Julie step out onto the front porch.

"Huck, you forgot your bag," Julie called out and Jake couldn't help but wonder if the arm Clay slipped around her shoulders was more for his benefit than hers.

Huck ran to the porch and Jake strolled slowly behind him, stopping at the bottom of the steps. He slipped his hands into the front pocket of his jeans and looked from the car back up to Julie. "Nice car," he offered.

Julie mumbled her thanks and Jake wondered if the flush he saw in her cheeks was from embarrassment or the chill in the air.

"She needed something new. It makes the perfect Christmas present" Clay said, reaching out with his free hand to ruffle Huck's hair. "And it has all the safety features to keep Huck secure."

"And a TV," Huck interjected.

Clay laughed and repeated, "And a TV, buddy."

"I told you it was too much." Julie mumbled and avoided Jake's gaze. He sensed Julie was uncomfortable with the gift.

Jake thought of his own beat-up pickup truck. No added

safety features there; he was lucky if the motor even cranked on increasingly cold mornings. He had gathered Huck, along with his bag, and had felt like a negligent parent as he strapped him into a truck so old it didn't even have airbags. He had slid behind the steering wheel and watched Clay guide Julie back inside the house.

Despair threatened to envelop him; a new car meant only one thing. Julie must have agreed to the move to Nashville. He glanced over at Huck and his heart ached. How could he be the father he wanted to be when the boy would be living hours away from him? He thought of the verse from Joel his father had quoted to him right before he gave his life to Christ. The verse promised that God would restore what had been taken from his followers. How was this restoration? The two people he loved more than anything in this world would be moving away from him.

He took a deep breath to steady himself. He reminded himself of the ways God had taken care of him in the past. By the time he pulled into his parents' driveway, he had decided he would trust God was working in the situation. Huck had jumped from the truck and run into the house eager to see his grandparents. Jake had stepped down from the truck and gazed up to the heavens. He had whispered into the darkness, "I trust you. Even when I can't see what you're doing, I trust you."

Thoughts of Julie, Huck, and Clay had filled his thoughts all night. When his parents had announced a trip to finish last-minute Christmas shopping, Huck had been beside himself with excitement. Jake had excused himself from the trip, having trouble conjuring up any Christmas cheer. When his parents had left with Huck, he had slipped his arms into his heaviest winter coat and drove to the farm. He had made plans to begin working on the porch in the spring, but the thought of taking a sledgehammer to something had appealed to him this morning.

He jerked his head up at the sound of crunching gravel only to see Julie's shiny new SUV pulling slowly down his driveway. He eyed the car warily and stood when it came to rest under a giant pine tree in the yard. Julie slid from the driver's seat and let the door gently slip from her hand. Jake took a step off the porch and began slowly walking toward her.

"Huck's not here. He went with my parents to finish their Christmas shopping."

She nodded and pulled her thick coat tightly around her. They stood several feet apart, silence stretching before them.

"Guess the rumors were true, I saw the road being cut through the timber down the road. I didn't believe you'd ever actually develop Shep's farm."

"It's not quite what you think, Julie."

"It doesn't matter what I think. I can't believe you would do that to Shep."

They stood facing each other, indignation burning inside Jake. She just assumed the worst about him without even letting him explain.

"Nice car," he said.

"You've said that already." Her voice was flat and her face emotionless.

He glanced around her to the car and then back to her. "Well, it bears repeating."

"Don't act childish," she admonished and he held his hands up as if professing his innocence. "I didn't ask for it and I didn't want Clay to buy it. He just surprised me with it."

She studied him and Jake could tell there was something else she wanted to say. He held his tongue from making any further comments on her car in fear that it might drive her away.

She buried her fists into her coat pockets and stepped toward him. "Rumor around town is that you got a job offer."

"Is that a fact?" He raised his eyebrows.

"A coaching job with a Division 2 college."

"Seems like you've been listening to a lot of rumors about me. Are you asking me about them, or telling me about them?" Jake furrowed his brow.

Julie shook her head angrily. "It sounds like a good opportunity for you, Jake. What you've always wanted."

Anger burst through Jake's chest and he forcefully dropped the half-rotten plank he was still holding. "Everybody in this town seems to think they know exactly what it is that I want. Please, Julie, why don't you tell me what it is that you and everybody else around here thinks that I want."

"To get out of here!" She raised her voice to match his. "To get out of here because this town was never enough for you. We were never enough for you." She paused, letting her words hang in the air before she added, her voice barely above a whisper, "I was never enough for you."

Embarrassed by her emotional outburst, she suddenly regretted making the spontaneous trip to see him. She turned quickly, marching back to her car. He called out to her back, stopping her in her tracks. "I turned it down."

She turned back to face him as he stepped closer to her and repeated, "I turned the job down."

"Why?" she demanded.

He took a deep breath, looked around the yard, sighed, and said softly, "Because it's not what I want."

She licked her lips nervously and he continued, "Julie, from the time I was a kid I thought I was destined to be something great, something special, to be someone that everyone knew and envied, but I'm not and that's okay. I'm pushing thirty years old, I drive a pickup truck that I'm not even sure will start most days, I am a part-time assistant football coach. My paycheck would probably make most people laugh. I live with my parents." He gestured toward the house. "The one piece of property I do own is falling apart and I am confident a family of squirrels has taken up residence in the attic. But you know what? I'm happy. For the first time in my life I can say that I am content." He paused briefly before he added, "The only thing missing from my life are you and Huck, Julie. "

"Jake, don't do this," she pleaded.

He ignored her plea. "I love you, Julie. I can't give you the material things that Clay can but I love you and Huck with everything I have in me."

"Jake, I can't do this right now." Julie roughly brushed the tears that fell from her eyes and hurried to her car. Jake's long legs caught up with her easily as he grabbed the door to keep her from shutting it.

"I'm not developing the farm. The road you saw cut was Mom and Dad's new driveway. Dad wants to retire and they wanted to build a retirement home out here on the river. I wanted to give the land to them, but they insisted on paying for it. I used the money to pay off some gambling debt I had." He reached out and touched Julie's face, cupping her jaw in his palm. "I've enrolled in online classes to finish my degree. I should graduate in May and I want to teach and coach right here in Bluff Creek. And I want to spend every moment that God leaves me here on this earth loving you, Julie. I know I can't give you new cars like Clay can or big fine houses. I can't promise you the life that he wants to give you in Nashville, but—"

"I can't do this right now, Jake." Tears flowed freely from her eyes. She reached for the door handle and tried to close it.

Jake held it tightly, refusing to allow her to shut him out until he said all he needed to say. "Okay, Julie, I'll let you go, but just know that I chose you. Over everything else, I chose you today and every day for the rest of my life. Even if you don't choose me, I will always choose you."

She sobbed openly as she wrenched the car door out of Jake's hands, slamming it shut. Jake stepped back as she quickly turned the car around and sped down the driveway. He ran his hands roughly through his hair. He hadn't wanted to make her cry, but he had wanted her to know the truth. He closed his eyes and prayed for strength. He had thought when he lost his dream of a football career that nothing could ever feel worse. He knew that if Julie took Huck and moved to Nashville, the pain that would cause him would be more than he could ever withstand on his own.

****

Jake waited as late as he possibly could before announcing to Huck that it was time to take him back to his mother's. He dreaded seeing Julie after their confrontation the day before. While he didn't regret anything he had told her, he didn't look forward to hearing her actually tell him about her plans to move to Nashville with Clay.

He groaned when he pulled into her driveway and spied Clay's car. Huck bounded out of the truck, but Jake took a few moments to prepare himself. Praying for peace and wisdom, he headed for the front steps. As he approached, Clay stepped out of the front door. The man bent down, whispered something to Huck while giving him a fierce hug, and continued down the steps in Jake's direction. Jake stood frozen as the man approached and braced himself to hear the news he had been dreading.

Clay stopped when they were within mere inches of each other and pierced Jake with a steady gaze. The minutes ticked by and Jake waited impatiently for the other man to speak. Clay opened his mouth, just to close it, and looked back to study the house. He finally turned to Jake and shrugged his shoulders. "You win, Jake. As usual, you win."

Jake's mouth dropped and he was unable to speak. Clay lifted his chin and walked steadily to his car. Jake watched him as he slowly backed down the drive and pulled away. He turned back to the house and quickly bounded up the steps; he didn't bother knocking on the door but threw it open and stepped inside.

Huck met him as soon as he entered, worry etched across his small face. "Something's wrong with Momma," he whispered, looking over his shoulder toward the kitchen.

Jake knelt down and turned Huck's shoulders so he could look him in the eye. "Go to your room for a few minutes, buddy. Everything's all right." He nudged Huck in the direction of his bedroom and slowly stepped toward the kitchen. He rounded the corner to see her sitting at the table, holding her head in her hands, softly crying.

"Julie? You okay?" he asked quietly as he stepped toward her.

She jerked her face up and the look of anguish on her features ripped at his heart. He quickly crossed the room and knelt in front of her, cupping her face in his hands, gently wiping her tears away with his thumbs. His touch seemed to open a dam inside her as she began to sob heavily.

"Shhhhh, shhhh now, sweetheart." He slipped his arms around her and pulled her into his embrace. "I'm here, you're okay," he whispered has he gently rubbed her back. She gripped the front of his shirt in her fists, leaned into his arms, and cried uncontrollably against his neck. He continued to whisper comfort into her ear. Promises to protect her and right all the wrongs in her world. Promises he intended to keep if it was the last thing he ever did.

He wasn't sure how long he held her in that position until her sobs became softer and less frequent. She finally raised her head and released his shirt from her grip. He searched her eyes and brushed her hair away from her face with gentle stokes. He waited, wanting her to tell him what had happened, but the suspense was too much for him and he gently questioned, "What happened?"

She took a deep breath, bringing one elbow up to rest on the table, pressing her fingertips against her forehead. He took her other hand in his, skimming his other palm over her hair and down her arm. When she still didn't speak he gently took her chin in his hand and turned her face toward him. He inched closer to her and said on a breath, "Jules, what happened?"

She dropped her face in her hand, her voice so muffled and quiet, Jake had to strain to hear her. "Clay asked me to marry him."

Jake's stomach fell but then when he thought of Clay's words to him as he left, his spirits soared. Wanting her to tell the story in her own time, he waited for her to continue.

She dropped her hands to her lap and met his gaze. "There he was down on one knee promising me all these things. Promising me that he would take care of me and Huck for the rest of our lives. He told me I wouldn't have to worry about making ends meet at the diner anymore or paying Huck's medical bills, and Huck would attend the best schools and have the finest education money could buy. He made it all sound so wonderful."

Jake nodded and when she didn't continue, he thought about his words carefully before he softly spoke. "If all those things he promised are so wonderful, why are you sitting here crying?"

"Because, Jake," she said angrily.

He waited for her to continue and when she didn't and then she refused to meet his gaze, he gently turned her face to his. "Because why?"

Their eyes met and they held each other's gaze for long agonizing moments. The love he felt for her swelled inside him to the point he feared he would suffocate from the magnitude of it. He pressed his palm into her thick hair at the back of her neck and let his thumb graze her cheekbone as he repeated softly, "Because why?"

As his thumb gently caressed back and forth across her wet cheek, something inside her broke, and tears began to fall from her eyes again. Taking a deep breath, she returned his steady gaze and whispered, "Because it wasn't you."

Tension left Jake's body in a rush and joy filled every cell in his body. He waited for her to continue.

"Here was this man offering to solve all my problems and promising me this charmed life and all I could think of was that I wished it were you kneeling in front of me."

A tear slipped from Jake's eye and Julie reached out to wipe it away before she continued. "In my heart, I wished you were on one knee in front of me saying the things you said to me at the farm. In my mind I could hear you saying to me all those things. It's all I've thought since then and all I could hear in my mind. So I told him no. I couldn't marry him because…because I had fallen in love with you when I was eight years old and I had never really stopped loving you, even when I didn't want to."

Emotions filled Jake's throat. As tears slipped from his eyes, he took both her hands in his and cleared his throat. "I can't promise you that it's going to be easy, Julie, and I can't give you all the material things he can, but I love you and Huck with everything I have in me."

Julie's lips trembled as she heard the words she had wished for coming from Jake. He pulled her closer until her forehead rested on his and he continued, his voice wrought with emotion. "I want to spend every moment God leaves me here on this earth loving you. I choose you, over everything else, I choose you today and every day for the rest of my life. I will always choose you. And now I'm asking that you choose me. Choose me, Julie, for the rest of your life."

She slipped from the chair to her knees in front of him, reaching her arms around his waist. He pulled her tight against his chest before pulling back. He searched her face before he lowered his lips gently to hers. She returned the kiss, trying to convey all she was feeling through it. When they pulled apart, both breathless, she reached up and touched his face. "I choose you," she whispered. "Today and for the rest of my life, I choose you."

Epilogue

Jake stood outside the locker room, twisting his wedding ring around his finger nervously as he watched the last of his players head to the field.

"Nerves getting to you?" Coach Doug slapped him on his shoulder, causing Jake to jump.

"Maybe a little," Jake admitted.

"Well, first game of the season always makes everyone nervous. It being your first game and the first game as the new head football coach, well, that's a double dose of nerves."

Jake grinned at Doug, and not for the first time since he had taken over as head football coach since his father's retirement, he thanked God for the man. They fell in step together as they left the locker room, discussing techniques, plays, and players as they swiftly jogged to the field.

Jake breathed deeply, enjoying the familiar smells as he stepped out onto the field that had recently been renamed Rawlings Field in honor of his dad's storied coaching tenure at the school. He scanned the bleachers looking for his family. His eyes quickly found Julie's. She raised her hand and gave a quick wave. He winked at her in return.

After their reunion at Christmas they decided that neither of them wanted to wait very long to begin their lives together. They were married on Valentine's Day with just a handful of friends and family surrounding them. Every day since then, he had woken up and thanked God for her and His provision for restoring all the years they had lost together.

His gaze moved over to his parents seated beside Julie. Jake wasn't sure how he felt about seeing his father in the stands and not on the sidelines. When Coach had announced his retirement at the end of May, Jake had never dreamed he would be offered the head coaching position. He had taken enough classes in the spring semester to finish his degree and had planned on accepting a teaching position at the high school and hoped whoever the new coach was they would keep him on as an assistant. Someone could have knocked him over with a feather when the athletic director had knocked on his door one day in late June and offered him the job. He and Julie had prayed about it and both felt God was leading him to accept it.

He glanced back to Julie in the stands and she smiled at him. He let his gaze fall quickly to her abdomen and then back to her face. She blushed and the corner of his mouth lifted in a grin. This morning she had told him that their family would be growing by one in the spring and he had felt a warmth inside him ever since.

Coach Doug, accompanied by Huck, walked toward him down the sidelines, drawing his attention away from Julie. Huck carried a football under each arm and sported an official Bluff Creek High School football jersey with the name Rawlings emblazoned across the back.

"I think our new ball boy is ready to go," Doug laughed as he ruffled Huck's hair.

Jake grinned and used one arm to pull his son to his side. Looking out over the field at his players, feeling his son at his side, knowing that his wife with his unborn child sat behind him along with his parents to support and cheer for him no matter what, caused his heart to swell. As Doug jogged to the center of the field, followed closely by Huck, Jake glanced up to the heavens and thanked God for what had to be the millionth time for the life he had blessed him with. Tears sprang in his eyes as he added under his breath, "Tell Shep thanks too."

Made in the USA
Columbia, SC
10 June 2020